THE
CHARMED
LIFE

THE
CHARMED
LIFE

THE CHARMED LIFE

Jack B. Yeats

Routledge & Kegan Paul
London

First published in 1938
by George Routledge & Sons Ltd
Reprinted in 1974
by Routledge & Kegan Paul Ltd
Broadway House, 68-74 Carter Lane
London EC4V 5EL
Printed in Great Britain by
Lowe & Brydone (Printers) Ltd, Thetford, Norfolk

ISBN 0 7100 7667 3 (c)
ISBN 0 7100 7871 4 (p)

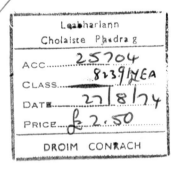

THE CHARMED LIFE

" THE MAN HAS AN EYE LIKE A HAWK AND A TONGUE like a courting dove, nothing comes amiss to him. I've heard him, with these ears, read the Angostura bottle beginning with the bearla, passing to the Franko and ending on the Gothic. The man's inspired." That was how he was described by a man who has seen, and listened, to many men with their heads in the fumes and their feet in the sawdust. A stranger introducing him to another said : " Allow me to have the pleasure of introducing to your notice Mr.——— ? Mr.——— ? Mr.——— ?—No matter." " Pleased to meet you, Mr. Nomatter."

That's a strange saying. Strange in a way as the call of the merchant on the sod to the people coming away from the Grand National in Eighteen Ninety-three. " Why Not the oysters ? "

The man sailing under the fluttering flag of No Matter had nothing strange in his appearance. In fact, a washing-away of strangeness was his long suit. He had at times, without any effort as far as anyone could know, a way of almost floating into the invisible. He was there. He wasn't there. A slow tick of the clock and he was there again. A shoulder coming forward, an arm raised, a bosom heaved, and he was hidden. That was all. Every sensible man is sure of that. Sure it wasn't that he was really gone—men don't go like that, not nowadays. Not go and come

I

back again. You couldn't run businesses on those terms.

There was one man from whom No Matter never vanished, that was his worn old friend, Bowsie. Bowsie was a medium-heighted man, his bones well covered. Winter and Summer he wore a long overcoat weathered to a green shade about the shoulders and the rotundities of his rump. Bowsie's face was smooth, his nose was long enough for sneering—but he never sneered. He had a comfortable chin and it was always cleanly shaven. His neck was round and the light yellow neckcloth, with small brown spots on it, was always fresh as a primrose.

Bowsie had not cast himself for a speaking part while on earth ; he listened well to all he heard. No Matter knew that, because when he put away the careless philanderers of thought and took to the macadam of human speech, he always whizzed his old stringy neck round to the right towards Bowsie and looked Bowsie straight between the eyes, and immediately Bowsie's eyes would give a step of a light dance, and flitter a brown ballet dancer, in brown flouncing skirts. In the middle of the oval proscenium of each eye she would flitter, with style. No Matter never indulged any Schoolmaster within in his hard thinking, except, on those meat-like moments when a train, or a motor-bus, or a steamboat, had to be met as it passed. Then the time-table had to be sought, and thought about. The result impressed upon the gluey lining of the mind in the place earmarked for such meaningless information. That was all the hard thinking of the teeth-setting brow-bending kind he ever used. The rest of his thoughts were communings with his inner ear.

He loved the wild and open spaces. " I love them

wild, and if they aren't wild, I'll wild them, and, if 'open' means free—then they are free to me. Through or over, I go in without a ticket, except a complimentary one. I give myself that one. I am Eternity's fool, and we neither understand each other. We don't have to." Do you notice, Bowsie, my child, how the meerschaum pipe in the middle of the colouring is about the shade of the water tumbling down that fall of water there coming towards your Lordship's feet. These tumbling waters come from the boggy flat tops above, you, and I, know pretty fairly the road they've between. But the way this little fall looks to each of us is quite different, and I haven't judged the difference by talking about my pipe dream. That only suggested a false bridge. That water isn't, in its smallest drop, like any old meerschaum pipe that was ever filled and smoked. It's a friend of mine—it has the quality of a dog's cold nose, and a bright brown eye—like—like an umbrella—like a muffin growing on top of a stick, like a mushroom on its stem. Early signs of a seafaring traveller. Everything he sees at home is like something he saw abroad. That's cultivation and extension of the mind. Amaryllis reminded him of Maude. I don't think Sir, Amaryllis wouldn't care to be reminding him of the absent Maude, and, if Maude was present, it would be worse. Amaryllis wouldn't mind her reminding her of a star, a planet swimming into his ken.

> D'ye ken Amaplanet, with her coat so gay,
> D'ye ken Amaplanet at the break of day,
> D'ye ken Amy Planet when she's far, far away.

That's all poetry ; but that's poetry for the cinema hounds to go a hunting on, and for Amaryllis to go the

same way. Just poetry in general. But if the seafarer said she was like some fine large form of a planet
with rushy fields, and fine dry ones, and rocks, and
lakes, with islands, and a wind always blowing one way
off the sun's cheek, except when it blew contrary,
Amaryllis wouldn't stand for that at all. Otherwise,
the seafarer wouldn't have attempted a detailed picture ;
something large and non-committal.

LIKE A STAR

Like a large mysterious parcel in a bran pie. It
might be Miss Frederick's old boots. But it might'nt,
it might be a crown of glory on a red cushion.

Bowsie, when you think of a crown of glory, what
do you think of ? Oh, no. I hope not. That up-
and-down angle effect with your finger, that's a cardboard crown. He shouldn't allow the gesture to take
the place of the true visibility of the object itself. But
he can, if he likes, jerk his pudgy finger upwards, he
can wind round and make the old spiral staircase
gesture. There's one thing about Bowsie, he never lets
you down. He always does the thing you expected
he was going to do ; expected with your toes, not with
your head.

Oh, Bowsie, please notice this high plateau and that
old-fashioned crowd. Though it's to-day we are here,
would you not, my boy, imagine it was long ago, any
old long ago. There is where the races that have an
unbroken tenure of their special sod, never change, or
only so gradually, as you cannot notice, except by
listing the differences ; the ladies' hats are at a different
angle, and there are more ladies. But these are changes
which have come, and gone, and had their dose of doing,
many times. Bowsie is being impressed ; he has turned

a little away from me to face his old round stomach to the sun. It's a very yellow sun, and seems to me a bit down the course, for even the time of year. Nice tangly sort of grass. Nice white rails to lean on. The ring makes a boomy noise. People are full of love for one another, if only they can get a couple of winners each. These young horses are magnificent— snorting up in the sky. They are very proud of themselves, that one, if he liked to go up in the air again and give another of those lamb kicks could hoist that sour little man off his back.

Bookmakers' tickets are very gay, the style of printing is good for the spirit. It would be a pity to have to return these tickets to the bookmaker, but perhaps I won't have to, perhaps they'll be mine to hold in remembrance of a good day. What is money anyway, in the bookmaker's bag it can't do me any harm. However while there is some let us buy food in the marquee. Marquee food has its own taste. A general tent taste but sifted over, it is the scent which comes from outside the tent: The scent of broad old river water rolling on its way, a lake water, a muddy grass well trampled, a grass dry over red dry earth, and boglands, with old bog holes, and old shawls, or homespun coats, and sea sand, and sea waves, all coming in at the tent door. And then outside the tent yourself, if you closed your eyes, languid, because this was the ineffable—but you aren't going to do that. You don't want to spend your days walking about the floor of a lake, with twenty foot of water over your head, buried in a scent. So the only thing to do is to snap your eyes open again, sharp, and look about you, and see something funny. The Maggie man's brother in the red coat, looking full of drink, and admired now, by

a man who looks as full, and his looks do not belie
him, but Maggie defies the world with a wooden,
solid wooden, bottle on her head, and the wattles
missing her.

Seeing funny things is a protection, but when the
curtain falls on fun, what then my children? Then
we, you and I, must take what comes. And here comes
Chance leading a horse by a hay rope, but the horse
in a sudden lurch of his stride breaks the hay rope
and passes by me like a wind. The man stands foolishly
with the broken rope in his hand, he says to me, " That
horse was the star horse of all the world and what will
I do now? I know what I will do." And so he makes
a slipping loop in the end of the rope, and the other
end he throws over a low branch of a tree, jutting out
convenient to his hand, he brings the end down and
makes it fast to a fairy's archway of a root that comes
above the ground, then he put his neck through the
noose, makes himself up into a spider's ball, and launches
for eternity. He signed to me to pull his legs, but I
wasn't ready to do that, so I went to hold them up,
to take the weight of his body off his neck, but lo,
there was no weight in his body, he was just grey air.
So I blew at him, and he went up among the leaves,
and I cut the hay rope with my penknife, and my
responsibility was ended. The horse came back and
stood under the tree with me and he certainly was
the star of Great Magnitude. His face was a rich brown
with a black nose, his ears were dark brown at the
tips, his mane was naturally waving and black as coal,
and his tail was its counterpart, he had a great body,
his ribs, to stroke him was comfort and security. Before
the saddle, though there was no sign he ever wore one,
and aft, his strength and symmetry was a wonder. His

black legs were as short as they wanted to be, his hoofs
were elegancy and strength. I saw myself reflected in
his dark blue eyes. But he was not thinking of me,
he had seen me I knew that. Then he sighed. There
in the forest glade he was alone with some old sweet
melancholy. He missed the great ones he had known,
they had walked beside him with their ribs to his, and
he had understood what was going forward with them,
forward and back again, occupying themselves about
many things, each an event, not a sum, or part of a
sum, not a problem, not arithmetic at all.

That horse had seen a warrior of old take another,
his own weight, by the hand, as though to shake it,
and then break away, and then take the hand again,
and with that one grip throw the other through the
whole half-circle of firm grass to grass, himself the hub,
the other great creature the tyre. That done the
warrior, the first warrior, showed the second just the
idea and how it was done, and was himself tossed
through the air. Can I wonder that great horse sighed
for those other ones.

Bowsie here thinks the strong almond-shaped young
woman behind the bar is every now and then looking
at him with interest and spreading with each look.
He thinks she admires him as a representative of the
Sons of Men. She is just wondering how anyone could
be so careless as to walk about looking so dirty in the
summer weather. Bowsie isn't as dirty as he looks,
he isn't dirty at all, he sloshes about the bath whenever he has one handy, but his hands get dirty, earthy,
finding his way about over stiles and roads with a tough
old stick held by the dirty curve, and he rubs his
hands over his head where the baldness is beginning

to come, and all over his sides he rubs his palms when he's pleased.

So Bowsie and the young woman attending are at criss crosses. He thinks she should be seen and not heard, and if she had her will he wouldn't see her, because she'd wash him completely, soap in the eye and all, and he couldn't open his eyes after the soap-suds began coming down his face. But he'd hear her because all the time she'd talk to him in the language which goes with slosh and scrub.

There's a Saturday—all cigarette ends and litter and dusty rubbish, and there's a Sunday—all the air dust falling in its own slow time, and there's a Monday morning ; the woman to scrub is coming up the stone steps from the tap. Her hour is coming nearer and nearer. Up the steps. She's got new brown sacking on her stomach, and wheezes, her clothes wheeze where they catch her where the Monday morning muscles begin to bunch. When she comes to the outer hall, down goes the bucket, swing goes the swab round in the early Monday water—and out she comes, the Queen of Sheba leaping from the Nile and landing on the rocky coast of Abyssinia. The swab comes down on the stone floor, and Monday's banner goes up to the truck, and we're well away.

Bowsie, could you whistle, artful blackbird, could you whistle a swab circling a bucket, sweeping into the air, and coming down on the floor, squelch, squelch, squelcho ? You could make an orchestra come up to it, if you had one, I believe, making pursy lips and knitting fingers at them, to hold them, until you had all the cheeks round, all the elbows limber, and all the fingers ready to jump when you threw down the gate and let them out into Squelcho.

Bowsie, you have great fancy, you can fancy your-self in many dresses, stylish without, contented within. You can fancy yourself this minute surrounded by people who are proud of looking as little like any earthly object, that anyone would think of calling " poetic ". You can fancy yourself as a hero of the old style in a creamy smock, all gold edges, and a crimson cloak floating behind you, and a spear in your hand, very fine and scoured on the shaft, but blue clear and very wicked looking about the head. And you can fancy yourself, with your gold filagree work boots and no stirrup sticking down into the middle of the back, of a large cream-coloured horse, and you're lead-ing yourself into battle. Just yourself, because you aren't able to fancy anyone grand enough to accom-pany you. As I look at you, gay old Bowsie, you are rising and getting bigger every way. Your fancy is yeasting you. Good bulk to you now.

We will leave the race-course by the plank bridge with its ancient rail strengthened for the races with a branch with the bark on it, made fast alongside the old member, lapped to it with a good stout cord of wire. The stream flows fast and if it isn't so very deep, it has the weight and gait to roll to the two of us over and over if we fell in and clutched each other. But Bowsie, I know, would never clutch at me, he'd be too proud, to drown in company. His greasy pride ; his pride in his own grease is greater than his madness of self-preservation. He is a man of the first class.

Through this bosky lane, at present fresh and green, no orange peel, no sticky bit of paper from toffee, no cigarette cartons. This is not the way the boys come chirking to the races with the girls. This is the road they take coming away, quarrelling every step with the same girls, and the girls upbraiding them for all the mistakes of the day. But we are ahead of them all, the tall elms are grand and green against the blue sky, just beginning to take on that more slaty, lazy blue of evening.

But one evening, a clearing-up evening after rain, going into a westerly sky to chase the spanish flag under the breaking cloud arch, we'll be dangling our legs from the back of a lorry—got a wink and a nod lift— passing fast along a road, we had struggled along so footsore not so very long ago. Certainly, sometimes, Time, little time, Big Time, is just fore and aft. Time is also above arithmetic, I am inclined to believe it has points round about it—as many as the compass.

This lorry is very convenient. Would you mind, Bowsie, would it be convenient to you to tell me, how you react to the future and the present. Do you feel, do you hope, are you just here, and not of here. Are you all over duckbackery ? You are in, I see, I note, on the floor of the lorry, far enough to push your round legs out in front of you and no more dangling. You are absorbing, from the walls of the empty lorry, the ancient smells of old hay, cement, carrots, tea chests, Demerara sugar, and new timber. You know that on either side of the road, and looping together overhead, are trees full of heavy green leaves. The heavy showers of the day have freshened their tops. You have no plans, but you are gently wishful for a good dinner. You think, if you were to bottle yourself up, that your companion wouldn't be able to read your thought. Not that you care, you aren't ashamed of your thought. If you wanted to be spiteful, you would stop thinking altogether. And you think of the man who took the thin paper bag, and put no thoughts into it only his own hot breath, and held it tight, full of breath, and brought it down bang on the counter, and didn't even frighten the little girl behind the counter washing the pint glasses. And while the bag was in the air the man knew his trick wouldn't come off, and so he made up his mind to be frightened himself with the bag. But, as it turned out, he was more hurt than frightened, for he hit the counter too hard—one nail, a polished nail "On the nail", perhaps, the "On the nail" where the publican rang the soapy-looking half-crowns. But spitefulness is the thing you are incapable of. It's unusual, I believe, but you must be unusual. Now, you begin slipping a thought or two, and you think "This companion of mine, ah, he's drawing up his legs on to the floor now in a sensible manner, not letting them wave and dangle, he's looking pensive again, and now he'll talk. If he was an old drake he'd quack, but if he's an old goose he'll gangle!" And then you remember that you never want to make personal remarks within your thought, except when you're over hungry, and you agree with yourself that personal remarks should be beneath you. And you decide to sing. Singing on an empty stomach empties the head you have found—

> The darling of the Gods,
> With his head in the hay,
> And his feet making trownsies
> In the stars Oh !

You know it goes very well to the rumbling of the road. And the lorry driver looked back just coming up that short hill out of the trees into the turn sharp to the right, and sky over sea beyond very glaring. And the little fat man scared, and no one could blame him, with the large fat woman beside him in the heavy open touring car, was into the hedge, and straightened out again, leaving his paint behind him. So near a thing, and he wasn't ready to die, but the lady was. If she hadn't the wolf instinct to snuggle close to her driver, she would have lost an inch of flesh and muscle over her shoulder and side, and perhaps her cheek and neck, to the hedge. It was a hedge cut well back, and very rasping it was a kind of a sweet briar.

Now, Bowsie, here's the town ahead, with the street not too wide to be comfortable. The lorry driver is so just and hurried that he can't wait for us to compliment him with a drink. What a change, leisure no more. But you have already forgotten him, you are rolling through the front door to the hotel, the coffee-room must be on the right up the hall, because the two windows on the right of the door have tin blinds with holes, and " coffee " on one, and " Room " on the other.

You are going into the house under the shade of the portico, between the pillars painted red one time long ago. You've managed to hollow your back to suggest a military career away back, and you are thinking it was perhaps a pity so many of the fair ones wasted time languishing for you—or was it Casanova ?

" Chops from the grill and lepping hot " is the word on your lips. High in a window opposite, a woman, no longer young, sitting at her window ; she had the whole wide drawing-room over the Grocer's. She sits on a small curly chair by the wide-open window and admires your back. It has suggested command to her. But she thinks it was a pity you'd sat so long grinding on a lorry lately carrying cement. They used to send cement in sacks made of sacking, but now they send it in paper bags. She notices them coming into the town, and she remembers when paper bags only suggested sweets to her sweet tooth. She draws her maid's attention to the cement powdering the Bowsie stern, and the maid says, " He should have spread his silk hankerchief under him." The maid pleases herself in being sarcastic ; she doesn't believe Bowsie had a silk handkerchief. She's ronga ronga, he's got a light washed-out blue-coloured one with large white spots. It's pretty and it's very large and very soft. Bowsie sometimes rubs round his neck inside his neckerchief with it.

The woman of the window was reared by a loving father for her mother died while she was a very young child. The father was a Sea Captain, retired. She had perhaps a dozen suitors, for she was her father's heiress, though what he could leave her was just a thing to make no great talk of, even in that small town. It was enough to keep one person in quiet and decency, if they had no great itch for moving about. The woman had had three lovers ; the first two the father never suspected, but the last, with the penetrating eyes of those clearing up the windows, thinking of the funeral visitors, the old sailor noted. He had him sized up accurately, but he was careless, and he couldn't believe he could have a foolish daughter.

The Maid servant had had one lover, just one, good-looking, curly-haired, rangy, well-meaning—an ignoramus. They got married in the Parish Church, and after a small while, he was not producing any money whatever, and he had a sensitive heart, and so he couldn't bear to think of Sall suffering hard work, with the extra impoverishment to her nature, of having to look at him wearing out the seat of his trousers, sitting on a chair lent the young couple by the bride's mother. So, after thinking for eight hours, he made a plan to make away, and in such a manner that he never could come back. He became a thief, he branded himself. He stole a horse, a large handsome horse ; he took it out of a stable in the inn called the Straight Deal. He rode the horse to a farm away in the North West of the County. He sold it for ten pounds, which, because of the grandeur of the horse, was quite noticeable to every-one as a false price—a price accepted by a horseman in a hurry. Why in a hurry, because he wanted to separate himself from the horse guilt as soon as possible. So the man who gave the ten pounds for the stolen animal got a tongue thrashing from the Chief Magistrate and the owner of the horse got the horse back.

The reason the bridegroom decided on stealing such a fine horse was because he wanted to take something that would make it absolutely impossible for him to return to his native town again. He wanted to have every excuse ready to bar every way home. A thing he never knew was, that his bride, in a long coachman's overcoat, and a hat fallen down to her jaws, was in the yard helping to push him up into the saddle, the night of the stealing. The other helper, was there, by agreement with the thief, to be able to swear to the ruffian. The witness for thievery was elderly then, and he is still alive. He was the confidant of the horse, not because he had any dealings with that noble and observ-ant animal, but just because he had been chatting with the thief in a small grimy public-house at the moment when the plan had finally come to full fruition in the thief's head. The witness was a man of the sea. Some Eastern place had been the little amphitheatre in which he had made his small square fortune. He had done it very quickly. Standing by a dark heavy gate made of a red, naturally red, wood, with a very twisted grain and a strong smell, a badger and wine smell, money had been pushed into his hand in a small sack. It was heavy and queer-hanging, so much so, that he had to put the loaded stick he held in his right hand, under his armpit and use both hands to hold up his sack.

He hadn't done anything valiant, as far as he knew. He expected to be fighting some sort of a rear-guard action out on the stones. But no one appeared to fix bayonets at him. So he supposed everything had turned out well, and he spread the money about his clothes, and wore the sack on his shoulders as a tippet, for even out there it was chilly at night. He walked down to the water-side, he walked aboard a small steamer. She was moving away and he had the satisfaction of pushing with his small foot at the old wooden jetty, sending it back from the steamer's side. He didn't know whether he was passenger or crew, and he had no notion of any kind of the value of the money he had found in his hands that night. He couldn't take the money out and look at it under a lamp—not yet. He slept on deck, with his sack snug round his middle. He didn't want to get a chill now, with money on him. By midday they tied up at a busy port, and this man, with the uncounted money, saw that his little sack had writing on it, which he couldn't read, but police people could, he had no doubt. So he went a long way down the further quays until he came to a dock full of floating timber, and when he found a piece of open water he filled his sack full of stones and sank it. Then he went and sat on a heap of white stones, with a flowery weed growing out of the top of the heap, and being so far away from any habitation, that no one, even with a telescope, could tell what he was at—he was dipping his hands into his pockets, and taking out a fist-ful and trying to count it. He was little wiser. The only thing he knew was that he had some gold pieces, and a main load of silver with a few rum-looking bits that might be old zinc. He jumped up and walked briskly into the town—there was a strong wind blowing off the bay—strong and warm. He dodged about the short streets which came down to the docks from the main part, until he found three money-changers' shops. He chose the one he thought would suit him best. It was half prosperous looking, and that was all right. But he could see as he sauntered up to the door that the clerk inside was a mixture of three races, and drawing nervousness from each. He went straight up to the counter, and gave a beautiful rosy panel a kick that stove it. The clerk reached in a drawer for a revolver. But our sailor smiled with all his teeth, as a jolly merry man with claws, but full of fire-water, smiles on who will be friends. The clerk was relieved. Point to the sailor. There was to be no fighting, no shooting, just a matter of business between two highmen.

The sailor emptied his pockets on to the counter and then turned quickly back to the front door, closed it and shot a bolt, leaving the money unprotected on the counter. That was a second point to him—the man is perfectly sure. Of course he doesn't want dirty robbers from outside slinking in. The sailor then carefully piled up the money in little heaps each made of coins the same class and value. He was sure he had their pictures well in his eye. Then he said " American money ". He was pleased to see the size and value of the wad that three-blooded clerk gave him. In the town where he lives now, they say he must have been a very industrious sailor to save enough money to live on all this time, for he had retired from the salt seas long ago. That was the man who knew that the bride hastened the bolting of the bridegroom, and he also knew the lady of the window had those three lovers, because he was a silent man—a shadow man—who moved about at odd hours, because he was retired from the sea. He was industrious ashore, tilling his garden patch often on a moonlight night. The towns-people said " Once industrious always—go thou and do likewise ". The townspeople knew very little of the sea, which is queer of them for the salt tide comes very near their doors. Just at the westerly end of the town, the road takes a sudden dip down to a bridge, and, if you were looking over the bridge, you might see dark water very close to the river-top, and you would say, " This river with its sedgy banks is very full." But that isn't river water, it's the salt sea. And when the tide is out you'll have just a small trickle of your fresh water on the river floor, and above it, up the sides of the trough, weeds that only grow with sea water over them, twice in the twenty-four hours. Half a mile away to the south is a stony beach, some rocks, a double horn of low cliffs, and then sea. No boats are kept there. The beach is not suitable. For bathing even there is no kind place. Five miles away there is a small seaport, and two miles farther a holiday town with sands for bathing. So anyone that requires a romantic sauce to go with his sea, can make a little excursion to the ocean pleasure town, or to the sea-port. It's only a small seaport for coasters, but cargoes rattle out and romantic shipmen and boys are always about there.

The woman of the window is very fond of the sea. In the summer she walks along the sedgy river bank to the beach and sits on the rocks in the shade of the cliff by the east side. But she likes best of all the early winter evenings just between the lights. She goes down a path under a hedge of many evergreens by the side of a small demesne, where, years ago, in the tall house, the old widow who runs it tried to make some money and amusement with paying guests, but gave up the attempt as hopeless. The evergreens are luxurious and glossy with friendliness to the woman of the window, as she walks under their shelter, dry under foot, to the beach. She comes out on it near to the westerly cliffs. She has a warm coat and she sits down on a rock, where the grass and beach meet, and she watches the sea towards the south.

She was never a traveller, but her father's stories of distant lands had held her, so that she bought an atlas, a fine spacy one, with colours bright, and she followed her father's old voyages, her long supple finger beside his short stiff one. Now, long after his death, she gets books of travel from the library in the seaport, and she follows all in her atlas. Every now and then she buys a book, which she thinks she will like as a reference book of travel—especially if it has a wide margin, because she has a bottle of brown ink and some very fine etching pens, and she likes to make peculiar little half-childish drawings of the inhabitants of distant places from the descriptions in the book, and from the words of her old father. When she is drawing, she always has her head on one side and when Sall looks at the drawings, she is the only one, except the draughtswoman herself, who has seen them, she also places her head carefully over to the artistic angle. Drawing and viewing, to these two, is the same thing. Sall is not impressed with her mistress's cleverness. It is only what she would expect of her—her father's daughter, her private means, her self-contained home,

and Sall to look to her. The two women have no
great feeling of faithfulness the one to the other ; each
is too much engaged.

Sall does not care for going walking to the sea. But
she likes a walk after making her household purchases
at the grocers or the drapers. But she likes the road.
Traffic is slight for the main road, the old coach road,
reconditioned, does not pass this way. So Sall as long
as she keeps to her proper side, is safe enough. She
likes the road, for on it her husband fled away. She
is grateful to it. It's a well-made road, and for all
the mile or two she ever walks, it is never muddy,
even after a week of soft rain.

Bowsie, a lady with the remains of much looks has
been watching you from opposite. She thinks you
look like a man who would have a steady job, with
a pension ; a bus conductor working for a solvent
company, or perhaps a conductor of a tram in the
city.

"No, she don't ; I saw her. She thinks I'm a
Prince in my own part of the country with cows and
horses and footmen in powdered wigs."

She doesn't think that, my friend, you know she
doesn't. She wishes she could think that, but she is
unable to punch up those fanciful romantics of the
thin paper small novels. She's a reasonable being.
She thinks she is, but she's cleverer than that. She
knows the only romance she can ever meet will be
unlike any that ever appeared in print, and the more
print she reads the more she knows it. However,
these are the chairs where we can sit presently after
we have cleaned ourselves and wait for those chops
you are going to order now. Go out to the hall and
find the waiter, he has a nose which could be con-

sidered red, if his whole face was not so full of rose. He is pleased to know that chops are what you want, for he couldn't recommend anything else except bacon and eggs. He is making himself flat against the wall in the little passage, from which you can see the kitchen, the big table, the big pot, and the great frying-pan, with the cook who hates all men who want to eat. She wishes she could make one great feeding of them that would satisfy them all, and their descendants after them—that's the men. The women she believes she could handle with her hand tied behind her back.

In leaning back, the waiter has pressed the back of his head against a coloured print of a coaching scene, with a foxhunt going on alongside the road, and a church spire in the distance. The print is in the old style. But was printed only a couple of years ago in the centre of Europe, and had age varnished on it, and the man who decided on the actual tint of the varnish, was a young man with a long brown face, who had never seen a coach, or people in red coats on horses jumping over fences after a pack of hounds. He didn't want to see them. He ate onions and caraway seeds together, as he stirred the antique shade into the varnish.

The day being soft and warm the varnish is loose and the waiter finds his head is smearing the surface easily. He had had his hair cut this afternoon, and dressed by the hairdresser, with a scented lotion, which made him think that he was an easy catch for bloodhounds. He likes the scent, but he isn't wanting in delicacy, so he smooths away the hair lotion from the varnish of the picture with his napkin, and he calls it a good afternoon's work. The chops are coming. They are here. But Bowsie isn't satisfied, neither am I, but I would take the

easy road, not Bowsie—his blood is up—he sends the chops
back to the cook with orders for her to blacken them, "give
them a grilled look, for God's sake ". And as the waiter,
most woeful looking, carries back the dish to the cook,
Bowsie begins retracting—he's sending a wheedling,
cooing noise down the passage into the kitchen, through
the door which the waiter left open. He wanted to have
the customer hear if the cook forgot herself.

Bowsie's words were intended by him to be "just a
teeny touch of the fire more, Madam, this gentleman
here has a delicate digestion. Crisped he must have,
or he perishes, Madam. He knows he's keeping you
from the pictures. But the first· one isn't worth a
Goddam. You're very good." But what came from
his lips is like a ghastly stream of artificial· silk coming
thin out of a hose, which some people say is one of the
ways artificial silk is spat out. Cook throws the chops
on to the fire on the end of the toasting-fork. She knew
that's what she should have done from the first, for she
sized up my bold Bowsie from the sound of his voice
which first sifted through the back of her kitchen door.
But she had to clear the fire, and afterwards put up with
a kitchen foggy with burning chops. However. " Now
to hell with the lot of them—Hotel Imperial and all."
She bangs her kitchen door just behind the waiter's
coat-tails. She rubs flour on her hands, and she rubs
it off, and then, in the box above the boots, she takes
out her make-up box and, it's deft she is, in that small
scullery of a bootery, and quick. She reddens the
nostrils. She brings out the eyes very bold. She tosses
a lock of hair down her brow and away to the right.
She ties the shining bright blue handkerchief round her
neck. She pulls one arm well up to the armpit, into her
check shower-proof coat, and then rolls herself round

into the rest of the coat. She has her tight shoes on all the while. She leaps out into the yard. Her star is up. As she comes out of the archway the town-owned bus is gathering speed, but she's gasping on the footboard, pulling herself together, under the young eyes of the bus conductor, who wishes her well. His father would have sung : " the full of the house of Irish love, was Mary Anne Malone ", but his son, more genteel, or more gentle, knows that even a pocket Juno gives, and expects, respect.

There are a couple of very good pictures for her—a long love one, nothing in it new, just the old sweet story of the designing, deceitful beauty passing out badly at last, and the honest, plump, cheery madcap coming in at the death. These films down here don't seem so long as they used to be, but the next one's full from the source to the sea. Men with long legs in black tight trousers. Sometimes the ends of the trousers stuffed in high boots, with stars on them, and when these men aren't going down to death underfoot, they are sending other men there. And the cook drinks blood.

After supper walk a mile. Bowsie here would sooner be sitting in his slippers in the corner of the bar, with the shutters shut, and the town privileged ones having quick short drinks—farewells to farewell.

That will come later for you. Now out along the westerly road towards the port, you know the road well. On the crest of the hill that'll make three-quarters of a mile out. We will climb up on the bank beside the gate and look out over the sea nailed down under the moon with the house, Crooked Dell, down below us on the south-east and the tops of the low cliffs before us. Keep in the shade and comfort of the hedge going up the hill.

Now, what do you think of that ? I wonder what he

does think, or does he feel no need for thinking. Does he just turn what his eyes see, or what his reason tells him exists, before him into some easily assimilated condensed, sweetly rectified, spirit, and then drink it, and it perhaps so volatile that it wafts itself away, leaving what some would say was less than nothing. But perhaps those leavings are without measure. Ah, Bowsie, it's you that has the capacity !

Look at that wide melon slice of bay ; see how the water lives where the moon spangles it, just like a beautiful photograph slightly blued. Can you imagine that sea full of ships of the old, decorated, broad-cheeked style, the ones of long ago. Three deckers looking one way and going another. Not as good-looking as a squadron of ducks until they say " quack " with their guns, and then, of course, if there were several of them, of different colours, that made a difference. If you couldn't imagine those old Junos of the seas, when you've seen plenty of lovely models of them, I'm sure we couldn't, either of us, call up the old early hawks of the seas. Open boats with shields along the gunwales and savage beaks on them. On water, we, you, and I anyway, cannot place, be it ever so gently or mistily, a ship from far before our own time. The unchangingness of water resents any wish of ours to optically delude ourselves.

Strange, deep thoughts, these, we might go further and fare worse. But we will continue a little farther along the level top of this road. And remember that while we talk of guns upon the sea, this stripe of it, it is likely, never heard a cannon fired in anger on its surface. For any marauding gentlemen, in showy, dirty linen, who came ashore here, in the middle of their men—that is, embedded half-way between the spear head and the heel, held their fire until they had the mouth of the cannon against the defender's mouth. And their cannon would only be pistols in their hands, unless one small gun was hauled ashore down a board, tilted an easy slope, the same way the board would be tilted if those gay soldiers of fortune were sliding porter down it to their own wide mouths. Perhaps they'd get their little gun on the beach, as if it was a performing pup, and all of them round it, stooping round it, and all talking to it, and saying what a feller it would be for slaughtering the simple Johnnie Natives, and they, the natives, could creep up behind them and kick them as they stooped. That would reduce their weight, bring it down a bit, so that when they turned round, turning in the same, straightening-up motion, the boys of the little patches by the sea would be ready to scythe the heads off them.

Pirates' heads, with saucy turbans on them, hopping up in the air in the night. Very ghastly—if you had any stomach you could not listen to such a moving story of a picture, Bowsie. I think your stomach, perhaps, is no tougher than anyone's, only more shameless. Don't laugh. " Ho, Ho." It's no Ho-Hoing matter to be differently conscienced in your stomach, than other people. Take care ; tread light. There are tacks sitting up on their flat heads for stockinged feet. Wisecrack number one ! But it's absurd to tell you to take care, you are so full of care that you are, in the full meaning of the words, taken one by one, full of care. So full that you are swelled out with it, and it's the care within that keeps you so round and smooth, and wrinkleless, without.

But glance with me along this level road to the westward, that's the way the bus went, and in the rattle of a few minutes, it brought the cook to the shining door

of the Star Cinema. Times long gone we walked this
road many times, and thought it was an adventure, a
contemplation, a determination, a doing and a done.
When we made the pavements of the town, we knew
we had come through something to make them. We
gave way for the poor townsmen who knew nothing of
the wild bracken and furzy country where we lived.
They and their little town. We kept together, you and
I, or however many of us there might be. We stood
about. We called as thickly as our voices would go.
We were watchful any sudden movement of the townspeople might be an aggression. We took no chances.
Down by the quayside we felt able to look about us
without fear, for there we were among men of the wide
world, travellers, men of the hilly sea, like ourselves,
distrustful of these townsmen with their yellow-lighted
shops. We were proud enough of the light from our
own few shops. But our thoughts were adapting themselves to circumstances and in comparison with the seaport, Bowsie, you thought, then, as I did, however you
may think now, that we were of the wild lands compared to the snuffy sugar- and tea-smelling shopkeepers
of the town—they and their mouldy doctors, lawyers
and schoolmasters, and daughters. Their sons, we had
seen them running through the fields near our little
town. Paper-chasing. And we have lived in other
towns, no bigger and no smaller than the one now at
our back, and it was always the same ; we felt we could
wriggle our ways through their small alleys and shelter
by their gables in a storm, and live, some hours anyway,
on their air. But the bigger town, the nearest bigger
town, was enemy stuff, the air was not nutritious. The
view was a view. The streets, and corners, had painted
names. The place would be able to show itself on a

map. But the little towns we knew and where we had
been owners in the spirit, they've no maps, only the
large-sized ordnance maps which say too much. But
there is for them some other thing " mechanised " some
would say, more mechanical than a map, a compass in
our brows. There, between the left and the right eye,
swinging between flesh and spirit, a breathless thought
is always pointing for us to one of our small towns.
Bowsie, my dear friend, Bowsie.

Through this larger seaport town, now that thinking
on the spirit has lifted us a little off the ground, we can
pass gaily on and, for the time, forget our old jealous
fear of the townsmen. We will even run round its
corners, winding into sea winds, or sodden with still
sea air, and nudge each other and say that the paint is
as wasted away, and bluey green, on the shop fronts
close to the old fish quay, as it was long ago. How
is it done by them that they should always have their
paint moulding away and yet not gone completely.
Perhaps they paint with mildew paint? No, it is the
painter's hand, that is white, and freckled and shivery
in a sea dew, the day he paints the fronts he never
paints the " Brandy " on the perforated metal blind ;
that is always incorruptible. It has an inner eye. But
no outer eye can see into the dark bar. Bowsie, you
will be wanting, I feel certain, to visit these haunts
to-morrow. But now turn your toes round again to the
eastward, and stately, as behoves men of vision whose
feet have to be watched going down hills, we will rejoin
our old little town, and you will be in your slippers,
telling common lies to the special trained listeners in the
hotel bar. And there will still be the small plated
teapots up on the shelf, and the two lemons by the
buttery hatch, two sentinels of the yellow light. Their

brothers were there before them. If you told me that over the years they came always from the same lemon grove, I could find it in my credulity to accept your telling. The stout proprietress in her black dress, with the velvet stripes on the shoulder-blades, will, in a little while, in a half-hour, be looking at the clock and saying " Time, Time, O time very much gentlemen," and handing out a silver cake-dish with ten small sandwiches of toast and ham paste. Late to make a new thirst. But such is human apprehension that all these old customers, called to their ebbing tide, will take each a fresh deep draught, against thirst to come. The proprietress had never planned these sandwiches, they were a tradition when she inherited the house, and she carried it on.

You are now away, Bowsie, on your flood of common lies, flowing gently towards the whirlpools and the rapids of your uncommon lies, your adventures in places you never heard of until some geographical memoried spectre of the shadows in the smoke breathed them on to your tongue.

These people don't believe you, as they believe that to-day is the day of the month they think it is. They don't believe you, as they believe that a large number can be divided by a smaller one. But when they go carefully along the nobbly ways to their homes, they will say to one another—you're in all their thoughts— " He seems a very comfortable-looking man." But while you sit in your slippers, with your back turned to the outer wall, the window, shutters up on the street. The memory of a shadow passes along that street close to the wall.

The woman of the window walked along there at this

time of a night long ago, and with her, conveying her home, walked a woman holding an infant child wrapped in an old shawl in her arms, and two men, one clumsy walking, a man of the fields, the other light on his toes, a man of the sea, the man who knew so much about the town. Water is dripping from the garments of them all. All are without a dry stitch except the shawl that wraps the baby round. There had been heavy rain all the day—spilling rain and the river was up, and the tide coming in. The water was within half a foot of the bridge arch. The woman lately at the window, wrapped in an oilskin, had been down seaward, and coming back she went close to the river to watch the brown flood slide over the top of the salt tide. There was a green island, green even in the night, the colour shone. On the island the woman saw a child, not a yearling yet, lying on the grass half in the sucking waters, but still its face and head clear. It was gently wailing a small cry. The woman did not run away screaming " help ". She measured the height of the water to the bridge—she knew the chance —she knew the bottom on the river was gravel—at low tide and with a summer stream, all would see the river-bed. She knew it well. She walked strongly into the river, only a rusty wire laid from post to post across the river was her hold ; the waters were round her body and they came in the centre of the channel she must cross, up to her armpits. The river-bed rose a little near the island and she placed her arms on the green grass, and brought them round the child. Then she roared " Help, help, help ". And her voice carried along the road into the street, through a window-pane, behind which two men sat by a cobbler's bench, waiting for the cobbler to make his way home full of porter.

And to listen to what they had to tell him of the politics which had changed since last they spoke with him. These men, the sailor and the labourer, came out at the trot to the " help, help, help ". They cried back " Hold on, we're coming " not knowing to what they came. Back on the bridge they saw—it was the hour of the night when men are stiff-legged, but these men were agile as angels in clouds, and they stepped down into the river, as though they walked into some noble roman bath of style. The labouring man saw something in the child's dress that he knew, a patch on a little shoulder, and he called " Mary Devany's child. It's Timmy she calls him." And there above them over the bridge side was looking, Mary Devany. A damming of the river with a falling log had driven a wave of it into her second room, behind the tiny kitchen, and there her Timmy in his cradle was found, and swept out into the night, the cradle was of wicker-work, and soon was half submerged and rolling. And so out rolled Timmy. It was the call of " help ", which meant nothing by the time it reached, through crannies, and round corners, to the mother ear, which made her uneasy and observant. That was all. No more than if a new crack came in the furniture on a dry summer night. But observation made Mary Devany look above her floor, and there, under the door of her back room, there was brown water. And when she stept down she stepped into water, and saw before her the shadow of the night of an open door, and then she heard " help, again ". She had run out of her house along a lane between high stones, then to the right, down a dip, and then the bridge. The labourer and the sailor called " All right, all right "—and kept calling " all right ", as they walked into the water on each side of the rusty wire, not trusting any pull of the weight on it. They shepherded the first woman and Timmy along back to safety and before they reached the shore, they had the mother in the water with them. She threw her shawl down on the sod and came in to them. Timmy was a good child ; he had the spirit that takes because it can give. To him it was just and right that four grown people should risk their lives for him. His own mother's life, yes, and the lives of three others, two of whom, to their knowledge, had never seen him before. They all risked their lives, for the force of the stream was savage and mild by turns, and the banks of Tim's Island was caving in and falling down ; though Tim's was its best point on which to leave an infant lying on such a night. As the four grown people staggered away back over the bridge, the labouring man, and the woman who looked out the window, were the palest. The sailor was grey-faced, and Mary Devany's paleness was broken on her cheeks, and up to her eyes, with crimson fire. She carried her child away from her home of danger, though her front room was safe enough. She carried him through the town to her sister's house. Her sister was almost a nurse—she knew a great deal, and she was well prepared for rolling little Timmy Devany in blankets, and she had always a good fire burning to make a cup of tea. Indeed, John Devany, Timmy's father, was sitting on a creepy stone having a sound sweet cup of tea, waiting to be joined by his wife, when it was the intention that the two sisters Devany, and a crony from across the street, would play cards for a melodian, which had been won on a threepenny ticket by a brother of the crony's in a lottery in the seaport. Now when Devany and Julia looked to the door, saying " Who's here ", they saw the four bringing the child, all in their clinging clothes, and smelling of flood water. And Timmy asleep in the glory of his little wet body and the dry shawl.

Sixteen years ago, to almost a day, that happened, and Timmy's a messenger boy for a bootshop in the sea town. In the summer-time, the Dolan family, who own the bootshop, keep open a branch shop at a pleasure resort, by a long stretch of sandy bay, another few miles to the westward. To that outlying shop Timmy goes, on a bicycle, on Saturday evenings, and he stands outside and sells tins of boot cream and bootlaces, and sees that no seaside swimmer fanatic steals boots from the outside display. It's a wonder they are able to keep that branch booterie open so late into the summer nights, for even with summer-time, towards the end of the season, Timothy Devany is often standing by his charges after the shop is lit up. Even though the sun is still throwing up the glow of its embers over the lip of the sea. Some double staffing, or owners working, keeps the shop business full tilt in spite of all labour regulations.

I suppose it is honest, for there are other shops in that pleasure town, who would be glad enough to see the Dolan family stay at home, where the parent shop stands. And if there was a screw loose anywhere, it's they that could loose it more and more and little by little, till the first puff of trouble would fall it out. Timothy Devany gets his half-day anyway. He views the world from the bookstall at the railway station to the end of the jetty which runs out to the eastward of the fish quay. He is now an orphan—alone in the world without brother or sister. His father and mother dead six or seven years. Even his aunt, who saw him, after his mother, the first woman to see him, after his saving from the water by the woman, who, Bowsie here thought, was thrilled, even perhaps only slightly, but still thrilled, by the sight of him rolling home into the hotel.

Devany knew the story of the night they snatched him back. He was very thankful to all who baptised him with romance.

A change in the river higher up in the valley was throwing too much of an accumulation of earth against the island, where young Timmy had lain waiting for his rescuers. And so the island was cut away by order of a Council. But Timothy, running about his native town, was always calling to all the townspeople to say to themselves a little good thought to romance.

Even Bowsie Munschausen, if you weren't fully occupied telling your stranger tales to these silly old topers, I wouldn't recall to you what that seaside resort looks like on a Saturday night in early autumn. I think, my thirsty-tongued friend, you'll have to remember soon that some of these topers read the same print as yourself, perhaps. You know, and I know these people want to believe that they are hearing adventure at first hand from the adventurer. But you know, if you'll give yourself a nudge, that as well as all that old dulcet preserved wise saw which says " you can ", all can, " fool all the people some of the time, or some of the people more of the time, or more of the people all of the time ". But all the fools aren't people, and there is anyway a second sort of fooling, a sort of making a temporary fool of oneself, and that's very nice, but it has as the speaker said years ago, about socialism, a miasmatic character, and in fact, it's a sort of artificial silk camera obscura in which your admired sits. And to stretch, my boy, the simile as far as it will go. It is

very easy to put a finger through it, and then the
ordinary, everyday, washy eyes see you for a liar and
a plagiarist. But on with the devilment and strife, and
talk fast for the portcullis will soon smack down behind
the heels of the last of " Time, gentlemen ". You will
put your head out of the door, as they go tumbling their
ways home, and you will look up at the sky with racing
clouds. The clouds always are racing when you look at
them by night. You'll look up and then—and then,
your thought prayers will wash your lies away.

But I now see clearly the whole stretch of the seaside
town as it was last Saturday night, when Devany stood
his ground by the trays, and shelves, of boots and shoes
and the creams, brown, black, white and tony red,
or is it Tony, and who was tony, some of it's foxy red,
and some of those shoes tinted so, are very foxy.

Tim Devany was standing in idleness, the season
being now almost done here ; that is, a live description
for the last of the good-spending visitors were a brother
and three sisters from America, and the steamer that
carries them to their present home there, is not long
out of sight.

Before Devany stretched the sea, and there was a
green streak or line in the sunset at which he gazed,
and that was a sign that to-morrow would be blustery.
But now the sea inshore is smooth enough. On Devany's
right along the pavement ran the shops and two hotels,
Ocean View and Mountain View. Both could claim
both, for if the front windows looked on the sea, the
back ones looked away to the mountains. They could
not be seen there at this hour of the evening, but on a
fine, clear day a blue nubble or so could be traced to
the nor'-west.

The road in front of Devany was strong, modernised

and steam rolled, it had no true footpath or building on the seaside, but a kerb marked where the road ended and the sands began. The sand came up on the road under heavy weather with high tides, but some bent grass kept most of it in its place, and what came over was shovelled back by a special band, employed by the house owners.

To the westward, low sandhills, more heavily cropped with bent, made a shelter, kept out flowing sand, and gave a feeling of security to the stationer's, and one of the hotels, as well as to the three grocers, standing side by side, clinking their glasses against each other, in the evenings, when the weather outside was unpleasant to holiday-making men.

There were no sandhills in front of Devany and he could sweep his eyes along a stretched horizon of salt sea and feel romance stirring in his joints.

That was last Saturday—to-night Devany is striding up and down the quay in the seaport. He has his arms folded, and is thinking of going to Hollywood and becoming a film star, before the bloom is off him.

Beyond the sea resort, ten miles along a twisted coast, there is a huddle of wooden houses, on the top of a low cliff. The biggest house has a lobsided veranda running round the four sides of it, and night and day, from a pole, which is against the south-west corner, the stars and stripes hang, or at this time of year, more often it is flying out stiff before a westerly blow. The flag is never taken in at nightfall. It is very likely the proprietor of the hotel doesn't take his boots off. The proprietor of the hotel is a Michal C. Hayden, Christopher Hayden. He loves the flag on his hotel, for he spent forty years of his life in America. He says so, though some of the time he spent in Liverpool. Bowsie here saw him there, he knows, fifteen years ago. He was attracted to him by his native accent, which carried through his seemingly exaggerated American accent. But it wasn't exaggerated, it was natural to him to pick up the accent of those about him. The underlying rumble from the native hills was caused by some formation of his throat and mouth, no doubt. Five years ago he bought a stretch of poor land on the top of the low cliffs, and with the help of two ballad-singer carpenters,—he had known them in his youth, before the call of poverty, of the hard road, had won them from their firesides. The ballad singers liked singing better than carpentry. But Hayden had a driving power about him, or he was able to look like a driver. He had so often, in those forty years, to set his shoulder to some wheel belonging to a driver, and appear as one himself to deceive a dog. He did not deceive the ballad singers ; they gave in to him because of a weakness in the will. The same which had taken them wandering with the green and white fluttering of ballads. It was not that they had run away from home. It was that they were away and did not run home the time they knew Sukey the kettle was beginning to sing.

There are ten small bedrooms in the hotel. It is called the Pride ; it was to have been the Pride of the Plains, that was Hayden's idea when he first engaged the lettering painter from the far city. The letters were large and thought compelling. Being of a bright glossy blue, outlined with black, with a pale yellow thickness. When the Pride was finished, Hayden thought the plains were so far distant, the plains of which he was thinking, that it would be absurd for his hotel to boast itself of them. He didn't mean the plains of Kildare, of course he didn't, he meant the great plains of America, where he imagined he had roamed himself, though he was only once on the very edge of them, and what roaming he ventured on very nearly caused him to be left stranded by the shack and water-trough where the thirsty engine drank. So Hayden thought of the Pride of the Sea and that seemed presumptuous, and then he smalled it to the pride of the Atlantic, and then to the pride of the Bay, and that he felt would put out the other hotel men at the resort and the seaport, and even irritate Miles Banyan, the curious tide-left-patched mariner, who had a small public house, in a village far on the tip of the westermost horn of the great bay. For Miles had once or twice put up an ingenuous wanderer who had the cleverness to make a holiday out of eating lobsters and watching birds flying about a marsh.

Hayden was a timid man when it came to annoying other people ; and the elements, he had the greatest respect for. The cliff-head sloped away inland, and sheltered his hotel as it was a one-storey building. It is true he had spent a great deal of money on a wind-mill pump with a high iron tower, the wind-catching wheel whirling sweetly round and round. There are no groans, and croaks, from it, for every now and then Hayden climbs up the tower and sluices the axles of the mill with grease. " Running water in every bed-room and three baths " are the Hotel Pride's pride within a pride. And though the proprietor often sleeps in his boots, from a memory of his wild life, he is a hardy and constant bather—dead cold water more than half the time. The arrangement for heating the water is working well only when there are visitors about. They may start coming in June ; they are here July, August, and September—every room is occupied. In September, sometimes, they imitate the proprietor and sleep in their boots, laid down on chairs. So much do they cling to their good-byes to the sea.

From the hotel a rough cart track, through an opening cut in the cliff, goes down to the shore. The track was cut long ago for the wrack-gatherers. On either side of the hotel stretch out half a dozen houses, two general stores, a cobbler's and a tailor's. Then some lodges belonging to people whose homes are in some of the inland towns. They come for the school holiday time—their happy children forming a chorusing background for the mature travelled little crowd of hotel visitors.

Many of Hayden's visitors are Americans home for a summer, and a few bacchanalian servants of the public on the eve of retiring on pensions. Snatching at life, in the fear that it may be snatched from them, on the brink of freedom. The public servants, in their conversation, are careful and truthful. The rest are, some of them, born liars, but all, taking something from the space and air about them, are under no trouble to found their anecdotes, autobiographical or otherwise, on any poor undersod of truth. Each has his or her guiding star by which they steer their way, each visit they have made to the old land, and some have been three or four times, is made to where no one who knows them in the country of their adoption is already fitted in.

It would have surprised me to be present while the carpentering ballad singers and Hayden were raising up the Pride. It was the Pride which was first started. When it was half finished, Hayden, cute enough, began the smaller houses. The first storekeeper and the lodge renters came the same season.

Hayden paid his ballad singers good wages and himself cooked the bacon and cabbage for the dinner in common. And he thought he would have been able to depend on the two as listeners to the story of his adventures in the States on his way to his fortune. But they were as little in love with lectures as they were with carpentering, so they sang and recited, verse and verse about, from all the ballads that they knew. When Hayden used to say " What's that from ? " politely to one verse, for answer, he'd be given a verse, or a couple of lines, from some other old song.

" I remember one time, I was in a little town in one of the Western States. I'd just got in, and I remember it was on a creek and there was a steamer, a wooden steamer, tied up to a pier, and just as I got in, she blew up. Why, the roar of her was like about a ten thousand buffalo bellowing one bellow."

" That's right :

Now to conclude and make and end, I take my pen in hand,
John O'Brien is my name—and flowery is my land.
My life was spent in merriment, when first my love I seen
For her abode lay near the road, in a place called sweet Gurteen."

" Right, right."

> " And I don't know the reason
> That slander is in Season
> Nor can we see the reason
> That it will be out of date.
> When truth was first left naked,
> Lest they should all mistake it,
> Or for a monster take it
> To obstruct the ' Christian Faith '.
> But their laws must all be changed
> Their ministry is deranged
> Or can it be hypocrisy
> That can never be exchanged.

> Shall this contribution
> Cause a second revolution
> And bring down persecution
> On our island of Saints."

" I seen an island once, in the Mississippi it was, it was a long island—looked for all the world like a battle-ship and the people that lived on it were battlers, I can tell you that."

" That's true, every word of it."

> In France once my Eagle he reigned most victorious,
> The Tuilleries were his chief royal nest.
> The birds of the country they loved and adored him
> Because one and all they thought him the best.
> When from Elba he landed
> With their wings expanded
> They flew to his standard and that speedily
> It was at Grenoble they raised their notes
> To the sweet tune of Vive l'Eagle, said she . . .

It was the tall one gave that out with full style and the harness rattling. Harnessed in poesy—he was. He, when he sang, or even recited, always gave the full volume of the sound he was able to command. And his throat was very supple at this time. The short one sang good and lusty. But in recitation he carried the words forward on a moaning whirl. But both gave the rhythm its room enough, and scope full and valuable. They could, if they liked, do the prose style elocutionary potato-voiced entertainment which they had heard in a circus ; when they went in under the tent edge. They never paid money to go into a circus. They came in for nothing always. But they never spoilt a circus, when they knew well they could have done so. They had many a good two-man song that if they once got into the middle by the pole and raised it. They'd stop any circus act. The double jockey, Turpin's ride to York, the Plunge of Death, or the Riding Machine or any of them. One time they stood in the city, by a tram-car, on a Saturday, raining fit to quench Hell, and they sang the people down off the tram into the street. And it was a man called Jimmy Buckley, and that was a coincidence, who took off his belt and made the ring for them, and of all songs they hit on it was " White Wings ", and that's hardly a two-man song. And when they were so politely, or as politely as they could, interrupting Hayden, their employer, they would consider, for the twinkling of a lip, giving him White Wings.

White wings they never grow weary.

> " Oh, Garryowen's gone to rack,
>   Her blood is on the outlaw's track,
>   The night hangs, starless, cold and black,
>   Above the shining river."

" Another time I was working in a druggist's in a little one-horse town, down, way down, south, and they got up a fancy ball in that town, and a couple of lads, going to the ball, came in to the store where I was. They were dressed like birds and they wanted some stuff with a name on it I'd never heard. I hadn't got any diploma. I was just a cleaner. I thought they were a couple of hold-ups, because I hadn't heard anything about the fancy ball. So I took up the bottle they used in the store for fighting the young boys that came in trying to steal the coltsfoot rock. I pulled the stopper out and gave it to the bigger bird to smell, and when he got his beak at it, it blew his head off. It was some prime smelling salts, I tell you, men ! "

> " What can't be cured must be endured love,
>   So fare you well, I'm going away."

" I tell you when the first bird got screeching with the smelling salts he fell back against his brother bird, and the other songster gave him a hook of the leg, just like a game bird using his spur. In a minute they were into it. I got the smelling salts under the counter safe. But just as they were rising at each other, with their second winds, in the middle of the floor, the Boss came in. He was a qualified man, most respectable, always dressed like a minister, and he put his hands on their breasts to force them apart, and if he did they went, I tell you, men, they went back, among the bottles and that brought them down. And there they were, a moving tableau. The Boss like a statue of ebony, the two roosters screeching and scraping their heels in the broken glass, and the stink of all those chemicals smoking on the floor. I moved out—I adjourned."

" You did right."

> " Tho' Garryowen's gone to rack,
>   We'll bring her golden glories back."

" He did right to leave."

> " My heart is sad and lonely, Johnny dear,
>   To think you'd leave Sally here,
>   For Auburn hair did my heart ensnare,
>   And your gimlet eyes bore a hole through me.
>   The night was still, the air was balm,
>   Still dews around were weeping,
>   No whisper rose o'er ocean's calm,
>   Its waves in light were sleeping."

" Druggists were always very respectable men ; I liked their society."

> " Oh, reg a geg geg
>   Let go me leg,
>   Or I'll dunt you with me horneo ! "

The night is advanced a good way, sitting here remembering in a hotel bar. Bowsie has gone out into the shades a little way to see his dumbfounded listeners a little farther than usual. The landlady is asking me if I require anything else. She gives a glance at the little shelf where Bowsie has left his last drink ; it is made with hot water, and he has left an old envelope on the top of it, and I see the steam moving about composing the sugar and whiskey vapours together. He has, whenever he could, been in the habit of so arranging a last drink for himself after a night of romantic story. It symbolises something to him. His ancestors have been composed of the vapour of symbols of their own. They learnt them at their mother's knees or while holding their father's walking-stick, while they lit his pipe on windy days. Bowsie, when he walks by a churchyard, always walks pigeon-toed. This is to keep them, those toes, as long as possible, from turning themselves up to the daisies.

The landlady pulls down the greeny-brown old wooden shutter which cuts off the bar of bottles itself, from the bar-room lonely. And I sit here waiting for Bowsie to come home. Bowsie's name means nothing to him. I gave it to him because I knew what a Bowsie was and he didn't. He, I guessed, would be too proud to ask me what it meant, and I was too proud to tell him. He thought it was something to do with an effigy that was blowsie floury, and an old mate.

I'm thinking again of the hotel builders—there they sat, the three of them, on old sugar boxes, the ballad singers, and the " returned yank " hotel-keeper—that would be if the stars were right.

"And it was a beautiful night, the stars shone bright,
And the moon o'er the water played——"

" I know, I know, I know."

"When a Cavalier to a bower drew near, a lady to serenade."

> "Since the year 47
> He lies in Glasnevin."

" I remember that one."

" You would to be sure, says Marshall Saxe, says he, says he ' Sire ', says he ' my liege ', says he the Irish troops remain."

> "We are the boys of Wexford
> Who fought with heart and hand
> To burst in twain the galling chain
> And free our native land."

" In Bodenstown Churchyard there is a green grave,
And wildly along it the Winter winds rave,
Small shelter, I ween, are the ruined walls there
When the storm sweeps down on the plains of Kildare."

" Then through the keyhole he loudly shouted : ' I've got Master here. But I'll give up keys—Heaven and all, when you set old Ireland free.' Now is that bad talk ? Well, in a sense, I might have heard worse. But at the same time, it's hardly blasphemy "—

> "Now, dear son, I am very poor
> The last shift of all I tried
> I never knew what hardship was
> 'Till the day your father died.
> I had to sell the little goat
> The day the bailiff came,
> 'Tis bad to be a widow
> For it is a lonesome name."

" Give me three grains of corn, mother." She said " give

me three grains of corn," so help us God. Three grains
and that only she said. "Give me three grains of corn."

"I heard a man once and him singing on the streets
of Baltimore. He was a coloured man, but he had an
Irish name, and no one but took pride in it, his voice
was so sweet—he was but young. He was a kind of
brown or golden colour; he sang 'The Mantle so
green' and 'The Round Towers of Ireland'. I am
not able to hold them in my memory. I was at that
time all for listening, and I never had the honour of
seeing those songs in print."

"But what do you want with print when you have
your good dinner eaten, and myself and my friend
here to instruct your memory :—

> "I am a bold rover—I travelled the nation all over,
> I travelled it over my fortune to try,
> To earn my living by cheerfully singing
> The praise of Erin I will till I die."

"Don't be talking."

"There's a penny for salt and pepper and twopence for mutton
    pies,
Three farthings for a beefsteak with a pair of rolling eyes,
There's twopence-halfpenny for a broom, to sweep away the
    dirt,
And a halfpenny worth of calico to mend your Sunday shirt."

> "Like a raging King of Troy
> All in your uniform."

"My father's a shepherd ; he keeps sheep on yonder hill,
And you may go to him and ask his good will
In truth I will, Lassie, I'll go instantly
All among the green bushes my Jenny meets me."

> "Though o'er my grave no banners wave,
> A pauper's plot you scan.
> Enough—you'll murmer o'er my grave
> 'He like a soldier ran'."

" As your hair grows white, I will love you more,
Though your eyes were brighter in the days of yore."

" The sun in the gorgeous East chaseth the night
When he rises refreshed in his glory and might
But where does he go when he seeks his sweet rest ?
Oh, does he not haste to the beautiful West.
Then come there with me; 'tis the land I love best,—
'Tis the land of my sires—'tis my own darling West."

" For the bosom of beauty itself might expand,
When bedecked by the Shamrock of old Ireland.
There's a charm that no Irishman's heart can withstand,
In the beautiful shamrock of old Ireland."

" There's a glade in Aghadoe, Aghadoe, Aghadoe,
There's a sweet and silent glade in Aghadoe."

" But, come, a bolt of work wouldn't do us any
harm. If we want to get a roof on the timber hotel
before winter comes and the Mills of God go grinding
the hailstones o'er the land. Master, lead on to the
workshop." And those two ballad singers, by always
giving their employer something to hold, if it was only
a joist upright, got the hotel built, roofed by winter,
and complete by early summer. That is complete, all
as far as the carpenters' work could take it.

Hey, Bowsie, I see you sitting there sipping. There
he is slowly swallowing his night-cap, and I am round-
ing off for myself the building of the timber hotel.
After the ballad singers had done their part, the plumber,
and the painter, and the glazier came, and by August
the house was shining, smelling of the shine, elegant
and enticing.

Regardless of everything, except a silent manner,
Hayden engaged the small and sufficient staff, and sent
cables to his friends in New York and Boston, and

Baltimore, who were to push off his first batch of visitors, well primed for nowhere but the Timber Hotel by the wild waves. Four visitors arrived together. The hotel motor met them at the railway station away across two wide bogs, and through a gap in the mountains. After the four they came in dribs and drabs. Two of each kind from England, they electrified the transatlantic visitors —their speech was so very near to the speech of the people eating hunt breakfasts in pillared halls, and stately homes, in the films. The first of all that came. They were the real thing ! The Miss Mullaines—Kate and Molly ; born in the States, but their father and mother had gone out in their youth. The sisters had been in Ireland twice already. Their black brows contracted over their deep violet eyes, and they shook their dark locks, sitting there in a motor squeezed together by the driver. They had seen the ocean through the beach road cutting, and taken in the wooden village, and the flagstaff with its sagging flag. They had what they had not yet had on their visits, a setting to fit their wild colleen hearts. If the balladsinging carpenters had been near, and singing, they would have stopped their singing mouths with kisses.

The half-light—the wiry grass rustling about them, the lighted windows in the hotel ; they were being lifted before they knew it, by some energy within, out of the car, on to the veranda of the hotel. There action came to their relief ; they clasped each other's hands and danced a few steps of an Irish dance, learnt all in a little room where, among the mementoes of ancestors long gone to their foolish account, a small old woman had held an Irish dancing class in Brookly.

Mrs. Kearney, the third visitor, was revisiting for

the first time in forty years her native land. She stood watching the sisters dancing, and she remembered before she married Kearney, and he was dead thirty years, she had danced a dance—the same, and she recalled the great noise that was all about her while she danced it, so vividly that she instinctively clapped her strong hands to her ears, though the silence there, now, was so great that the tapping of the sister colleens' light feet hid any other sound to all but her. When she was dancing, it was on the deck of a steamboat, on a bay, and green flags were waving. Three fiddles were playing for the dancers, and the sound of roaring songs were booming under the sounding boards of the deck above. And by her the wide-open door of the saloon with the shining bar and the bar-men in the white jackets, and the high drinks tossing, and the independent singing. But she liked the quiet place as well as the old battering memory.

The last to leave the sandy road and gracefully lean against an upright of the veranda, was the fourth visitor —the Judge ; they said " the Judge ". He told them to. He had seen a Judge—he got a good view of him·; the place he stood in was arranged so that the Judge could have him well in view, and the jury too, and so our Judge—Judge Goldlock—got a good look at the Court.

It had been a close call—though he wasn't guilty, and he left the Court no worse in reputation than when he went in. But he was guilty of several other things, so he waited until late in the evening, when the Judge was well rested, washed, shaved, and had done full honour to a supper full of little dishes—very pungent. Goldlock asked to see the Judge alone ; locked

the door, showed he was unarmed, not that the Judge
cared a thrawneen about that. He felt so full of good
food that he did not believe in the bullet that could
pierce him. Goldlock said he had an Irish grandmother, and that he had come to make a clean breast
of it. He said he was thankful for the fair deal he got
in Court from the Judge, and he said justice was main-
tained for he was not guilty of that crime. But he had
another crime on his conscience, and on the Judge's
word that he would forget it as soon as told, he would
tell it. The Judge grunted and Goldlock told him a
good ringing story about a crime, which he just thought
up for the Judge's entertainment. It was a showy
crime—life taken, but so that by no possibility could
an innocent man suffer for Goldlock's man-killing.
The Judge was impressed and pleased. Before he had
thought much, he was lighting a very nice cigar offered
him by the confessed killer, and then the killer was
gone and the door closed behind him before the Judge
had thought of asking Goldlock why he confessed at
all. He wasn't called Goldlock then, the initials of his
name then were J. N., and every Christmas he used to
send a pretty card to the Judge, and in Roman letters
on it, such things as " MAKING GOOD ", " STRAIGHT EVER
SINCE ", and always signed " J. N.". And it was perfectly true—Goldlock never did any single illegal act
after he left the Judge's supper-room. He christened
himself Goldlock and kept the Irish grandmother.
When he sent the Christmas cards, he gave an address,
an accommodation address, box such and such a
number. Well, there came a day and the Judge died,
after letting off a whole bunch of prisoners, who were
surprised. Soon after he was gone a notice appeared
in a great many papers—" If ' J. N.' can remember

what was the Judge's last mouthful, and will call at a lawyer's office in Washington—he will hear of something to his advantage ". Goldlock called, just as quickly as he could borrow the fare and run to the lawyer's office. The door of the private office opened ; he went in ; it closed behind him. The lawyer, a wide-faced man, a leonine face, but amusable, locked the door and then, coming very close to Goldlock, said : " Well, Mr. J. N. The last mouthful, please," and Goldlock said : " Dill pickle and banana ". The lawyer said : " You win ", and handed him a long comfortable wad of bonds. He called himself " judge " as a memorial to his benefactor, and he was proud and glad that he had been so many years on the narrow path, for he knew that this money would keep him, now his tastes were refined and quiet, in a really beautiful peace. All the anxious wrinkles fled from his brow in one hour. He breathed in thankfulness and smiled happiness. He lay back in a barber's chair and had eve smoothering that a barber can give a middle-aged man, who has worried long, but knows the prices on the primrose path come very high. He looked when he came out on the street again like a Faust who had sold his soul, and then found there was a crack in the document and got it back again. He was an absolute success.

The Judge came to the Timber Hotel year after year, and sat on the veranda later into the autumn evenings than any of the visitors. The other three first footers never came to the hotel again. They came to Ireland many times. Mrs. Kearney, until she could come no more in the body, for the last time she had her trunk packed, and was waiting to call up the Express Company to take it away. She sat and rested in a chair and died there. She had expected her end about that time. Though she knew if she got on the steamboat and was alive there long enough for its prow to cut the water on the Irish road, then she would get her refreshment from her own land and live to return again to New York, that she might die, not in a room of death, but looking through a doorway into such a room. And so, as her eyes filmed over, she saw the doorway of her small apartment open with a faint blue light flecked with yellow sun—and she was gone.

Kate and Molly visit different parts of the country every year. Their faces are getting lined before their time with the emotions they so wildly fling themselves to, when they feel Irish soil beneath their feet. One or two grey threads have shown above the Irish brows, but not for long. As soon as seen they are dissolved away into darkness, and so it will be as long as black dye, to restore the original colour, is on the market. They are the colleens of colleens.

But the Judge comes no more—his face there, like a Cæsar on a coin, used to look so splendid in the evening light on the veranda, taking its place, a standard of beautiful line, among perhaps a dozen profiles of every angle that forces character forward into view.

The last visit was perfect to the end. The chauffeur drew down the curtain ; he helped the Judge with just a touch under the elbow, and a hand about the waist ; he helped him into the hotel motor, that was taking the last visitors of the year to the railway. He had never been helped in or out before on that coast. The chauffeur knew it was farewell by the largeness of the tip the Judge gave him. The notes were folded up into a tight wad, and pressed into his palm, with the Judge's last handshake, and there was a slight squeeze within the manly grip.

The Judge is alive yet and will be for many years. But he takes his rest now where the grandmothers themselves were cosmopolitans, sometimes in the mountains, sometimes by the sea. He rests because he is tired, tired of sitting in picture houses. That is his occupation, almost his business. He has never failed to see every new film he hears of. He tramps from cinema palace to cinema palace—it keeps him fit in body. And the stories he sees before him on the screen are nails driving nails out, so, though they tire him, because the excitements play on the cords of his heart, they do not clumber his heavy load.

Among the mountains, or by the seashore, he gazes for a time at nature, and becomes a tree, or a wave, for half an hour, every day. He has given up all the trouble of setting his profile to look the Judge, and is often now very chatty. English tourists when they see him want to listen to him at once. They think he must be some old Indian fighter or trapper, or cow-puncher king, retired. But the other guests see in him the tree-like, wave-like pulsation which makes them think not of a Judge, he has let the title slip away from him, but of Law itself.

Ah, Bowsie, you're for your bed at last. I was gathering goats' wool. To-morrow, bright, and fairly early, we walk west.

The street is nice and dry as we pass along it. We meet the Woman at the Window. She is stepping from the pavement in front of us. She has been to the grocer's to buy a small tin of salmon ; it will make a light lunch for herself and her Sall. She eats tinned salmon because her father loved it best of all kinds of fish. He had preserved some of the labels from the earliest tins. After his death she found them in the old chronometer case that stood on the table, always by his bedside. She is stepping away to meet a middle-aged gardener-faced woman, who has just got out of a governess car, which has hay in it for warmth. She has given some of the hay to her pony to amuse him. She has just let it fall on the cobblestones before him. This lady is trying to think that the good old days will never come again, and that she is a landmark sinking in the sands of more democratic days. She is as well off as ever she was in her life, and much happier than she was ten years ago. Every day she sheds some old antic. She talks deep, and high, by turns even still, when she first comes into the town to do her shopping. She knows she is only giving pleasure, without envy, to those who hear her, so soon she will drop into the same tone of voice as all the townspeople here, which is sweet and deep.

The town bill-poster is now politely standing with his mouth ajar listening to her talk. She is only talking about it being early for frosts, and a new pair of artificial silk gloves she is going to buy herself, because she still enjoys dressing up. The bill-poster stops and listens to her because he stops as often as he can when out posting his bills. Bowsie, where was the first place we saw an advertisement of Mullen's Boots ? You know it wasn't farther out of the town than the fence, by Prospect Gate. Well, that's not three-quarters of a mile from this street, and the last to the west will be just as far as the dip after the second hill by Lasho's Wood. That's a mile—so all the bill-posting he can do won't take him more than two hours, and he wants to spin it out to look like half a day.

Well, Bowsie, over the bridge and up the hill and farewell little town. Bowsie wouldn't notice, but when he kicked a stone crossing the bridge, it made a noise that carried back along the street, and the Woman who looked out of the Window turned her face and looked towards the bridge and remembered, as she always does when she thinks of the bridge,—the bringing of young Tim from death in the Deluge.

And Tim, in his place in the shop, the parent boot-shop, in the seaport town, has put his hand in a dark pigeon-hole, behind the box of labels for the special parcels sent away. His hand brings out a small worn paper book and it opens at a page, opens of itself—Tim reads :

" He recoils from his doom, and would shriek out his despair, only that the malicious water prevents the opening of his mouth. But the water seems to rise more slowly now. Can it be that the tide has reached its flow ? A ray of hope, like a gleam of sunshine, through a rift in the stormy sky, darts into the man's mind. He cherishes the idea that the worst has come, and watches with breathless interest the motion of the waves. Ah ! his chin is un-covered, and presently the water only washes his shoulders. Saved once more as a brand from the fire ! And where-fore ? To do good in his day and generation, or to work iniquity and clothe himself with crime as with a garment.

He has read these sentences many times, and could have easily committed them to his memory, so healthy and strong. But he prefers not to memorise the words, that he may come for refreshment to the reading of them. He tries to smooth away the irregularities of the cover, and knows that the book must have been eaten by the mice long ago, if some reader of a generation past had not spilt with a lucky hand a bottle of eucalyptus oil over the pictured cover. In damp weather the eucalyptus scent fills again the book's little cubby-hole.

See, Bowsie, how friendly Lasho's Wood looks laced with the morning sun. Look into its serried depths with thankfulness. Did you not, in your unsteady youth, once cool your burning forehead against the damp trunk of some monarch of this wood ? A king not more than two feet in diameter, but a king among these stunted perishing bravoes who have fought the good wooden fight against the winds in a rocky place so many years. This wood is as old as either of us. But, age talk is queer talk. Now we have a gentle declivity suitable to our course, let us rattle our brogues. I would ask you for a song, but I know you would sing too lusty and too long, and when you lost the words, you would heave away again with the refrain. So I will put off your stave for a better occasion. In this white cottage where we turn to the left, we know, until a few years ago, an old woman lived, who had been, in her youth, a teacher of a village school, when she wasn't herself learning at the dancing school. She taught out of a book which had pictures—A picture of " An Apple ", an engraving showing the roundness of the apple to perfection. And all her pupils remembered all their lives what an apple looks like. There was another engraving, round and solid of " Fat Ox ", and her pupils who had never in their childhood seen a fat ox, carry always his pictures in their memories. Some of her pupils became citizens of power, politicians, advisers of the advisable, even orators—but to her always they were round apples and fat oxen. She was a woman who never laughed. She had other plans. She believed until the last few years of her life, when romantic wishes died, that she should spend a glorious autumn in a glittering palace, surrounded by wealth falling into her lap from a cornucopia long prepared for her by her indulgent fairy godmother. And when these years began she intended to laugh at all that had passed before her.

As we pass along this road bearing more towards the sea, we notice the trees on our left with the moss-bordered small stream are of a more luxuriant growth than those of Lasho's. The green mound behind them hides them from the sea fury. But they do not impress us with the same dignity as those crouching wrestlers of Lasho's. However, these are soft and soothering, and it takes all sorts of trees to make a world. That was a thrush who flew there above the bush ; his waistcoat had many more specklings—more regular than yours. Yours, I know, are the specklings of many breakfasts, and his are the specklings of God.

Here, when the road narrows so suddenly, stands the grey arch, very dangerous for motorists. But only an odd one comes this way ; they bear to the right by the ex-schoolmistresses's cottage. This arch has a name— the wrong name. The name of a man who lived here-abouts and imagined this arch looked like his gateway. He was a Justice of the Peace. He loved his title, when he had lived in this country five years continuously, from the first arrival, as a sporting tenant, they made him a J.P. for he had a house in the dip on our right. Here is his true gate decayed, as his body is, long now. But next to his J.P. ship, he loved people calling this arch after him, though everyone knows it was put up by the Normans ; they had a castle by it, but now the stones of the castle have gone to build these walls beside the road, and a small farm-house between us and the sea. I doubt if anyone, except an inspector travelling through the land, because he must, has any respect for this arch. Since the invention of matches, they have been struck on it, but not one with affection. The special Normans who built here left a memory of consequentialness, which has the people, within twenty miles, anxious to show how free and easy they can be. The narrow-built little whistling man, with his whistle of tin, when he gets within this radius of easiness, plays neither as a mendicant, nor as a great artist down on his luck. He does not play as a person who had ever seen a better day, nor a better hour. He stands on the pathway by a door, and after he has played one tune, money, or a mealy potato where there is no money, is handed to him not as a reward, but as a something that belonged to him all along.

Of course, if this open-handedness got known to all the roadsters, the country would be reduced to poverty by the hordes of entertainers. But those that have felt themselves so snug within the precincts keep it to themselves, and chance travellers ignorantly pass through the district without taking a fiddle from an armpit, or a Jew's harp from a pocket. And the people look at them with their bold, free and easy glances, and let them walk through and away.

To-morrow, Bowsie, if you consent, while you stay in bed, or sit up in your room, wrapped in a blanket, I will take your clothes to the little tailor in Quay Street, and he will freshen them up with petrol, and iron them. And the smell of petrol will soon fly away, when you get out with them again, and walk about up and down across the end of the fish jetty. You won't know yourself, and I know you will put away your old overcoat and get out your collar and necktie. I know you will pretend to be disgusted with your out-of-a-bandbox appearance. But I know you will be purring with delight enough to charm the fishes out of the water, being wishful to leap all over you slithering their sides on the petrol slopes.

But, come, put the best leg forward for two or three steps. From now on the road slopes down to the port, and we have our destination dangling before us. From up here on the high storey part of the road, we can see the top of the town laid out before us, and look right into a brown street. That's New Garden Street; it has country carts as well as dingy motors in it. The people who live there have no connection with the sea. They would not be connected with a sea-faring family by marriage, unless the bait was very luscious. The street is not new, and never more than led the way to gardens. It wasn't called New Gardens at first. It was called first of all " The Warriors' Way "—and did for Victory or Defeat, or Revenge, and a turning out of invaders. It was a bloody-minded street always. Most of the houses have been rebuilt, perhaps houses built on ruins time and again. But in half a dozen cases, the smooth cruel doorsteps are the original ones. Where wrathful feet strode in and strode out. It was a battling street, where fire was only used in fight, to burn out a nest or to boil up pitch, for top of the wall children to drop on the crowns of attackers, or it was to heat up iron bars to drive away the wild beast men, or at any rate, to make them leap about, the way the

pantomime clown used his red-hot pokers at pantaloons.
When gunpowder came it was often an empty street
while extravagant, arrogant folly threw away good
bullets down its short way. No bullet from the attackers
ever got beyond the bend where the hammer-head of
Shop Street and Quay Street met, for there the sea-tide
men's flood carried them to meet the traders' blood, and
any attacker who got so far, pistol, musket and all, was
caught in a rock cleft and pounded. New Garden Street
was always a dry street, and its people have the tindery
character of a droughty place in a moist land. Sparks
fly quickly, and soon the place, both sides of the way,
is full of the roar of running fire. It is the only street
in the town which has a constant sound, always ever in
the quiet of the night, which some ears, or any ears,
unobstinate, can hear. It is continuous, like the
ticking of a clock, though the sound is not in the least
like a clock tick. It is more like the noise of the sea
in a shell. Nothing startles anyone in this street.
Years ago, a runaway horse with a car rattling behind
it, having pitched the driver and the passenger out in
a heap of stones away in the country, came galloping
through the town. And the next day every citizen of
Quay Street, Shop Street and Post Office Street was
talking about the noise the runaway made, and comparing notes about the excitement the noise created at
such an hour—three o'clock in the morning. Some of
the sailors in a ship by the Quay heard the noise and it
was a watchman on a steamer who went ashore and
found the horse, with what was left of the car, still
hanging to him by a trace and a shaft ; eating the grass
on the fish quay. But in New Garden Street all burst
awake, as the galloping rattle came through. All rose
steadily from their beds and stood ready—the teeth

stripped. But next day in their own street, or about their business of work in other parts of the town, they had nothing to say about the mad gallop of the night. Some people say the street is always drier than any other street in the town because there are cellars deep down below. But no living person has ever seen them or any entrance to them. Some say they can detect a hollow sound in the street. But a lot of streets have hollow sounds.

Shop Street and Quay Street are promenade streets. No one would be able to promenade Post Office Street, the gradient is too severe going up or coming down it. But Shop Street and Quay Street, making a continuous curve, and with the shape of the town's hollow, fill quite a pasear, especially on a summer night, mild and still. Then we can all stroll all along the roadway, as well as on the pavements. The motor drivers here are well trained. They don't come scuttling through this town at any old pace, even the two or three motor-cycles owned in the town do not trust to their din to make a way for themselves. They sneak home slowly, and carefully, and when the armoured and padded owner gets out of the saddle, and pushes his companion into its receptacle, silence falls on any group which happens to be near. They are impressed and a little disap-pointed, as if the lady and the tiger had finished that ride of long ago with the lady leading home the tiger. We will stroll about the road as we will, and stop and talk in sugary, dry, or just low deep voices. Young Tim will be in his bed. He has to be on the floor of the shop early. The bootseller believes, for himself, in staying out, in conversation, the middle watch. But young Tim folds his arms across his chest and sleeps soundly, thoughtless of the warring personalities pacing in the shuttered streets below him.

You are out of heart, at the moment, Bowsie, to feel that all our walking this morning, you have only had me for company. You would have liked to see some other human being. You don't want to talk to them, or hear their voices particularly just now. But you come very near, this moment, hating my appearance —only my appearance. But, patience, gentle roadster, we have been, ever since we left the schoolmistress's old cottage, on a by-road. But now we are coming to the cross-roads, where sheltered by the high bank, where the road is a deep cutting, you will see the late country people going into town, and the early ones going out. Couples talking to each other how nice it is to get your business in the town, your trading, done early and so get away to your home by the bog among the little rocky hills ; and there to hug each other, to think that you have about you the lands, the rushy lakes, and the crooked potato patches, that you understand and that understand you.

At the same time an occasional lingering on in the town all through the day and to dusk is worth the ennui that hangs on waiting about. And then to the cinema. The Star where just a turn of the wheel may give you a story, where a man in heavy boots shows up well against all these light-booted heroes, who would be foundered, before they'd walk three miles beside a cart on loose-stoned roads.

Now, here we are,—the two streams, the comers and the goers. It's market day, my boy ! And you'll smell a frieze coat that was never fully dry since the wool left the sheep's back. In the town the country ones will be standing about, on pavement and roadway, with their stout sticks, and we, and any townspeople who can afford to leave their counters and desks at all, will have to walk round the country people. There's no question of fighting ennui to-day. The town is theirs. At the same time they'd like to be able to get on the roofs and take the slates off, and see the towneos in their lives. The useless part of their lives, that is useless to the country people, but still it should be amusing to see them sitting glum and wise looking among their sideboards, and the knick-knacks, and their looking-glasses, trying a piece of new wallpaper to see if it'd match daughter's dress. But some of them are just like ourselves, not too bad, cold and hot by turns, wishing us well on our roads out into the mountainy ways, saying " The blessings of God on the country ones. They keep us going."

But, Bowsie, as we drop down step by step into the town, and soon we will go down to sea level because we must, both of us, we meet an outskirts entertainer, a ballad singer. He is not, I notice, in a glance, at all like the two carpenter-joiner ballad singers who built the Pride Hotel. He is a tall hawk of a man and he sings with a caw, in the old fits and starts style, that only a few of the old ones understand and appreciate.

He is singing the song of the shirts sardonic. It is a hot-air song, and he wishes he had started on a song which suggested something more than the shedding of life-blood. He wishes he had hired a poet in one of the big cities to write him a song about bidding farewell to money, throwing it from you before the

> Com noym noym noym
> Yon ynom
> Unists have come

He has no accomplishments, his singing is purely gifted. He cannot write down any ideas that come to him, indeed, he cannot read either. Though he holds a ballad, if he is selling as well as singing. But that is just his arrogance. He believes, if he liked, he could read. It is not quite fair to say he is unable to write— he can write his own name

—JOHN DAVEY—

yet it is doubtful if now, getting on past middle age, he could make the alphabet. Once he could do it. He did it many times for a little long-necked child he had— his son, John David. John David Davey. But John was taken away from him when he was five years of age, by a sister of his wife's ; taken to the great America.

And this boy, grown to be a man, is quite a successful, even a leading man in a town of fifty thousand people. He is no respecter of persons, and is a strong light among those who run a resting-place for tramps, bums coming in from three states. But he never will see his father again ; he saw him for the last the day before his aunt took him by the hand, and trotted him down to the railway station, explaining that she was taking him to Limerick to see the shop windows. She was a liar always. She loved lies—she thought they were friendly to her. When John David saw his father for the last time, he saw his back lurching down a leafy lane. He was walking on the grass by the hedge, to save his feet, always rebellious to a hard road now, for years, leaseholders of all the old roads of Ireland. But when he went down the lane, he was bound for the fair of Ennis. He thought he'd get cattle to drive ; he was a poor cattle driver. He had no system of his own. He could not master the traditional style, and the cattle either didn't understand him, or understood him too well. He knew his sister-in-law loved lies for their own sake, and he did not believe that she was going to show John David any shops in Limerick. But he did not know she was going to show him shop windows in New York. If she had told him so, he wouldn't have believed her. So she felt no compunction in not telling him. Nor in not telling him that she had driven his wife away from him and from his son, her only child, by abuse unmeaning, just the noise of it, and a network of lies, all matted about some central thought, like the rails about a railway terminus. Into that great black arched terminus, John Davey's wife had gone, so now John Davey was singing on the roads. He leans, with an old-fashioned elegance, an elegance learnt from carrying his shoulders back and his head always high, against a motor-car parked in the gutter, outside the long ironmongery and farming implements store.

The owner of the motor-car is getting into the car and now he wants to be revolving the wheels, and bumping away to his home beyond the bogs. He does not cry out " hi " or " by your leave " even. He throws a new trowel down loudly on the floor of his car. John Davey hears him and steps farther on to the pavement, and the car owner can go what way he likes. John Davey, when walking, carries that high glance, because he has never had to stoop his face to read, and because he loves to watch the clouds bunching and lengthening themselves above him.

A ploughed field of beautifully straight furrows saddened him, but the scattered furrowing of the skies continued their wild journey through his chest. His eyes will gaze almost into the sun at summer noon, because they are so unstrained. Their lazy strength unimpaired with print. He loves to look in a book-shop window, passing on his business through a town, and to think that of all that pile of books he has never read one. If some wind tossed him to the foot of the great pyramid he would be full of a gaiety, like a child's gaiety, when he knew that he had never " even masoned a stone ".

A little farther on our right a man is sitting by a dingy, red, short-legged table, piled with tin cans, and with tin cans below it. The table is in the gutter, but the man sits on a stool, half on the pavement, half in the gutter. He leans back at times so as to impede the comfortable passing along of those behind him. Sometimes, he plucks a man by the coat, or a woman by the skirt. When he does so, he points at some particular object among the shining stock. Just what he thinks most suitable, judging by the material of the coat, or the skirt, should make the most appeal to the buyer he holds. He isn't blind, but he does not trouble to turn his head. Sometimes, he will point to only part of the object he aims to sell. A very fine tin-can lid. Or the handle of a grater, by which it can be hung on a nail. It is believed by some romantic people that he makes the tins himself. An ancestor did. But this man buys them from some factory.

Now, they shine and radiate their blue flashes, the brightest, far the brightest, show of all the market day. They shine now, and will shine when they go to the homes of their buyers. Well scoured and handled, they will shine like swords in a pantomime, until one

day, a little girl will bounce one of them down carelessly on a rock, and it will be dinted. The young
girl's brother will beat out the dinting with a clear
round stone, but the can will refuse to hold water or
milk ; the grater will grate the hand that caresses it.
And the tin will be cast away. We will turn our backs,
bite our lips and count a same count : Oney, twoey,
threey, fourey, Hokus, Pokus, Allicum gloriay, and
when we turn round again the tin will be a rusty old
joke on a stony briary lane.

Come to think of it, Bowsie, why wait till to-
morrow about having your clothes freshened up. Turn
round here to the flat-faced Imperial and so straight
to bed. While I rush your clothes round to Leonard,
you can give out that you've got a headache or letters
to write. Don't make a lot of bother about it. The
day's still young and you'll be much happier spruced
up. Don't act a kind of pouting Jeff with me ; I
have not got the high-handed style suitable for a Mutt,
and you know it. Give out that you are working out
a scheme for breaking the bank somewhere. Give
out that you always rest in the afternoon—since
the races. Don't put a notice on your door saying
" speak softly do not shake floor—doctor's orders ".
Because there's sure to be some old traveller of the
wide who'll think you've got D.T.s in there, and he'll
be quivering to be at them with a big stick and a
plaister.

Here you are now up the stairs, Number Nine—
empty, isn't it ; in you go. No pyjamas, of course not.
Not till the 'bus comes along with our bags, and then
we'll have to fetch them.

Do you want a newspaper to read? Terry, is there a newspaper down there? Here you are—now, don't over-read yourself. I don't want any of the paper to wrap up the clothes. I'll throw them over my arm as if I was carrying a light overcoat.

Is Mr. Leonard in? "He's been at his dinner, but he'll be in in a minute." There he is talking to the Harbour Master. If I hold up the trousers so, he will catch them in his eye and see that there is work to do. Here he comes—the door swings in on the sob of cord and weight.

Iron these well, Mr. Leonard, but don't damp them too much. After all, my friend doesn't want to get the rheumatism just at the moment. Is there a scentless petrol you can use for the cleaning? Well, he can toss a threepenny bottle of "Helio Essence", you think, through them at the moment of getting into them, and get a counter-scent, and would you advise a hair-dress with unguents as a crowning glory?

It shall be done, Mr. Leonard.

Yes, the strollers in the Rialto to-night will be enjoying his society; every whiff, a meal in the æsthetics. He planned a few turns on the fish quay to mix the ozone with the others. Would you recommend that? It's a pity that those brown-coloured suits are not so very fashionable down here just now. If the iron sat too long on a crease, the burning blent with the suit's own shade, and would be passed over except by a very eagle eye. I see it isn't burnt; it was only beginning to toast along the knife edge.

What if I take a turn up the street, as far as the post office, where I have a plan to buy a few postage stamps. I think it is a good thing to always carry a couple of stamps with you. Some people might want to pay money to me, and I'd like to be quick with the receipt before they can change their minds. I suppose the post office is in the same place.

" Yes, they built it to last."

Yes, yes, Hibernio gothic—a pure round tower would not have suited so well, not enough wall space for the telegraph boys to lean their bicycles against.

Yes, yes, as you say, I'll " shuffle off your doorstep " right away, and return.

The post office is indeed a smooth article, without allure. I suppose no one buys postage stamps for any reason but the poets' reason for singing—because they must. They might number them all with a different number, and give a prize to a lucky number, every now and then. Getting near the day for announcing the winning number people would be in such a fever that they wouldn't be able to bring themselves to put a stamp on a letter. Perhaps giving away to their correspondent a fortune, and so the letters would be all delivered unstamped, and the post office would make a great thing out of the fines.

But the cool grey walls of nice cement repulse my frivolity. The white waxy flowers with the dark green leaves in the postmaster's sitting-room window do not appear to notice me. They watch the telegraph boys to see that they do not begin any game that looks like pitch-and-toss. The view from up here is good. I see the mounds inland behind the town, and I see a signpost with three arms up on the ridge. To-morrow, perhaps, we will climb up there, and follow on where the western arm points the way to America. Down the slope, immediately in front of the post office, I see into part of Roland's Lane. It's very full of jobbers ; they are pretending to have dissensions among themselves—they are full of mire.

I am inside the post office now, and I walk across the width of it to enjoy the baked smell, where the sun is beating on the southerly window, and shining down on the window ledge and the floor. The girl behind the counter gives me my two stamps, and takes my money. I feel as if I had stolen an incident from Bowsie. If he was buying the stamps the girl would reverse the order—take his money first—then give him the stamps, and that would be because, as soon as he got inside the door, he'd begin rolling his eyes about. And this girl, who is young and probably new to a town office, would watch Bowsie as if he was a licked finger moving on a window-pane. But I should perhaps now be moving slowly back to Leonard's.

I will lean here on the low wall above a sloping cabbage-patch balcony with cobwebs on the cabbages, which leans down to a buttressed wall of Roland's Lane. But the buttressed wall is too high for me to see into the lane. So I can only see the smoke rising from the jobbers hidden. I am moving slowly down the hilly road. At the very bottom, I must stop ; my feet refused to move on for an instant. Side by side they hold me, that I may view, in a small shop window, a large advertisement card. It shows, in proper colours, a grand high bottle of whiskey with sun shining through it, and by its side, its reflection. Soft amber. The bottle has a full blossoming upward glance—the card is propped up low in the window. It seems to belie the cold grain which first thought of it. It says, " Love me—love my reflection ". I am hurrying now ; I am inside Leonard's, and Mr. Leonard has just finished his work on the Bowsie suit. He is holding up the trousers, to show how straight they fall, not a sign now of " over-at-the-kneesness ". Mr. Leonard will not hear of me carrying the clothes listlessly falling over my arm. He wraps them up, with a touch of tissue-paper over them, in some new brown paper. He ties them with thin queer string. I pay the price—it seems little for such a transformation. I trip back to the Imperial. I'm flying up the stairs. I'm hammering on Bowsie's door. He unlocks it. He is looking at the clothes ; he approves of them. He thinks them mag-nificent. He hangs them over the· end of the bed. He walks back from them. He lays them out ; the coat above the trousers, on the bed—lays them out as though a flat man reclined there. He is so lost in his admiration for their sparkling quality, that he is putting off the moment when he must get into them. I realise that I have wronged him in the past—Bowsie is not vain. He thinks more of these clothes, now freshened, than he does of himself. But I must not let him get low-spirited. A low-spirited man is poor company in narrow streets. I resisted buying many stamps, so I'll have Bowsie jumping into his clothes, and now let's make tracks to where the bottle in the advertisement looks so good. I will buy, for fear he gets chilled, a half one for Bowsie, and for myself as next-of-kin.

Now, Bowsie, walk in your flowery garden of scent. I will not go back on Mr. Leonard. I have here the threepenny bottle of Helio. Smell it before I pour. No. I won't splash it—I'll just dab it and you can take the bottle and add a new dab whenever the old dies away.

Now, to the pier-head for more air.

We are pacing up and down the jetty, gazing out on the flat bay ; the wind has dropped and a fishing boat with sweeps out is coming steadily but slowly home.

They have a few hundred fish ; they expect to sell to the country people—and so they will, indirectly. They'll sell them first to fishwives, who will take them to their tables at the edge of the street, where Roland's Lane taps Shop Street. There is a wider piece of roadway there where the steps go up to Look Out. The fishwives will let the fish, dead as door nails, fall about in the roadway, and they'll smear them about with old newspapers, all in a secret process, unrecognised by themselves, of taking the ocean queerness off the fish. People from inland places are thought, perhaps, to distrust wild fish even in death ; liking them better tamed by handling. The nearer the brink of the sea the more the people wish for the fish they eat to wear a warrior look.

Now, Bowsie, the greater strength of the petrol has flown away, only the subscent remains. Come, let us pass back to the town. The fiercest part of the commercial side of the market has melted before the sun of human fellowship. Let us be there to see.

I have no doubt you have never read the few notes about the town which are given in the guide books. If you had read them you would find perhaps a mention of these Look-Out Steps—and it would be wrong, the natives say, that is those natives who nurture still a peculiar memory, there are two or three always living in every town. They here have told me that the Look-Out Steps lead at no time to any look out, as pictured by the ignorant, a high spot with old men and spy-glasses, sweeping the sea. No, sir, these men of strange memory say that the name springs from a time when housewives who lived in the houses, whose gardens are above the high wall on the left of the steps, used to empty the unwanted contents of pails over the wall down on the steps. They would call in the air before the empty-ing or perhaps at the same instant, " Look out ". A more tricky memoriser told me late one moony night, when the shadows were very thick and he refused to walk up the steps, that the custom was pagan—a libation to the God of Steps, and the words spoken were not a warning. They were " luck out ", and the gesture was the throwing out of ill luck. He said he knew you, Bowsie, but I fancy that was only his agreeableness.

Ah, my Bowsie is afraid of owning up to knowing any odd ones. He has always hoped to preserve his individuality by vagueness. This man of look outs was probably just carrying on the tradition that every town should have a few, who would attempt to carry on some cultivation of wit, or perhaps just a reassembling of wits, learnt from a bigger town.

Stoop here, my friend, and look into this dark cavern of a draper's. See the woman from beyond the hills buying a print dress suitable for her daughter. You would imagine she would choose something to keep her daughter in her quiet servitude to her home. Nothing of the kind. You are all wrong—this mother is choosing as gay a trail of flowers and bramble stalks as she ever wished for herself in her plunging youth. She was a plunger. Yes, on a long rein, held in the left hand of her own mother, a tall broad-faced woman who had seen churches raised on stony grounds, where no habitation of man had ever been before. Unless some one reared a skinny tent before the glaciers came and ground away the surface.

Far behind the shopping woman is a conceited

commercial traveller, with his samples spread about. He knows he has come to do this business of getting orders at the worst day of the week. But his conceit makes him come, testing his coaxing, intimidating, salesman's power, against this small-town shopkeeper's irritation and resistance. He argues that an irritated person, who is irritated in spite of himself, and not for the pleasure of indulging in personal specialisation in irritation, is so glad when some burst of sunshine through the day's agony comes like a glimpse of rest everlasting, that he becomes wax to the salesman, who is alert, and has his right exhibit in his hand. Some article let fall carelessly on the counter, a thing that will sell itself on sight with a bumpety-bumpty-bumpt, and can, if it's wanted to, be dropped in the window unpriced to make the townspeople gaze and long. A thing that the shopman's wife and daughter, if he has them, will respect, and respect the shopman for having secured it.

This traveller writes articles in the journals of his profession on selling. But he always keeps something back. After all, when the line which stretches over the torrent will only bear the weight of one, and two travellers stand on the rocks watching the thin rope of escape sway—then we come to tossing for the chance. And when you come to tossing, is it your duty to tell all you ever learnt in the tossing schools ?

The traveller pares his nails. That's an artful touch ! He keeps the talons short, in appearance. If he had a vulture's beak, he would cover it, if necessary, with a cardboard nose of kindness.

In this draper's, there are other shoppers beside the good-natured mother. Two assistants are waiting on them. One of the shoppers is a wife buying a necktie for her husband.   She wants it to be bright, and classical enough for it to draw attention to him that will show that he is well done for a Sunday and a holy day. But not enough to make any woman look his way twice, and not enough to make him look at himself in the glass more than twice.   It's difficult.

Oh, Bowsie, don't say that.   Don't say that when woman chooses a necktie for her husband's throat, the man, and all that stand within sight of him, should first be chloroformed.   With your new, or renewed, clothes on, you should not be in your bitter mood. Look up—smile.   We will pass farther along Shop Street, taking airy appetisers for soon we must eat.

Now, let us back to the Imperial ; we feel hunger at an early hour to-day.   Four o'clock.   Why ?   Ah, because we broke our fast earlier than usual.   I had forgotten in the coming and going mysteries of the streets.

This is a meal that will stand to you for some hours. The potatoes mashed, with the American masher.   It was from America I always believed the early ones came.   Do you remember how like soft macaroni they used to push the potatoes through, falling in a nice heap on the plate below.   This cute lump of bright yellow butter in the middle of the heap is good.   I am sure you agree it's a good mixer, and we are good mixers too.   You and I, Bowsie, are admired without envy.

He likes that.   He is too lazy to wish to excite envy. If the Feast of Love is Music—then Laziness is its dish.

Let's be funny tourists with Terry.   Let us pull his

leg. Ah, my ancient friend, you don't take to the sport, and Terry is not in a humour for giving his mime of The Paddy Waiter giving the Micky Free answers to the tourists. Terry is tired. Market days tire him, now, though he is but young. He has only been three years a waiter. He was not bred to the calling. He comes from that corner of the town between the cockle heap and the Custom House. They tried another before this Terry. They brought him in from Garden Street. But he couldn't bear the harness. He flittered it, where it touched him, in forty-eight hours. Then he went away home, by the yard through Muroo's Store into Bucket Lane, up the wall there, along the top of it, and dropped down into his mother's yard. He put on his own Sunday suit then, and paced up and down in front of the Imperial, defying them to take him. His mother said he had been well fitted for waiting in a foreign land, where he was observing how it was done for two days, until he mastered it, and he only left the café because the Turk said he'd sell him for good money to the Arabs, for a camel boy. She said he would not have gone down to the Imperial, but that he was on the dry strand, between two storms of drink. She said he was one of Nature's gentlemen. It disgusted him to hear her say it, but she was his mother, and she had only picked up the saying from some stranger passing by her door on a dusty day.

I propose, Bowsie, now that we each take a stroll apart—one to this low headland, the other to that. West or east—choose ! You take the westerly head—good. Though I had thought of it for myself. But I gave you choice and I stand by it. No changing now.

We will be pleased to see each other's small dots of heads, on bodies that will look like sucked comfits across the blue and tinkling waters of the bay. Each of us will commune with our own nonsensical souls, which at these times will not be said nay to, but peak up in their squeaky little voices, which it amuses them to think are like the human ones. Good-bye, now, and for the present ; take care of yourself. You may see me illuminated by the sun shining behind your back, and through the pink of the ears. While I will see but a silhouette, a little gloomy silhouette, relieved only by the round blushes of the ears.

Ah, he has arrived at the point. His was the clearer way. My road led up the muddy hill, where the rain of two days ago softened the earthy way. Under the shade of the fuchsias. Well, I have cleaned my boots on the short grass, and when I go back into the town, I will fall back a little to the east, and get on the dry road which leads to and from the lighthouse. My side of the bay is the most civilised—I have a wooden seat to sit on, and there are two cigarette cartons, dead and empty. Over where Bowsie stands marking me with the sun on my façade, there is only a stone to sit on, and black and dried wisps of old seaweed spotting the grass.

Between us lies the bay—the baylet briskly palpitating with a new breeze lately sprung up. There is one large yellow motor-boat at its moorings. One small motor-boat, painted with a green streak, is moving about aimless. The owner is trying out the engine ; he left it neglected so long.

Between the yellow boat and the quay in a space of water bound within the westerly point and the fish jetty, perhaps twenty small boats—rowing boats, and power boats, are flocked near each other, bouncing there, looking careless and unafraid. I sit down because a weakness comes to me before the ocean which I know stretches away on my left. Bowsie will not sit ; he will look about him, and walk up and down, and think about a home he once had on which the sun never shone, and where every day was too long. Then he'll shrug his shoulder and forget—forget everything, while a comic strip of some ridiculous adventure, of coloured figures, bouncing before him in cloudland, will pass before his eyes, comatose eyes.

The equinoctial gales have come. They came before the equinox—he remembers that, and he is peaceable now, so he leans his shoulder against the tall shoulder of the stone pillar raised in the old days to mark the place, where some old battle hero fell down in the victory of death ; final, no more of the weary sweetness of comings and goings between Hybrazil and here.

Bowsie is squinting his eyes far out at the ocean's creamy edge. He has ceased to be a wilful being ; he is a receptacle for flying fancies. He fancies now he is looking straight into the cluster of the houses by an east coast shore town in America. His eyes have unpuckered their edges ; he is as nearly asleep as ever he is. He never sleeps, if you and I sleep. The state of drowse in which he sinks is no more related to the sleep of other men, than a visiting-card is to a circus poster. We come first with our bill-poster on his bicycle. Then every strong tree, and gate, and smooth wall, announces us.

Our tent is pitched in the Green. The band climbs

up into the gold car, the creamy and Isabella horses are yoked and the triumphal car is fed with the corner boys of the place in false heads—our circus has come !

But Bowsie leaves his card, the corner turned up, on Morpheus, and then away with him about his business —rested and refreshed. He is magnificent in pivoting his own world. I buy a newspaper from a boy. There are three newspaper-adventure boys in the town. They are each ten or eleven years of age. They do a small business. Their life would be heavy in under-foot charges, boot leather, only they are without the charge, for they are barefoot. This boy has marked me from afar. He has offered me the paper without any special recommendation. If I asked him he would read the best of it out for me, without expecting any payment. He has only one paper—he dropped it in the clay coming up the hill. It is an English paper, specially printed in Manchester perhaps, for the Irish trade. It has only lately arrived here by the train. I begin to read it, just anywhere. The boy sits beside me. I know by a slight fluttering of his ragged sleeves as he claps his hands over his knee, that he has seen the figure of Bowsie—stone of the stone on which he leans. The boy is thinking now about me sitting by him. He thinks I'm a poor affair ; he thinks I have an inside like a sheep and a head like a bird. That is what he wishes to think about me. But he is watching a race, before the breeze, of a piece of new yellow shining wood, perhaps a foot long, the side out of some grocer's or fruiterer's case. The side it is of a mandarin box. The wood is racing a shining tin box, that once held mustard, for the beach, the space of shingle and boulders which lies by the stream's mouth, to the inside of the long quay. The tin can catches the breeze better than the wood. But floating light and high it is always turning about and running up into the wind. While the timber comes whaling along. Some accident of the shape or thickness, or a nail acting as a rudder, keeps it on a steady course. Now, some eddyings of the water, caused by the stream, and some baffling wavelets, spring up, and are tossing the wood and tin around and about, so that the race is an argument. My newsboy turns his face away ; his interest is gone. What started so fair as a trial with causes known, has blundered into the pitiful little politics of inshore tumbling.

The newsboy springs up and as he steps away, a child again, towards the town, he whistles into the air three bright clear notes—a farewell to the headland, to the breezes and to the old sheep's stomach. He himself is for the left-over excitement of the market. " God be with the old times, when I seen them fighting on the pavements." He thinks he'll say something of that kind when he meets the other newsboys on the corner which faces the cinema. But he has to pass his mother's door, and his creepy stool by the fire is standing waiting for him, and the fire has a red glow coming from it. And now he sits down. His little lamb stomach calls for food. His mother stands behind him, and leans on his shoulders, and puts down her hand with the mug of tea hot and sweet, with a piece of bread and butter balanced on the top, and a little sugar on the butter too. When his tea and bread is finished, he reaches down by the edge of the cupboard, where he had a short piece of green ash sucker. His market-day insignia. He and the other newsboys always carry sticks on the morning of market days. Newsboys grown to manhood and dead and buried did so here before them. But now it is late in the day, so this boy puts his stick back in the corner, and fingers in his pocket an oblong of wood, wrought into a shape which has no meaning until you see it grasped in a determined hand, and then—it is a parabellum. It gives him pleasure to have it with him on a tough corner, where, for every generation, there has been an upstart boy, trying to form a gang to put terror into the breasts of all the other boys of the town.

The terror corner is up Hill Street—a short street at right angles to the quay. The corner is an old Indian meal store, partly now a tenement. It has a gate dark, sunk, and two corner stones. Opposite the meal store is an extraordinary thing—an empty public-house ! Decayed, its licence gone long ago ; its lamp glassless and twisted. Its walls, whose pillars once shone painted marble, now show a smeared blue and green that makes the passer-by think of fogs and deep-sea moans. The windows were boarded up in an age gone. The place would be full of rats if there was anything left to eat there. Even rats won't nest in a derelict gold mine because of the name.

The terror corner has no ambush laid to-night, for late last week the newsboys arrived by the chance of their feet in the dark, all together, at that corner. The sortie band was weak at the moment, the romance of their life in the dark was at such a low ebb that only half the band were in the shade of the archway, and they had been standing about uncomfortably for ten minutes. The newsboys arrived, fresh and lively, on their toes. Each had the idea of springing past the dangerous corner, and without loss of dignity, arriving at well-lit Quay Street. One came from the side door of the Imperial Yard, one down the hill, and one from Bucket Lane. They ran into each other. But between them was the tough band, caught in the centre of the road, where they had sprung to attack, scuffle, and maul. The end was as though the rays of the star had turned and beat against the star. The tough band lay together, heaped, and the newsboys strode boldly down to Quay Street.

The tough ones then, the idea came quickest to their leader, agreed to pretend that they thought they were still gripping the enemy, and they pulled each other about, and cried out battle calls " up the hill men " and " stick 'em up ". After a little they spring apart, with expression of feigned surprise, as they discover they have been caught by the old trick, and left fighting each other. I believe now they will be reorganised under another leader.

The newsboy who sold me the paper has a business to be about soon now. He has to get into the cinema, and that without paying any money. He brings this off twice a week ; he must, he is driven on to it because the programme changes twice a week.

This is the last night of the first programme. Being the night of market day, the townspeople will be too jaded with the day to make up a large attendance, and so the young man in the paybox will be inert, and will be smoking a great many cigarettes, and the newsboy will be sent to get more, and as payment for his trouble, be let slip into the hall, where the girl with the electric torch will not waste electricity on him. She has been instructed not to be lavish wheeling the torch about, as if she was stirring a pudding. He has to vary his way of getting into the hall. An argumentative picture lover, who is faithful only to the stars, and does not take the trouble to read the posters, and requires the young man in the box office, almost under oath, to give him the programme, causes a commotion. And the newsboy slips by. Once, in the early days, he used to allow himself some silent song of self-praise, after making a successful entrance. Once, stooping low, working his way down to a good seat, he pulled the loose end of the girl usher's shoelace, and so her shoe came off, and rattled down the steps,—in a moment when the pictures on the screen required every nerve tensed.

This newsboy cinema fan is quite different from the ordinary fan. He hardly remembers the actors' names. He has made for himself a group ; they carry the names of characters, and any personage that appears, in any story, who sufficiently resembles one of this group, goes by that name to this boy. So all films he sees are a continuation of the lives or characters he knows well. It is well it should be so, for he is of use in his house and generation. The boy's mother only gets into the cinema hall about once in three weeks. She has to pay. And the boy's father, even if the money counted for nothing, does not wish to go now. He went two or three times, and was unhappy. He is a man who has been an excited man. Things happening near him, or far away, have moved him very deeply. He has never been even tipsy with drink, and he was unhappy at the cinema because he felt, as he felt when in company with a man full of drink. He was not able to take to himself any of the drunk man's curiosities and excitements. But he sits by his wife, and listens, twice a week, to his son's story of what he has seen, and heard, at the pictures. In this he is quite happy. He has never been to a doctor. He has always been earning wages ; they are not very large. He is very muscular, though he is small. All day he wears a sacking apron, and drags about bags of sugar, and flour, and small crates and boxes, and pushes them on to a hand truck and wheels them along. In the lofty grocer's shop in the store of which his work lies, his short figure is well known. For, at intervals during the day, he pushes his loaded truck through the groups of customers. He is all bluey white with flour then, but recognisable. He comes and goes in a gnomelike resistless way. He rarely has to speak. His employer, the man who owns the shop, is afraid of him but likes him. And he likes his employer, but he would like him not to be afraid of him. He has seen, in the darkest inner cavern of the shop, a returned American, " Yank ", in the last decade of two hundred pounds slip to the clayey floor in a spasm of drink. He balanced the handles of his truck against a stock of meal-bags, and stooped over the prostrate man, opened his shirt at the neck, peered into his face, and left him to his friends. When his work is finished, and he has washed and put on a clean muffler with blue stars on it, and brushed the flour from his trousers and his coat, and got into his boots with the black shine on them, then he is the pride of his wife, his son and himself. He stands at the corner of Quay and Shop Street and watches the townspeople who pass up and down. He is old enough to have reminiscences of other days. But, unlike the men who stand beside him, he never speaks of them ; his eyes are all for a to-morrow.

When I meet Bowsie in the town again—our periods of reverie gone down to join the rest, the shopkeepers are shutting up their shops. That is the unlicensed shops. The licensed cannot close for a while yet, and when they do close, only very few mutterers will bother the street as they go home. Changed times from the days down here, when the imitation mohawks and three water Rakes of Mallow would come howling through the streets. One, at least, of those old amateur rakes lives on, a professional man—he has a wheezy voice, and one eye that looks out blamelessly ; the other has a tilt. But, as he dozes off in his high bed, he is glad that the three other whooping Indians of his youth do not come back, and stand drawn up by his bed-side, upbraiding him with not having made enough noise.

We pass by a small, sunk, brightly lit tobacconist's. Bowsie goes in ; he is going to fill his pouch with good plug tobacco, and he hopes to get it cut up for him, and he hopes that, when his footstep sounds on the shop floor, that it will not be grandmother who will come out, but granddaughter, busy, cheerful, and comely. Grand-daughter it is. There is no other customer waiting, so it is not too grasping to ask her to cut up the ounce of tobacco for him. And she does so with the strong half-moon cutter, and she grinds it all up in the pads of her hands, and Bowsie thinks some old Eastern ancestor of his kept slaves, and the fairest Fair Circassian handled his tobacco for him. And his ancestor is so long away that Bowsie feels small, and sweet, and sad. And instead of chirruping over the granddaughter's head as it bows over the tobacco, he moves to the front of the shop and leans his round fat chin on the edge of the low partition, by the window, and looks down on the pipes, and the cigarette-boxes, and the shining patent lighters below him.

He comes out in the street to me, and looking away over the house-tops, he says " Beautiful moon ". But

he is wrong, the moon won't rise for a long while yet.
The light he sees is from a cottage above Look-Out Steps.
The light shines on a bunch of mallows, which look
like a sky cloud from where we stand. I had already
been taken in. One of the bank managers passes by,
walking briskly. He greets Bowsie. Bank managers
know Bowsie. The manager plays no games, so he is
taking a brisk walk out to the westerly point, where he
will march up and down six times. He trips over
nothing. Even in this dark hour, he knows where all
old ropes and spars and stones lie. Three times marching full pace—then one slow circling on the point,
then three more swift marches. After that, he will be
passing this way again. Therefore any good thing
that Bowsie can do himself, any kindness that he can
show any human being, let him see to it now, let him
not postpone nor defer it. So Bowsie takes me affection-
ately by the hand, and leads me into the far dark end of
Willy Dempsey's where we each make a small drink
last a long while. Dempsey's face is heavy, and his eyes
sunken and dark, under the lamp hanging above.
He can only look at us ; he is tired with a long day
and the strange conversations he had heard going on in
front of his ear, bargains, litigations, threats, his mind is
confused. He is glad when we go away. The bank
manager is coming into sight. Bowsie stops him and
introduces me to him. We walk slowly along the
street, the very centre of it, only once having to break
our ranks, to let a motor-car through, with the wife
of the other bank manager driving ; she had golf clubs
with her. We talk about European politics. I like
them to talk about. The bank manager knows the
geography well. Bowsie is vague, and pretends to be
as innocent as he is able to look sometimes. It remains

for a time an ideal conversational interlude. I air my views, the bank manager airs his geography and Bowsie aerates the whole cloudy gloom overhanging Europe with his picture of the peasantry. He leaps rivers, mountains, always bringing along his Sally Eva, and his Joe Adam. He believes Sally always wears black velvet stays over a lace chemise, and a skirt of rainbow plaid, a flat straw hat on her head with a bunch of grapes in it. And Joe wears long plum-coloured trousers, with a gold stripe, a pale blue shirt, open at the neck, earrings and a tall silk hat. Bowsie's imagination introduces the tall silk hat. In a moment of jealousy of his own creation, he had to turn his Adonis into a figure of fun. However, at times he lets him toss the hat into an olive tree.

John Ogle comes out of his office. He is a solicitor, and not a good gossip. With them mums the word except when they are demummed at six and eightpence for each and every demummage. That's what they say, but it isn't true—they are discreet, and Maurice Ogle will not even invent gossip of the living. Though he can give his reminiscences of members of his profession in the town long gathered to their fathers, men who acted again the part of the cloaked and defying Daniel O'Connell. They should have had footlights set in Court before them. To-day they might have been floodlit. Do you think, Mr. Ogle, that Mr. Bowsie here would look well floodlit ? No, Bowsie, don't pretend that your ways are subterranean ways. You are a vivid stained-glass window through which the sun is pleased to shine. But here is John Murphy, whose family first named the potatoes, and with him, or on his heels, Mr. Love, " a name to conjure with ". When he was Mayor the outgoing Mayor introduced him with these words. Mr. Love didn't see anything in them at the time, and has never been able to understand clearly since what they have to do with him. There has never been a conjurer in town in his time. Of course, he knows what a conjurer is. And if he was to ask anyone, his daughter for instance, to explain the saying to him, he would understand at once. He is an intelligent man, and he was a first-class Mayor. He never troubled anyone, and no one troubled him. If the saying had been " 'Tis love that makes the world go round ", he would have understood that, without having to ask anyone to explain it to him. He is a brave man, and showed it when Black and Tan bullets rattled in these streets. But so did all these. His business is very small ; he has an agency for selling typewriters, gramophones and rubber stamps. He has a small boat to sail about in. She will soon be laid away for the winter. He is a widower, his daughter keeps house for him. She has had a far better education than he had. He knows Bowsie—has seen him several times about the harbour. He has no distrust of his round flat face.

Murphy, and Ogle, asks Love of the weather prospects and, as one speaking from inspiration, he gives them to-morrow, and the next day, and the third day —" blowing smoke out of the Atlantic nail down the slates ".

We six, making a broad front, pace slowly along the street. The talk hovers easily over America, the U.S.A. Mr. Ogle has been there on a business visit, a business to do with a search for heirs in Ireland, for America's dollars whistling for an owner. Murphy has also been there—for some years. He might have been blown there,

on a fleecy evening cloud, for all the information he
gives of the hows or whys that governed his being there.
He is a very deep-chested man, and his hands have
worked for him.   He is a sombre-appearing man.
What he gives to the conversation is sombre, and short.
He says he has seen men die of work in America, and
well-fed men too.   He believes that men's hearts can be
broken with work ; especially if they move too quick
under a load.   But he generally is asking questions.
And he remembers what he is told, if it is a fair answer
to his question.   He knows from Love's weather prog-
nostication that in three days there'll be pandemonium
all around the bay, and he will take all precautions
necessary to the protecting of his property.   His mind
returns to the idea of man being capable of falling on
death in harness ; because some one of us, nodding
towards the figure of a labouring man slowly moving
home, says " That man there would not be liable to die
of over-working himself ".   So Murphy answers quickly,
" No, he wouldn't, but there are some who are liable
to it.   It's the way they set themselves under the lift.
You would see a weight lifter shift a bar bell, and you'd
see the way he'd get under it.   It's lazy done."   Mr.
Leonard comes out of his shop, pulling the door to
behind him with a bang, which sounds angry in our
quiet street between the houses.   But there is nothing
angry about Mr. Leonard ; he is a little fretful in himself, because he wanted to turn into the cinema, and
see part of the programme, anyway.   He has not been
able to get there earlier in the week, because he has been
unravelling his accounts.   He wishes there was any
honourable way in which he could sell off his bad
debts, as he used to be able to sell off his waste corners,
and edges, of cloth.   He wanted to turn into the cinema.

But the sight of six men strolling and talking must draw him towards it, and he joins us. And now we fall into another stage. Three in front, and four in the rear. Those in front discuss the old times. Those behind the times yet to come. Neither use their own imagination. But each one who speaks, speaks from the lips of his friend next him—mentions events with a shape that he knows his friend believed they took upon them. And those who imagine the future, imagine it in the mind of the man walking on one, or other, hand. Everyone notices that he is being plagiarised, and is flattered, and smiles secretly for his mind worked before him is so perfect a mimicry that it would deceive almost himself. But not absolutely, that is why he smiles. His friend must be inspired to speak his thoughts so well, he must know everything, everything but the secret spur, with which he spurs his flank.

It is getting on into the night, and townsmen are coming out and walking in twos and threes, passing us with remarks about the mildness of the night. The air is so still that in the passages of the houses, the hall of the Imperial Hotel, and the roadway, the temperature is the same. A band of four young men, walking abreast, came towards us walking along Shop Street, near where we make our turn, and begin to stroll west again. They make an opening for us to pass through ; they fall back, two towards each pavement. We say " Grand evening. It's holding up well." And they say " Pleasant for getting about ". That's all, but they eye Bowsie as if he was a kind of a Mocktowser pawing along with statelier hounds. Where others seem to walk with joints, Towser Bowsie rolls along.

At the crossing where Post Office Street and New Garden Street meet almost face to face, where Shop

Street dissolves into Quay Street, the townsmen begin to come to a stand for a while. Our original group has broken up, and I am with a tall, dark, middle-aged man with a flat-crowned hard felt hat. He has a grey cropped beard, and I know his appearance well, though I am not sure of his name. He is, I think now, a brother-in-law of John Devine, whom I had heard of often. It must be so, because the woman with the broad unwrinkled brow, with grey-sandy hair, who stands beside him, had a dark blue eye, which I was always told John Devine and all his sisters had. This woman is the only one who is out with the conversing men. Other women pass out of doorways, hurry a few yards along the street, and into another door. Sometimes they linger a moment, where a little sweet shop has a light still burning. In one end of the town, the houses have electric light—at the other end they still have oil lamps. But the work is going on steadily, and soon every small house will have its electric bulb, and we will be a little brother of the Great White Way. If electricity and lamp oil were to fail now, from hidden store, in boxes, on shelves, out would come the candle, and then we would see a transformation ; for those hundred women, who stay at home, or slip so quickly by shortening their walk on the street to its minimum, would come out in clusters to see the candles light each other across the roadway. And our ponderous, slow and stately talk would be broken into by sparkling uneven beams of candlelight. But Bowsie would fall away to the rear, and keep in the shadow of others. He is not for candlelight ; he is for the natural twilight —well, the natural twilight that might be viewed in China when China was most padded, most small-footed and fattest.

John Devine's sister, and her husband, stand where I
first saw them, in the shadow just before it is broken by
the lights at the door of the cinema. They do not walk
about. From time to time people come and talk with
them. I hear them talk of old racehorses, and old
steamers. The style of the names are not so different,
the names they remember. They have travelled into
Europe. They stopped in Paris, and saw a cab coming
back from a duel, and one man in the cab had his face
close to the window. The face was very white. It
was early in the morning, and these two were, as I
had forgotten, just young people at the time and impul-
sive, and dark blue eye was sad about the white face
looking out of the window. So her husband ran to the
cab, which was slowed down in the traffic, and balanced
on the step, whipped out a large flask of whiskey and
pulling off the cup, filled it and pressed it into the mouth
of the white-faced man. He was restored to a ruddy
colour in a moment and gave forth thanks in the most
beautiful French John Devine's brother had ever heard,
or was ever to hear.

The cinema is closing. All together, the audience
come out into the street—not a large audience, but all
young ; with a harum-scarum skip and a run, they
come down the steps and scatter for their homes. A
few stand about the entrance. We hear an odd exclam-
ation, at the value of the film shown. But the cinema
audience have supped, and so they soon have all gone
to their homes. They go in the four directions of the
ways that part where we stand, but very few go up New
Garden Street. From there it is a prosperous day
when many of the people go into the cinema.

The streets are now our own again. Above us, and
to the right, in an upstairs room, two windows are open,

and there is a subdued light. I had forgotten. It is a small undignified club.

At intervals, now, I am standing a little by myself, and not listening to any conversation. I hear the sound of a billiard ball poorly slithering against another. I know some young man is trying to forget himself in angles, and failing.

We are all standing at the moment in little groups along the streets, when two cars, full of young men and women, come into the town. They have been away to a dance at the Pride Hotel. As the cars come along the street they stop and a talking passenger gets out, stands a moment at a doorway, and then goes in, opening the door with a latchkey. The dance has only been an early dance—a sort of preliminary canter ; this is the correct term before an important all-night dance to be given in a few days. A farewell to summer long gone. The owner has never attempted a large ball, but he has seen great dance halls in America and has no fear but that he can stage a night's entertainment, unbeaten, unequalled, among those sandy hills.

" Perhaps when the heroes, and heroines, of old walked about the land just as they liked, and you were as likely as the night was long to have wafted on you a flock of bright, tall, men and women from Hybrazil, for a dip and a dive on earth a while. Just to make Hybrazil blaze sweeter and also to do a dance hall a good turn. And there is no manner of doubt they'd bring their own fiddlers with them to rest the old earth ones.

Well, it's a poor heart that never rejoices, and maybe, even now, if they saw a good light, they might take a squint in at us through the window. Keep looking

towards the window and smiling. If the night is calm
(I'll pray for that) it's the best night for a dance. But
if it's a storm—and well it might come, though some say
we'll have calm weather up to Christmas. If it takes
the roof off, still I'll be here for a while—the undefeated
old Owner of the Pride ! ! "

We have the roadway again to ourselves.

Devine's sister, and her husband, have opened their
door and left us. We are talking to anyone who happens
to move a few paces towards us. We are talking about
safe things, happening in far-away places, rebellions
against any form of authority are not mentioned. We
are not witty, or brilliant. But we wait for each other
to finish a sentence. We never now take the words
out of another man's mouth. We think of each other's
feelings. And not a bit too much, for our feelings are,
at this time, very tender, and easily disturbed. Bowsie
is still the youngest of us in the chronology of the heart.
Youth has left us stranded waiting for the return of to-
morrow's flood-tide. If we walked, and stood about, until
the first workers disturbed the morning, we would see no
more of youth. For in the town, where the domestic
startings, and returnings, on the roadway, are known to
everyone, it is known that no wild motor-bicycle will
break into our night of quietness. They are locked away
safe in their sheds, reserving themselves for the larger
dance in the Pride. Motor-cycles, when bought, not new,
are treated with cajolery by their purchasers, and not re-
quested to put forth efforts too close together in time.
Sometimes, confined within their cages, supported on
jacks, their engines are run into limberhood. But some
masters prefer to put them on the road untried, having
their trust in the luck of the moment. Some of their

old vixens cry aloud, and it is the rage of the chained
spirit on the treadmill, when go it must. They start
in the hollow of the town and you hear them snorting
and blaspheming the hill, and even on the table-top
of the land you hear them, the perspective of sound
reeling away into distance.

Our night is calm in promise and we are walking
slowly. A man I had not noticed before, seeing me a
little apart from two on my left hand, turns towards me
and slowly, by taking short and fumbling steps, brings
me to the rear of those I lately, for a moment, half
accompanied. The man is of the medium height. He
wears black clothes, an old-fashioned morning coat.
He wears no hat, which is curious in his case, for
he is a middle-aged man, and only young men here
have thrown away hats and caps, some of them have.
The man's face is of an ivory whiteness, with grey
shadows, and bright red streaks on his cheek, as though
finger-tips had brought his carmine blood to the surface.
His hair is grey and closely cropped ; it is strong and
thickly stubbed. He is clean shaven and carries a cheerful jowl, denied by his eyes, which are deep brown, for
they are careworn, and would if I could see them under
the penthouse brows, be of great mournfulness. I can
see, by the way he clutches at the lapels of his coat with
long strong fingers, that he is nervous and anxious. I
don't know about what, until I make two or three
attempts to begin a conversation about the bay, and
about the land, potatoes. I notice that he does not hear
me, so I know he wants to talk himself. He tells me that
he has been in Spain, and it was a long time ago. He
does not seem to care anything for what may have
happened in Spain of the last few years. It was a long
time ago when he was there. It was always a hot sun

country where he was. It was curiosity that brought
him because of the oranges and the dried fruit, and the
sherry that came over from there. And he took a
passage with a captain of a boat. He was not able to
speak to the Captain, but the Captain could speak to
him. In Spain he deliberately let the steamer sail away
and leave him in a small port. He thought the people
would trust him best if he was in a small place, and
would teach him the language, and see that he came
to no harm. And so he came to no harm. And so he
loafed about the quays and in the streets built one above
the other. He was not given to any heavy drinking
habits before he left home, and the place suited him
well. " It was like a town you might hear tales of.
The little wine shops were dark and cool, and in there,
wine plenty and cheap, and a little bread and salt,
now and then. I lived on a low diet but it was enough.
Every little while I had a blow out—not in my lodgings.
It was in an old sailor's home by the water-side I lodged,
the old man and his wife had no English, and they lived
very frugally, so my few shillings a week were like a
bonanza to them. Every now and then I'd go up the
highest street in the town, and out at the end of it,
where there was a garden, with flower trees growing,
and a restaurant with a table under the tree's shade.
There I'd have a strong hot stew of, maybe, goat meat.
I was keeping well within the money I had on me when
I came, and the town was so honest that I had no fear
but I could lie out all night on the quay wall with my
wallet open by my side, and I would wake up, as rich
as I lay down. You could tell the town was honest by
the way the people looked at each other. They never
turned and looked after me in the street, not even the
children made a laugh of me. In a moment—the

moment I stept ashore on the quay, they took me, not as one of themselves. I don't think they could have done that, sir, but as a man made of bone and flesh, with no harmful wish to them.

One Sunday after Mass, I was standing by the gate —the place was very white and clear up there. It was standing, the Church was, so high up in the town, any sailorman way down in the Mediterranean could see it by day, by the white wall, and by night, on account of the light over the door. It was a fine light then, gas it was. Now I'm sure it is electric light. Well, I was standing by the chapel gate listening to the people wishing each other the morning sun, or giving away some gossip. I liked to hear the Spanish roll out, though I couldn't even guess at a word. But I was lazy and young. I had not been so many years from school, but I thought I knew nearly enough. I was standing there and I was just in the act of lighting a cheroot. I was always smoking then—they were cheap enough. I was standing there, when a young girl, a young woman, came out through the gate stepping down where there was a step between the gate-posts. There was no way for a cart or carriage to drive up to the door. Anyone that came in a conveyance had to get out by the kerb, and walk through the gates, up to the chapel door. The young woman, she was very small, or she looked small, for it was a part of the country where most of the Spanish women were tall. Like a tall Wexford woman, some of them were. The young woman was walking very nicely on the gravel, and immediately I thought it was a shame to have her walking on rough gravel, and I looked at her face. She was small, when she was on top of the step, and from a rise up in the path from where I stood, my face looked straight into hers. And

I tell you, and you must not doubt me, that she bore the most lovely face any man ever saw on a woman. It was brown and her mouth had a sweet smile that was always on the move. But I saw her eyes, and I had never seen the like, nor have I since. Deer's eyes they would say. I never saw a deer. They told me I could see a deer if I went to the Zoological Gardens in Dublin, or wherever I would be. But I would not go. Her eyes were as if they would float to you from her face, so that they would be outside your own eyes and looking into them. I was afraid to look at them deeply after I saw them that once. Young man, do I make you ashamed for me talking about a young woman of so long ago? I would not wish to make you ashamed. It is a bad thing for a young man to be ashamed. Ah now, I do not put any shame on you. I often now take in my hands a paper with photographs of beautiful young actresses, with their eyes looking at you, and you can see the photographs wished to take eyes in a way to make them lovely. And I think looking at these that some days I will see eyes that might be those of perhaps some child, of a child, of a relative of that young woman. But I have never met the right eyes yet nor never will. She was a grand woman then. She passed across the street and down stone steps and I stood dreaming that a bird of the sky had flown away. After I had my dinner eaten I got a board and I wrote on it with a pen and ink, " *Spanish Teacher Wanted* ", and put it in the window. The next day, the Monday, I heard someone talking on the floor in the first room, talking to the old woman, and the voice was so sweet, and yet holding, that I thought of the eyes I saw by the chapel gate. And I went down the steps to the floor and there she stood. The young small woman of yesterday. She had a little book in her hand. It was an old book, and it had one cover gone. She held it to me, and spoke in Spanish. I shook my head and took off my cap. She put the book in my hand and opened it for me, and she leant to me to open the book. And she got the page she looked for, and she showed me " Spanish Teacher " in English, opposite it what I know must have been " Spanish Teacher " in Spanish. And then she pointed to a sentence " Good morning, I wish you luck ", and said the Spanish. I saw there was a mark in ink by the sentence, and when she turned the leaves over and said another sentence, I saw all the book through, there were sentences marked with a scratch of ink. But she had never marked them, for the ink was so old, and worn out. I could see she wasn't old enough to have marked them. I stood there with my cap at my feet, where I dropt it, watching her lips and throat move when she spoke. After a few minutes she sat down on a little long stool fixed by the wall, and I sat beside her, and she said a sentence, and I said it after her. I seldom read the English of them, I just said them after her, as we went along at our lesson. I forgot the old couple sitting on their chairs on each side the hearth. But I heard the old man make a move, as if he turned himself in his sleep, and I looked up at him and I saw he was awake and crying. I saw he was trying to hide the tears with the big strong hand he had, holding it over his face. But I could see the tears coming down the old side of his face and I looked at the old woman and she was crying too, but she was cleverer. She was by the way of look-ing into the fire, and rubbing her eyes, as though the smoke was coming into them, and I, young and vain of myself, thought it was tears of laughter at my saying the Spanish so, that they wept. But then I could tell, in a moment, that there was no laughter by those tears. That lovely woman that taught me was all the time looking down on the book she held, and I would try and get her to look up, by throwing my head up and talking as if I was talking to the rafters. I wanted to be seeing her eyes, but when she did lift them, it was in a shadow, for the house was shadowy, except for the light that came in by the doorway on the book. And I didn't see her eyes again, as I saw them by the chapel gate. When she stood up to go I took the book, and tried to find something which said " What should I pay for the lesson ? " I had to do it, had I not, sir ? But she moved her hands about, and said " to-morrow " in Spanish, and showed me in the book that it was " to-morrow " she said. I had heard " to-morrow " in Spanish myself, and I thought it was a funny saying. I thought even I could say it myself.

The morrow came, and there was another lesson for me, and then the night came down and there was a man, a priest standing on the floor waiting for me. And he had no teaching book, and so he spoke to me a few words in Latin. It was like what I had left from when I was at school. I couldn't follow him for a long time. But he was a very patient priest. And at last, he got me that I understood, and I wished that hour that I was a dead man on the ground, for he told me my sweet Spanish Teacher was a mad woman. The next day she came again and she had the book, and new marks on it. She pointed to the words " Queen " and " daughter ", and she pointed to her breast. She was saying she was a queen's daughter. And she showed where she had marked the " son ", and she pointed to me, and to the words " King " and " son " and so I was a king's son. And she pointed at the word " marriage " and I was to say it after her. I, a king's son, was to marry her, a queen's daughter. And I didn't have to look up, for I knew the old man and woman would be at the tears again, and the priest stood by the door and he had tears too. But I wasn't able to cry. My mouth was bitterness of sadness. I took the young woman's hand and kissed it as if I were well used to that graceful act, and she went away, walking most straight and fair, and the clergyman by her side. And then two men from about the harbour came, and one took my box on his shoulder, and they led me down to the quay. And one of them took a torch of wood from under his coat, and he pushed it into the watchman's fire until it was blazing. Then he waved it about. Then he threw it into the air. And a whistle blew from a steamer off the harbour, and those men took me down the stairs to a boat, with three men in her, and they pushed out into the sea, and they put me aboard the steamer. I never saw her before ; the Captain had no English. But he took me away. "Good night now—may you prosper in your way."

Now in a moment, he's turned from me, a second quicker in the turn, and I might have thought he vanished. But he turned by the house which bends at the corner of New Garden Street and Shop Street, and I turned my sad curiosity to follow, and I saw him. He opened, with his quick key, an oiled lock, in a door in the very bevel of the corner. I always wondered if that rounded corner, cemented and painted brown, was part of the long draper's shop on the right. But now it seems to me by the glance I got into the narrow hall, as this man opened the door, that there should be no communication with the shop. The glance I got of the hall showed a look of comfort, with a deep carpet on the floor, and on the stairs. A heavy closed smell came out—not unpleasant, for it was cedary, as of a scented polish. The door closes ; the narrow window of the room above the door is flooded with light. The man has switched it on. I see him now. He puts a heavy book on a small gipsy table by the window and he sits down to read. Then he rises again. He thinks he is in the public eye too much. So, very slowly, not to be impolite, he draws down a yellow blind ; and now his silhouette appears on the blind. It has a plump appearance. Some trick of the angle of the light has given him a docile calm shape, which he, I know, never had at any time. I wonder does he know how public stays up there his shadow. I am standing here in the street to guard his shadow. But he must have turned, and realised, that the sunk and plump flat copy of himself was by his shoulder, for he has dragged on to the window a heavy curtain. I heard the great wooden rings swish along the pole. There must be an inch or so of window open at the top to let out the sound. And now, hearing that so clearly, by a delusion of the senses, I think I hear the man turn the leaf, and I think I hear his long soft breathing, though I can't see him any more.

But here comes, walking towards me alone, Bowsie. He looks very dashing in his ironed clothes and as I live, he has a pink rose in his coat. It is a paper flower, and it has a paper leaf sticking out behind it—like a rabbit's saucy ear. Bowsie must have taken it from one of those flittering young girls who went by a long while ago. I think she had a bunch of these false flowers to decorate the sides of a looking-glass. So that her face would look out at her with flowers on each side of it. Bowsie, with one of his small audacities, asked her for the rose, and she handed it to him, back handed, the way she'd give one of those indiarubber imitation bones to a small dog.

But now I see Bowsie close to me—his perky figure belies his face. He looks dispirited and wan. Someone must have been telling him a sad story. Perhaps he's slightly gassed with the cleaning materials about his clothes. But that cannot be what is the matter with him, for I detect now none of the odour of the cleanser. It is all gone down the wind. Perhaps it's nothing but the hour, and who knows what emotions may have torn through poor Bowsie, walking these roads in the calm night. Someone, perhaps the tall, dark, forbidding-looking ex-captain-looking man I saw him walk with a long time, may have told him of adventures with sword and dagger, cloakless, on some exposed and lonely strand. I know the man is an ex-civil servant of other days. But still he stayed on till he had the right of long holidays, long enough at any rate for adventures.

When Bowsie hears a tale of sword-play, he has to clasp his hands together, to keep himself from stretching out his arm, with an imaginary sword in it, and whistling through his teeth—the music of the sword in the air. He knows that sort of thing is never done by such as he now. I know nobody has told him a tale of requited love, they wouldn't dare. He would pluck the pink rose from his coat, and throw it on the ground, and dance on it, if he didn't know that that kind of thing is never done in the world of to-day. If Bowsie is in the world that others live in, he appears, at times, to be moving away, and then coming towards the beholder, everlastingly. He goes away, into some ancient air, so choked with dimensions, that it's a jamb and no movement. Then, in a flash, he's back again, gazing straight towards one, with his face flashing with clear bright light, and coloured darknesses. Bowsie isn't " right ", if other men are " right ". What's the matter with you, Bowsie, you look as if you'd had enough. Says he, " I have had enough, and so have you. A man must turn in sometime—a few of these leggy devils will never turn up a corner. I have the spirit but not the legs. I could talk with them, if I liked, till rosy dawn doth appear, but for the leg, the left, it's not what it was, since the bicycle accident long ago. Those were the days. Bicycles, those false man-haters, invented by man for man's undoing. Then man first became mobile for a few shillings, if he was content with second hand. Man had already the horse, and the camel. But the bicycle came and it was its own propulsion. The alibi of the body was within the reach of all. But away with mechanical folly. I have the power of the alibi of the spirit, and that's the one that counts. But let us give the road the go-by. Here the Imperial door is on the jar, push it gently, with the finger-tips, not the elbow." I do what he bids and we pass up the old dark brown stairs to our rooms. We ought to both be asleep before the dawn, anyway. We are the only visitors in the hotel so we can let our boots fall as heavily as we will on the floor. The only way to get the full relief to a tired foot is to slam off the boot, and, with glory, stretch the toes, and limber them. The staff we need not think of—none of them can be brought awake except by the name shouted at the keyhole. There is one man—a yardman—who shouts the names, because, in a distant land, long ago, he threw the dice for five, and as he rattled the last pitch he said " One more five and I'm five's men ". A fifth time they came up five. So he makes five his hour for arising. When he reached the age of fifty-five, he expected to die, and was ready. Now, he's afraid to say it for fear of making people laugh, but he in secret expects to live to five hundred and fifty-five. You'd say, if you didn't know him, that he was mad. You'd be very simple to say that. He is perfectly sane. We do not hear the five-o'clock man call up the people. Not that he calls them up at that chill hour. He gets up then himself, and is shaved, clothed, and booted in good and sufficient time. We left no orders for our calling last night, and so we are left to sleep out the morning, if we wish to. But hunger wakes us both, and we hit the hungry trail, both simultaneously, at ten o'clock, each coming into the coffee-room by different doors, with far-away dreaming looks in our eyes. Bowsie rubs his hands together, and signals me to strike the bell. A maid, in a pink cotton dress, with deeper pink patches on the elbows, waits at the door for our breakfast orders. But bacon and eggs are almost waiting for us. When the maid comes back to fish out the marmalade from the cupboard, we ask her where is Terry ; she answers in a tone that suggests that Terry is an amusing study to her. She announces that Terry has a headache. We saw no one getting a headache last night. Terry may have been sitting up all night playing cards. Bowsie says that he has never known the hotel waiter who was a thorough-going card player. He believes that shuffling the dreadful creatures who stay at hotels gives them all the interest in chancy life which they require. I would agree with Bowsie but I am not able to on an empty stomach. Just now, at this moment, in comes Terry himself. He looks a bit rattly about the eyes. He does not sleep in the hotel, and he may have slept, by an open window, with the five-o'clock morning breezes blowing on his head. He is not one of those old timers who wear nightcaps. For generations, in the Western World, men thought that they would die if they left off wearing their nightcaps. Perhaps they were right. Terry had sent a message round to the hotel, telling of his headache, and the messenger, going back, told Terry that we were up—and so without ostentation of feeling for us, he came from the rack to see that we ate well. Bowsie searches down in a deep breast-pocket, and finds a flat phial with some white pellets in it. He puts two on the palm of his hand, and throws them into Terry's hand, and tells him to swallow them. Terry, dumbly obedient, swallows them. He takes a tumbler intending to pour some water into it, and wash down the pellets. But changes his mind, and pours a small quantity of dark brown sauce from a sauce bottle into the tumbler and tosses it down. Bowsie looks at him with admiration, and tells him to sit down. Terry, being a little nervous, and looking for somewhere to sit, sees a high hassock by the fireside, and plumps down on that. Bowsie says " Stay perfectly still for five minutes. Do not think, let all that pass you by." Terry does as he is bid. While he sits there the maid comes in with our teapot, milk, sugar and hot water on a tray. She sees Terry sitting there and might have given him a saucy morning greeting, but our presence—Bowsie and myself—sitting, our white hands crossed, hanging limply from the wrist over our crossed knees, gazing fixedly at the sitting waiter, gives the girl pause. She is impressed. Bowsie glances at the clock on the mantelpiece, notes the time that has passed, decides on giving the man of ache another three minutes. Then when they have passed, he claps his hands together and shouts " It is gone—rise up, Terry, you are well ". Terry jumps up, snaps his fingers in the air, and darts through the door which leads to the kitchen, singing out as he goes—" It's gone, it's gone, it's gone ". In a few moments he comes back, serene, carrying our bacon and eggs before him. Bowsie sighs deeply and falls to. I can see nothing to sigh about, and I am eating well. After breakfast we wander a while in the town, loath to depart. We look through the windows of the banks, and by peering over the concealing blinds, we are able to see the clerks at work. They carry heavy books by each other and consult on figures in the books.

In each of the banks while we watch we see several petty-looking customers about their poor business. The busy hustlers, who carry their money before them like a corporation, are, it's likely, not about at this hour. Later, if we could wait, we would see them, we feel certain, with their thumbs on great wads of cheques, and postal orders, paying in, and one, drawing money, the rolls of notes in the hip-pocket, or in some lining pocket of the waistcoat. Yes, he will go over in the corner of the bank, where nothing can see him he is sure, but the framed advertisement of the insurance company. And there, forgetting that the glass on the advertisement, in certain lights, is a looking-glass, he packs away his notes, all in the chamois-leather pouch. Something of the first wearer of the leather might give his notes a jumping hint, for the chamois jump from peak to peak.

We both, Bowsie and I, have the same thought looking over blinds into banks, that if it was ever so, holding up a bank, would go with us, against the grain of the nerve. The younger clerks have a glossy look, which give us the idea that, if it came to shooting, bullets would bounce away off them and back to us. Only in the most fantastic shades of our imagination, do we see ourselves with a revolver in the hand, and never, certainly, letting it off. Even held in the hand, pointing at a banker, we each know that it might seem to tremble. Not that it would matter. An obedient man will stick up his hands before a trembling revolver, as well as before a rigid one. But afterward it would seem scandalous.

But we cannot wait. We must climb out of this town. There is sun on the high ground now, and we will soon be in it, for the sun will shine for some hours to-day.

Up New Garden Street, then up beyond church and cemetery. Then to the left, for a while, between high banks. And then, high on an open moorland, where the sun is ours for its full worth, for this time of year. It's a grand sun. Bowsie is looking neat, and imposing, still. He has the artificial rose in his coat. But, passing by a furze bush, an idea comes to him. He takes the rose from his coat, and fastens it securely, with its wire stem well twisted, to the topmost spray of the bush. Bowsie, with that poetic droop in his eyelids, says, " Wave there, noble flower, and long may you wave over the little young things of the wild— under the rose."

So far we have neither met, nor been passed, by any person on feet or wheels. But now, up from behind, a Ford car comes, and arriving beside us the driver asks us if we go with him. But we wave him on. We are for the footwork, boy. He drives on with our portmanteau beside him. He is going to the Pride Hotel, where after many hours we will arrive. We are now at the highest part of our road and we can see the Atlantic rolled out before us. We stand quite still by the roadside.

A man, on a bicycle, comes towards us and passes us. He is a policeman. I wonder does he know that we look over the blinds of banks, and let our minds run on holds up and their possibilities. But I think he wasn't bothering very much about us. He was resting between crime tacklings, detectives and criminals must rest or they would die out.

Bowsie, I know, thinks a sea coast is no frontier. That man, when full of skill, walked out from headland, out out, over the sea, and could not be gainsaid. And where he stopped, and turned, that was his frontier for the time being. To Bowsie, a hedge inland might be a frontier, but a sea verge, never. I suppose, at this moment, there is no man in all the world kinder than my friend, gazing on the melting into distance of the sea's bright gay surface has sent his mind to think good thoughts for everyone. Yet, in a corner, when he has been rolled in the clawber twice, by a stiff fate. Then I have seen him fight back. Yes, from his back to his stern, from his stern to his knees, from his knees to his feet, and upright. I've seen him flatten fate against the wall as if the dirty coward attacking was nailed there. And I've seen him come out a victor, as if he had a lien on an old star.

But now as I look at his round back, I know he's neither defying nor defeated, he's woven with the sun and the sea haze. In a while now he will move.

He makes the move, and, as we are going downhill

—it's a good time to smoke a pipe, so he fills it and lights it, and the clouds bring him back to this shadow land.

He says we are bound for the " shuttered summer resort, camphored for the winter ". He is proud of words like these. He uses words as if he was using them just for the second time. Like a deaf and dumb man, restored to hearing and speech, who has to constantly pull up his fingers when they want to interrupt ; and, finally, sinks into a broken fingering. Bowsie takes a pleasure in the words, as he speaks them. Most people listening to him think of him with a slight sneer as an amateur. But I'll bet those who talked to him in Gloamy Street last night never thought of him but as one of the right kind.

Now, on the low land by the sea we have before us, many miles away, Shutter and Camphor Town. Sun is shining there. From the foot of this hill we are now on the country undulated with smaller hills away, and here, and there, a sheltering wood, hardly bigger than a copse. Some yellow thatched houses catch the sunlight on their roofs. And even the taller slate houses, here and there, catch a beam where they slope to meet it. Some small rivers meander to the sea. It is low tide, so we have their multitude of mouths, wriggly about the strands. Where we cannot see our road, from where we walk now, we can know where it is by the bridges.

Bowsie knows, between us and the shuttered town, there are two houses of entertainment. There may be more, but they are unlicensed, what some people one time called Shebeens. But now the knowing visitor of the Western World would call them " Speak Easies ". And they are so situated that no one could lurk within a mile of them, without his presence being known. There are no hedges to hide detectives. So any customer can roar out as loud as ever he likes. He will attract the notice of no one but the sea-gulls. Bowsie is in a mood which can never be satisfied in this country. He is in the mood to visit the second of the licensed public-houses, and drag a table out in front of the door and sit on a stool by it, under a tree whose leaves are turning yellow. And he will wish that we should sit there side by side, with the landlord for companion, and sing old choruses while we carouse. Certainly, the exercise of walking and the light strength of the autumn sun would keep us fairly in comfort, for a time. The landlord wouldn't enjoy it so much as we would. But he is a stout man and wears plenty of clothes, except in the height of the summer when, if the summer is good, he is constantly bathing where the sea comes in among the rocks and he has plenty of places where, with sand under his foot, and water up to his breast, he can lean against a rock with his arms folded on it, as on a high desk, and gaze over the surface of the sea, and think of the great sea animals which disported themselves in the oceans long ago.

The landlord would bear with it—that sitting by a table, in the open, late in the year, and so would I, for a short time. But Bowsie cannot do it. For his fancy must have it that he is dressed in full rolling breeches of old crimson velvet, and a blue coat with large flap pockets, and silver fringes and lace about his neck, and big boots, turned over on the top, and a shadowy hat, and a sword, and pistols too. And his hair in ringlets hanging about him. And last, but not least, in the hat, a feather, perhaps thin and worn, like an old pipe-cleaner, near the hatband, but curling, and gay, towards the tip. In fact, a Charles the Second Squire of the footlights. But Bowsie knows he may bring his fancy with him right up to the moment when he sits down on the stool behind his table, but, when he turns his face towards the horizons of the land, that are about him, he knows that his plan cannot strut there. It will not mix. The very essence of the atmosphere disintegrates his figure of fun, and an Irish moth walks through it.

Bowsie must think of something else to loose his make-believe humour on. He might be thinking of himself as a ballad singer. He would enjoy, between whine and roar, intimidating an innkeeper to give him a halfpenny. But, as if to sweep the idea from him at once, from a little brush of trees, at the hill's foot as the road comes up, up come my two carpenter ballad singers, swinging boldly towards us. They have not been as far as the Pride. They were not in that humour. But they did a little trade in Shutter Town. For the handful of permanent residents and the few hang-on-to-the-last boarders were glad of the company of their songs. Now they have been drummed out, or they drummed themselves out. They have always done this of late years in any town they stopped in, if only for a night. Whether they took much money, or little, were taken by the people as innocent lambs, or goats with a bleat. They have always drummed themselves out by marching through the town in the morning singing a song without any known words. But sounding of diabolical defiance. A rogues' march of farewell. They make no collection of money afterwards. They do not stop their march. But clear off on the high road for their next bivouac, leaving behind them a brimstone stink, as the lightning, when it arrives with the thunder.

> Ookie kan, Ookie kan, Ookie kan,
>   kan, kan.
> Ana Kackey ackey ack
>   kack, kack.

The ballad singers go by us moving fast. They wave their arms to us ironically suggesting a Fascist salute, with a fling in it. I feel proud for a moment. I think they know me as in an obituary "Who's Who" of the roads. I would like to think they knew me. But I know now, I had just hit a lumpy piece of road, and was going with a slight halt, and so they recognised me as a footsore wanderer. But Bowsie, in spite of his disguise, they soon penetrate the stilly festive appearance of the pressed clothes, they knew him as a two-footed wanderer, with four good splits in the hoof and prehensile toes. But they did not stop for the sake of either of us. Having turned our faces, to laugh to the ballad men, we turn them back again towards the plain, and an endearing spotlight of sun shines on the rocks, lying out, surrounded with the sands, where the bathing publican laved his body so often this last good summer.

Bowsie passed the first public-house, with his nose in the air, abnegation twisting the muscles of the calves of his legs. He walks as for a wager, and I must keep up with him. He soon saunters again ; it is a dangerous time of year to get very hot in. A cold breeze may blow out of a quarry—there is one quarry on our road—and freeze the limbarised oils of the body. First the quake, then the shake, then the shiver, with a very quick step, short length cropped. Then the bed and the blankets piled high. Always they honoured the shaking warrior with the new blankets, and the smell of new blankets on a sinking soul. They never had new blankets in Tir na nog. The thought of a sick man brings a doctor. I hear a rattle behind us coming quickly near us, and then it goes by us. A doctor in an open car. He would, if he could, have it more open still. He'd have the whole engine uncovered, so that he might keep one eye on entrails always, ready with his lubricant or his stick-for-a-spoke, to encourage or detain. But, if he's a surgeon, he does not love to break any bones. So he does ever keep an eye glued to the road ahead. He has his car so trained, so handy to the wheel, that he can circle her out into the bog, and back again, so swiftly that she never gets quagged. He reserves all her greatest speeds for these swoops from the road and back to it.

A son of Bacchus, lying on the crown of the road on a dark night, admonishing it with a single finger, is safe from the doctor's tyres. If he were as safe from all motorists he might never have to sign the grim pledge.

The doctor—there are others, but this man has made this country to the south and west his own. He asks for nothing better than to be on its few roads and many bogs and sandhills, for as long as he is able. He garages his motor, stern foremost. She must always face the road, and on a frosty night, there's heat there. Though the doctor may be sleeping by a cold grate in a chair, and in his boots. His bell is as easily rung as a fire-bell, and his car might be like a fire-engine, only that he carries the fire with him. He snips a little piece off his life and gives it to the very far gone, and holds them back for a while. He is prodigal in

all things but in this. With these pieces of his life—
he does not give them where they can do nothing—
he knows they will come to the last snippet some day,
so he gives when he is certain, and he is always right.
We fall well away to our side of the road, to give him
the whole crown for himself. He gives us a toss of the
head. A foolish man might have offered us a lift.
But not he. He knew by our backs, when he first
saw them, that with us it was walking time. To most
people there is a time to ride, and a time to walk, and
to some a time to move, so that it is movement, with
a direction, but nothing else. The doctor walking, or
in his car, is moving always on a way. I have seen
him, on a gloomy night, just stepped out of a stalled
car, to move half a dozen miles to where he must go,
and he seemed to step from the car to the road, without preparation or thought, and to move away keeping well down on the roadside, as though the road,
on its fringe, carried some spirit of propulsion itself
that lifted, and put down his feet again, and kept them
straight from stray stones, until he reached the house
where he was wanted.

Bowsie, I say, out of nothing, you would never
make a clerk in a bank, you have not got the necessary gloss. Did you notice how glossy those were this
morning? I don't mean their clothes—some of those
were wearing a sort of half sporting jacket. I mean
about their heads. Smoothed out, in round figures.
All figures should be rounded towards you and me.
Ten thousand pounds are far, and away, better than
nine hundred and ninety-nine pounds, nineteen shillings
and elevenpence.

Bowsie is agreeing with me, with his Japanese " ho,

ho " laugh, but his thoughts are far from glossy money. He is thinking of the shining sea, and where it leads to. He is thinking of the first of the higher land, on his right hand, hanging listless by his leg over the sand and the bogs, and of the time when the sea rolled up there, with boats on the top of the waves, and men and women in them, and all singing in time with the rumbling of the great round boulders, rolling about at the waves' edge. They were already rounded then. He thinks he would have suited those men and women in the boats, coming ashore from an island that was sunk at last. And he turns round to look back at the two ballad singers, just a speck now in the distance, and he tries to think wisely about them, so as to know if they would have suited those men and women in the boats. And he thinks now they would not have suited them, but they would have entertained them. There among the round stones, with their ballads.

Now, here comes number two inn, with the bathing landlord standing by the door, laughing at something he thought of when he saw us coming his way. When we are in his shop, we ask for biscuits to crunch with our bottles of stout. And he calls them " Crackers " because an American visitor, on a bicycle painted a bright blue, and hired to him in the city to the east, called them so. If a mediæval visitor had asked for mead, he would have said : " Here is his fellow-goats' milk with a glass of cognac in it stirred with a cinnamon stick." He has a nanny goat always, though he has also a couple of cows. He keeps his goat because a special occasion may arrive for goat's milk at any time, and it is never wasted. There is a fair old woman who lives in a small cottage propped between sandbanks, by the side of the lane between the road and the sea, and she will have the goat's milk before the cow's. She has great faith in nanny.

The landlord has seen us both before. He never forgets an outward appearance ; he does not collect memories of souls. But though he has seen us before, and knows there is nothing romantic about the diadem in which we sparkle now abjectly. He says "What news ? " with a throaty voice, that tells us well that the news he is thinking of is the news of the great wild world, beyond the rivers and the seas, where swordsmen take their longest weapon and ride round in a circle marking it with the sword's point, and then stand in the centre, with daggers in their hands, and call any woe-to-be-gone giant to step inside the ring. A desert country—a step-on-the-tail-of-my desert country. But we are too filled up with the deep-sea air, and then this porter, to be able to offer any kind of vivid story, even from the newspapers.

We gaze at our landlord, and he gazes back at us—all stupid with the heavy salt air. We had not noticed it as we came down the hill, but now on the level, some eddy caused by the few rocks, and the filling of the tide into little ditches, and a sudden dropping of what little breeze there had been, has filled the whole dip of land with a drowsy greyness breathed out from an ocean's throat. The back door of the shop is open out into the small yard with chickens and a small family of ducks. And it seems as though the strong air floating through from the road, and out at the back, held up the house as if it was straddled on the solid emanations of the sea. The chickens are listless but unafraid, not as they would be under thunder. The duck nearest me twinkles his deep perverse eye at me. He focuses it for me so that I can see straight into it,

between the forms of Bowsie and the landlord, across the whole depth of the shop.

After a time we begin moving about the floor, which has a drift of fine sand on it, towards the door, and the road again. Having said so little, we shake the landlord's hand. It was a good thought, for he, too, was feeling that he had offered no entertainment but his question " What news ? " He shakes hands twice with Bowsie, once in the shop over the counter, and once while he stands under his lintel. He thinks Bowsie needs it, and he gives it, just as he would give a second straw to a drowning man, if he was so chained that he could do nothing else.

Now we are on the road again, it is lifting a little, and now the sandhills are standing up tall, on our left hand. They have cheated the strong sea air from tangling about us, and so we are able to see each other with clearer eyes. We look straight at each other as we stride out strongly. We are both well impressed with the outward appearance of the man we have walking by our side. Bowsie has not even lolled on a gate so his pressed clothes are still in their festal state. But his dark mind is displeased with me. He expects, on this road, to have for companion a being who hides within an earthly shape a most stately soul. And his knowledge of souls is limited. We come to the highest part on this low road, and it is only the top of a hillock, but from it we can see into the sandbanks, and over them. There is a small secret flash with reeds round it, to the north, close in to the road, and as we came abreast of where it should be—some small bird of the reeds flies out, and with a fuss of squealings of imitation fright, and to warn his friends, dashes across our automatically moving knees and

Bowsie forgives me, for ever, for not having the casing of a spirit compensating at the moment his own. And from that moment, we get on better on our way. Now, we have a stretch of road on the higher land, and a breeze is falling across our path, from the hills to the north. The sea gases are driven back before it, though it's only a mild, and irregularly puffing, breeze. Bowsie is talkative ; he tells me of his victories, or more often his runnings up, in foot races at school, and as a young man. Four miles was his best distance. If he could afford it now, he would have a cinder-track on his estate, just in front of the high paling which kept in the artificially wilded boars who would live in his private forest, not for the purpose of having them hunted, but that they might go back to nature. He liked to go up to the top of the ladder and watch a fine old boar sharpening his tusks against the trunk of an ancient oak. On his cinder-track he would watch young men, as good as ever he was, racing their four miles, and every lap he would jump up and run twenty, or thirty, yards with them, alongside them, with a high-stepping meticulous action, none of your sloping along come-day go-day. He says his mansion, with pillars, will be in another part of the estate, with another palisade, between himself, his guests, and the wild boars. He does not believe that they could get over two fences. We are passing by a twisted elder bush, and Bowsie begins to throw himself about in argument. He says that it is not arithmetic which makes him believe two fences better than one, because in this case there is no reason why a nimble young boar, supple enough to mount one paling, should not mount another, unless the first had taken too much out of him, and if the palings were the same height. " Then why do you suppose I have two palings ? " he is asking me. " I believe you think it is just because I think that two hostages to fortune are twice as good as one, which is arithmetic again, unless the idea is that fortune considers one an idea and two an importunity, in which case, fortune might like to give me a slap over the knuckles. But that introduces fortune into a moral point of view." But I am quick here with my word. I point out to Bowsie that he has named the elder bush long ago " The Bush of Argumentation ", because, while passing it, he was always starting a shadow-word fight. Bowsie lowers his crest, convicted out of his own bush. He wipes his mouth with his hand, and forgets arguing with me—for always.

Over the land on our left, zigzagging round the marshy patches, comes a young sheepdog, he came from a long whitewashed house on a hillock. He is a friendly dog, and looks at us with an inquiring look to his head. He is worried a little about some obstinate sheep, which has strayed away from the higher lands. He thinks to find her on the end of the sandhills. Even in his young life he has known sheep go a good way to pasture, on a small piece of bright grass—no larger than a quilt. He is looking for this one from a difficult sense of duty. But Bowsie looks at the dog's long nose too quizzically for the creature to remain all the time in school. All work and no play would surely make Jack a dull boy. So this Jack paws a piece of blackened dried seaweed ; throws it into the air, catches it in his mouth, and races away down the road with his tail waving. A little way, and he stops, and we watch him gambolling from side to side.

After a time we look back and we see the dog still on his gambolling ground, and he has received the reward of the playfulness, for we see a grey, and leggy, sheep climbing over a bank, and going towards the antic dog. Where dignity had failed in a sheepdog, plain foolishness had succeeded. Curiosity, and admiration, had drawn the sheep to come to the shepherd.

Bowsie feels that he did it, that, but for his encouraging glance, as of one emancipated wanderer who had passed the Bush of Argumentation to another who had never bothered about the bush, the dog would have remained a worried dog. He had done a good work and encouraged the mitching spirit. He thinks, now, that he himself, in his young days, might have mitched more. But he forgets to regret, in planning new duties, which he will never perform—to travel the wide world—to see all the great buildings of the East and the West—to master languages—to learn to be a sailor before the mast—to train his memory to perfection—to learn to play a light waltz—to learn to be a perfect gentleman at all times, cool, except when his cheek is flushed with indignation, and rightly so. But even that flush will be under his perfect control. One message flashed from his brain will stop the flush, stop it at the neck. I know you thus far, Bowsie. You glory in your mitching freedom from ever getting within a distance of all these named duties. If you had a little Jew's harp now against your teeth, and could play it, you would send forth a farewell to duty. But it is well you haven't the harp, for the solo would complete your sense of freedom in one performance, whereas now, as long as you live, you will always freshly hug another duty not performed.

One more up, one more down, and up again, a twisting turn in the road, with a small ford at the foot of the hill, and stepping-stones on the right. And then we will see Shutter Town before us.

As we walk along we are wandering about on the roadway, walking carelessly, where up to this to-day we paced sturdily, side by side, keeping an even distance from ourselves. Now, our day's journey nearly done, we weave about, bump into each other, and use up the space of the road ; one time going pigeon-toed, one time splay-footed. Until we come to the ford, and there the stepping-stones must be crossed with care. They are fine, square, strong, steady blocks of stones. But the moss grows well on them, and over them, and we see that, ever since they have been put in position, those that used them stepped off and landed in a space no bigger than a span. Neither of us know how long these stones have lain here so solidly. We both think that crossing the running water will give us the fear gorta. And so it does. We both feel finely hungry in a moment. We crossed plenty of running water, for there were ten stepping-stones. And though the river was low enough, there was a brown, twisting, lively bunch of eddies about the miniature cliffs of the stones' steep sides.

Up the last short hill, and before us lies Shutter Town. We thought it might have grown, and spread out grandly, since we last saw it. But it is not so. We count six new buildings, and two of them are sheds. The town still is just a large village, but it's letter E shape, one street facing the sea, and three short ones at right angles, each of these short streets, with no more than a dozen houses in them, gives it something of the unexpectedness of a gold-paved bonanza, the shape of which, in the days of old, the days of gold, the days of forty-nine, set for ever, while this civilisation lasts. One main street where authority draws itself out as long as possible like an elastic band, and like such a band is liable to snap back very small, if not held firmly. The short streets at right angles have gaps among the houses, and garden plots. But the main street had no gaps, nor has it here. The ironmonger, who has a licence for the sale of alcohol. The post office. The older chemists. The public-house, which sells groceries also, the Island View Hotel. The stationer's and newspaper shop. The baker's shop. The bakery is in one of the short streets. The View Hotel, it had at one time claimed an ocean view, but the salt spray, coming over the sandhills, mixed with the sand took away the " ocean ", or melting it to such softness that the proprietor's little boy, on a ladder, which his father and mother held, high up, on the house's front, painted out the " ocean ", and came down again. That is a few years ago now. Not so very many for the boy is still young, though he is far away. He is on the backs of horses all the day's hours. In the Southern States of America, he rides races for a rich owner and a sly trainer. His mother often thinks of his little legs encasing the fiery bodies of huge black horses, who snort as they gallop. She always pictures the horses as black and tall, and she has forgotten that her son's legs must be longer than they were when he left home, with his uncle, to try his fortune in the America where his uncle had lost his so often. Still, her son has not grown very tall. He'll never be fat and heavy. The great horses, some of them are black, excite him too much for his flesh to ever rest long enough to swell and thicken. He always had good bones and in his bones he will die. He has hardly any muscle, just whangs of leather. He rides the horses by his will which runs, as a wish, through him into the horses, and drives himself, and them, on together. Horses fly under him, and he wins too many races for people not to pull their noses and talk about the " devil's luck ", and " evil spirits ", helping on " their own ". But there is no evil in the victories of these horses and this man. They both wish for victory.

We are close to Mullin's bootshop where young Devany works once a week. But he is not here to-day. The shop is only half a shop, one blind being half down. The boots and shoes in the window are in some disorder. A grey and white fat cat is sitting proud amidst the disorder. He made it for himself, not because he could not pick his way as delicately as he liked, but because he liked playing with the laces of the white canvas summer shoes. The cloak of puss conventionality worn by cats had made this one think lightly of canvas shoes so far in the year as now.

Our hunger is now acute. We enter the View Hotel, and we eat well, in a back room, without a view, but with a fire. The proprietor brings in our meal himself. Not because he loves to be " Mine host " waiting on loved guests, but because he sent the maid, the old one who stays on through the winter storms, and calms, because she knows no place better, to the bank. There is a bank round a corner. The landlord of the View says his wife is away in town. A particular picture she wanted to see. The landlord doesn't look the Jovial Boniface. He is a brown-faced man with heavy lines driven into the sides of his mouth during a long illness. He, apropos of nothing, tells us of a certain winner for a race next day. He gives no reason, nor does he tell us who told him. He dreamt of this winner. He has had these dreams of race-courses before, and this one was less vivid than usual ; but he is determined about this one, so much so, that when we have gone away, or finished our dinner at any rate, and the maid comes back from the bank, he will take his motor from the yard and drive to three towns about in the district. In each he will place his money with a bookmaker. A turf accountant. There is one even here in Shutter Town. But who would take a dream-certain mass of money from a neighbour's child ? Neither will we take the man's money, so we give a few shillings each to the landlord, to use for us, placing it where he thinks most fit. We believe we are in on a vision and empty our pockets of all our ready money but a trifling sum to jingle until to-morrow about four o'clock, when the landlord, our friend in bets, will know the result, and hand us our winnings, in perfect confidence that his bookmaker will not fail him in settling to the minor pennies. I never have seen a man so confident. I can see it in his back now, for we, Bowsie and I, are standing by the hall door watching our friend shaking up his span new car for the road. He spins her round sharp to the left—an inland running road will take him to the town, where his first victim must take the money to-day, to bite the dust to-morrow. Bowsie and I, with a fleeting thought for fellow-men, hope for a moment that these victim turf accountants may have a full bag fed from those who have no dream certainty, and to-morrow afternoon will be down the course. But what about these other sportsmen, are they to lose their money to soften our consciences. Too late, or too soon, our landlord carries our money. So we are

too late to take it back. But " too soon " never that.
Never a thought of possibility of defeat to-morrow.
To-day we may be neither mice nor men—in seeming,
but to-morrow, we are men stuffed with our winnings.
We wish, for a moment, we had been more full of ready
money for the sure venture. But now we know the sum
was the right sum for the event. The event opens to the
moment. The height of the sun which opens the daisy,
is neither more, nor less, but sufficient. Two daisies,
we. We will stroll about the layout of this town.
Five minutes walk to the north-west, up a small hill,
and then a sedgey place, open and wild enough. Back
to the front of the town, a look-out towards the west,
and we know that will do for the next day. So we
turn back along the face of the town, the way we came.
Turn inland, up the two remaining short streets. One
ends in a quarry of poor soft stone, and one continues
over low rolling hillocks towards the north-east. We
have left the last cigarette carton, so we are out of the
town. We are satisfied ; we return. The dusk will
soon be falling. The gramophone shop is about to give
its public concert. Children and old men are at the
door just at the moment, when the opening dialogue
begins. We are there too. We timed our walk to the
country's fringe well. We have passed into the half
sleep of the town's life at this time of year. After a
while, we will go down to the less metropolitan of the
grocer's, and there we will find the grocer sitting on
his counter to be near the lamp, reading his daily paper.
He will give us helpings of it, a large double sheet
each.

We are with him now. I have the financial sheet ;
I am reading it, as if it was of the greatest importance

to me. I read of a far-away world. When the night has fully fallen, the road we walked along to-day will seem a far-away track, though our shadows walk there still. But this world of money, and ups and downs, is exciting to me, as an account of a bull fight in China would be. Bowsie has got a sheet with some minor criminal proceedings, a farewell supper, some notes of condolence passed in silence, all members standing. But now the grocer has finished as much of his part of the paper as he cares for, at this time of day. He puts it down, turns round, and using his stomach as a lever, gets his legs clear of any boxes that are propped behind the counter, and drops to the ground. The floor behind the counter is lower than where we stand, so, the grocer surprises me by disappearing, except for his head and shoulders. I had been in his shop several times before and never happened to see this peculiar phenomenon before. At other times we had been further down the counter nearer to the door, where perhaps, the inner floor is raised.

The lamp leaves all the four corners of the shop in darkness, and clothes many shelves in an air of murk. I am thinking idly how unexciting it would be if some genie from out of an Ali Baba jar, or a tea chest, should jump up on the counter and run along noiselessly, like a pet of an old cat. The grocer says to me : " In my father's old shop up in the town, we had an old cat, and when the father was reading the paper, he'd come along and sit looking at the back of the paper, and you'd take your oath he was reading it. The father wouldn't turn the paper over until he asked the old cat if he'd finished with his side. They're very knowing." I see his eyes turn, looking along the counter towards the door, and there, sitting in the shadow of the shop desk, with its green paling, is a small white cat with pale green eyes. He is looking at us three. Bowsie asks the grocer if he has any of those old Henry Clays he used to have. The grocer goes away and comes back with part of a box and Bowsie buys two. He hands one to the grocer, and lights the other himself. They are strong and beautiful ; the grocer finds a small tin cigarette case, with a broken hinge, in his waistcoat pocket, and offers me a cigarette. I take it—light it and let it go out. No customers come to the shop. I sit on a box, with a tinned salmon label on it, and see the mists of cigar smoke gathering in that deep shaded, low-ceiling'd shop. The sky over the sea has turned, while my back was turned, to a clear, bright, fleckless green. It is as peaceful a green as ever I saw.

I remind Bowsie that we are for the Pride Hotel some time to-night. I should not have done that—it has brought Bowsie back from some fairyland where he and the grocer were discussing safe, dead and leaf-moulded, politics and a Happy Land of pure personality. Bowsie turns to me coldly and tells me I should telephone to the Pride to have our suit-cases taken back here to the View for to-night.

I go along the street face to the hotel and telephone. So we are settled—the lorry will take a spin this way on its return to the port, and leave our luggage here. I believe Bowsie would have been ready, and glad, to sleep in his clothes. Indeed, this day's tramping, and lolling about, has taken their first bridal flush away. By the way Bowsie rubs his hands down his thighs I know his clothes are becoming familiar to him again. By the time I get back again to the grocery, Bowsie has said all he wanted to say, and listened to all he wants to listen to. As I come in at the door, framed,—I know I am, in the clear green sky shine, Bowsie gives his peroration—a farewell to dead politicians " wrapped in their cere clothes ". Old copies of the *Freeman's Journal*, giving their firm speeches in full. That's what he pictures when he says " cere clothes ". But he is unwilling to hurt the feeling of the man he talks to, to whom those long columns of speeches represent " A golden youth fled ". So he says " those cere clothes are the green unsullied flags of those old days, before a lot of young fellows thought they could improve a decorative effect by substituting other emblems for the Harp, the Round Tower and the Old Dog. No matter what they say, there were good men in those days, good-night "— he was going to say " to you ". But with the affection-ate sympathy of that rounded type, to which Bowsie belongs, he substitutes " my old friend ". The shop-man is pleased, for he has reached so far along the road that he sees the end, and he knows how few grey flannel shirts he will buy for himself. Every year he waddles up the street to Lowrey's shop and buys three. And gives away the old ones to the man who wheels about the little truck with the sacks, and boxes, balanced on it. He himself likes the rasp of the new shirt-band against the stout bristles of his neck. He knows quite clearly that Bowsie is too young to remember, except in a haze, those old political figures of solemnity. That in his own day were alive, and swooping from one great meeting to another. In the roomy wagonette, which made a platform at some times, at others, came easily alongside the board platform on the barrels, and like a ship by a quay side, discharged its cargo of Treasure Trove. From Parliament, the House of Commons, the floor of the House, in frock coats and with top-hats they came. Two long railway journeys, a sea crossing between and a long drive in the wagonette, and yet these Warrior's of the forum, by the black majesty of their bearing, and the full loaded speech, might have stept from the seats in the House to the wagonette. Without a ruffled lock of the hair, they stept out on to the platform in the market-place of a town of the south, or western fringe, of Ireland. Bowsie has never seen them like that, but the shopman has.

Bowsie and I walk along the side walk, with the grit of the sand under our feet, and Bowsie is very tired of me, walking again by his side. So he turns quickly to the gramophone shop. It will not be closed for a long while yet ; it may be open all night. At all times, the man who owns it leaves a small lamp burning through the night to show them, if at any dance, the company should want a new record, they can get it from him. The bell above his bedroom door rings. He lights the candle on the chair by his bed, rolls out of bed, and always automatically, throws his arms out in time to catch the falling gramophone, which, on the chair, had sung him to sleep with a new-old favourite record. He has never yet failed to catch the gramophone as it topples towards the floor. The records he appreciates are never the very latest ; they set his teeth jangling, nor the very early ones ; they make him ashamed. But the ones in the middle distance come into his heart and comfort it. For in the middle distance of his own years, he re-members he had hope. The gramophone man is fixing a new needle, as we push into his shop. There are three young men already in it—two sitting on the counter, one sitting in a low armchair.

The gramophone man starts the machine, and turns away his face. Some uncertain purring comes up to us and then chains of golden syrup seem to float in the air, while through them, at six-foot intervals, crates of china fall to the floor and smash into stars. Bowsie presses his hands against his chest, throws his eyes up to the floor above, and says he lives. One young man whistles through his teeth in opposition. The others look downwards absorbed. Bowsie turns to me, his travel-stained face, for listening to the records, he has travelled far down alleys of calm, but oftener of teasing, memories. He says " Do we eat ? " And so meekly I walk out of the shop and lead the way back to the View. In the stone hall, propped against each other, pathetic, yet friendly, are our two suit-cases. We eat chicken, and bacon, and potatoes and apple pie. The hotel had known we would stay. The Boss is back. The money is on.

Bowsie rises up over his plate, fully fed, and blesses me. He is no more angry with me for being about, trailing by his side, like a broken boot-lace. He even sings a little under his breath " Maid of Athens "—an old-fashioned song for Bowsie ; a song of a day, and Bowsie himself, is out of all dates. Hard set for interest, any crumb will do, he makes his own and pecks it. He takes up now a fashion magazine. A cover design that might have come from the studio of a designer, who was ready to follow Picasso—if he was let. Bowsie is unperturbed. He gives no sniff, as he will give no sniff, when the ninth great wave rolls him over, and away, with the last sound in his ears. The sand and pebbles of the shore, swished down by the falling sweep of water. The hotel man is ready to give us the full account of his visits to the turf accountants. And how, at one time, he was followed by another car—mysterious, long, black, and raking, no doubt, and how at a cross-road, he fumbled at his pocket, and as if by accident, left on the road a leaf of a note book with the words :

> High Span
> Ketcheree
> Embroidery.

written quickly with a shaking pencil.

It worked well, for, as soon as the following car came up to the paper, the men in it got out, and cogitated on the words. They thought they were names of horses to back, and so they might be as far as the hotel man knew. They came to him at the moment. The delay gave him the chance, he said, to shake off his pursuers and now the money is on nicely, nicely.

Well, here we are, in the back room away from the sea, and looking out into the yard, where the light from the window, shines into the open shed with the mud-spattered car, limestone mud, which has served us punters so well. " So well ", we hope we will be saying that to-morrow afternoon.

Bowsie is expansive now, with his whiskey glass held in his round hand. We washed down our dinner with hot, strong tea, and it is not always the best soup to go with chicken, bacon, potatoes, and apple pie. Bowsie tells us of his visit to Venice, with his mother, long ago, and, of how he took the long oar from the gondolier, and in the early morning, tried to swing the gondola on a corner, and took the wrong road, or read the rule of the road, of the canals, wrong, and a gondola, Bowsie said (" A Fire Engine Gondola ") took him off his perch, and threw him in the canal, and he was saturated for his breakfast. He tells the story well enough to make an undignified figure of the young Bowsie. But it is a rambling, disjointed, story, without the true raconteur craft or show. He did not trouble to keep the water even under and about him. For all we listeners might know, part of his adventure might have taken place in a dry ditch. He is finished, a depleted story maker. The hotel man takes up the running. No Joe millers no Percy anecdotes. No old Almanac stuff. But tales of the adventures of two friends, a shoemaker, and a publican, dead beyond contradiction. Most of the adventures are pictorial, and moving, as if our landlord had pre-invented the cinema. These stories are all of the years before the cinema, and I never detect in the telling, the slightest influence of the screen. I do once or twice, think, if my theatrical memory was more certain, I might recognise some grouping from an old stage.

The small shoemaker, bobbing up and down, in the barrel of water, in the deep night, believing he is in the bay. Or the publican in the dry barrel,· or the cart without the horse and the reins round a branch of a tree and back to the publican's coat tails, in the dark of night. Almost all the adventures required the darkness of night, or the darkness of the mind before a deluge of strong drinks. In these days, when man walks the earth bright, and alert, for all his waking hours and sleeps with one ear to the floor, for fear his neighbour's gramophone might be chasing a new record, jokers must not make any plans where the confusion of alcohol is necessary to make the victim easy, and willing. The story-teller has run himself to a standstill.

The room is full of smoke. The landlord gets up, and pushes down a couple of inches at the top of the window. The door opens and his wife walks in, with a plate, on which are sandwiches. She is a tall, narrow built woman, and was crouching, for three hours, in the cinema to-day. She is full of the dramas she saw, and could tell them well, but she won't. She would tell her husband and myself, if I was the only other in the room. But she could not describe a drama before Bowsie. The cushioness of his lumping figure is indicative of a deadening of resonances,—a buffet to a buffet. But her plan of the stories of the plays she saw, is sharp and swiftly darting, forward and back. And she will not attempt to loosen more than the plan of her stories against Bowsie's heavy ramparts.

Bowsie and I go off to bed. We are both dog tired.

My window opens inland and there is a little ivy about it, which catches the morning sun. I know I am not so ravenous as the strong air should make me. I remember the sandwiches last night. They must have been a stay to breakfast hunger, because I am shaving slowly, and carefully, and so is Bowsie. For it is long after we have been called, with one dead thump, on each bedroom door that we arrive at the open hall door together. Bowsie is looking very fresh and pink. Against the door jamb is leaning a tall aged man, in frayed, and shining clothes. He is tanned the colour of a Red Indian. We have heard of an old timer sailor, derelict for ever, on this shore. On the beach, at summer, giving advice to visitors in the launching of small boats, and he knowing nothing about small boats, for his great manhood was spent in tall, magnificent, reckless ships, bounding round the globe. Bowsie at once speaks to Red Tan, and to hear as much before breakfast as he can, bursts lamely enough, for Bowsie, who can pick his words well when he likes, into the blue sea. " Morning, that's a nice clear morning, better than some of those you've seen, not so far off the Cape, or sliding through the easterly islands." And old Indian Red says quickly :

" Bet, your life on that, coming out of the China Seas ; every rope squealing. Into it like you was on a pond with the old man sweeping the crest of the head, of any man, loitering near him, with a belaying pin. Like it was a pond, I'll say, and it the deepest hole of a sea in the world, nor ever Marco Polo saw, and sucked down half-way below in the troughs of the waves. But not breaking, you'll understand, too thick to break. Like as if they was made of old green bottle ends. Like mint jelly. Thick I'll say that. And as you say, sliding through the islands. Over some of the flat ones, I shouldn't doubt. And the old man eating his moustaches up into the Indian Ocean to get a slant. And then down before it with the masts like fish-hooks hooked forward. And all the same sail we were born with. All new stuff, stiff like as it was nailed. We tightened everything with a tourniquet. Swooping down the Indian Ocean, and between Tasmania and the Australian main. Then up, short hauled, through the South Seas Islands with the bonitos hopping out of the sea, to let us have the road. And the old man all combed up, and greased, expecting to be home in a matter of hours. No sense of lives or men's lives. We went through two purple hurricanes like as if they were cheese. And for three days after that we were smashing through spray, green spray, lumps like big snow, the wind just forrard of the beam. The old man rubbing the spray all over his withered old face, as if he was going to shave. Coming up by St. Helena, I was all for going ashore, and seeing some soft bread, and Napoleon's Memorial Museum. But the old man was all for on, on. After that I fell into a deep sleep, and when I woke it was the Old Head of Kinsale, and I was glad. I had a pillow on the fo'c'sle head, a silk pillow, what I'd won in China, in a raffle and I never lifted my head off it until we made Liverpool.''

A fair-headed young girl comes tripping out of a side door, beside the newspaper shop. The side door is of a passage that leads to a little house, in the yard, behind the newspaper shop. The young girl, without bothering to look our way, cries : '' Come along to breakfast ''. And old Tan Face turns swiftly round on his heels, and strides away, and disappears in to the door for breakfast. And Bowsie turns to me and says '' Was that the right, man ? '' I say, I cannot say, I have a doubt, but I am content to leave it as it is.

After breakfast, we idle about a long while, looking at old papers, where the sun comes in at our hanging bow window over the door. The day is the loveliest I have ever seen in this county. The sky is mildly mother-o'-pearl, and the air, that drifts in at the hall door, and up the stairs, is like milk. But the sun is in no way reduced by the sweet moist air. For it is strong with a diffused strength ; and when it beats on the bow window it bakes the old newspapers lying about, till they smell like tinder. We hear the landlord's feet heavily falling on each step of the stairs. He is coming up to us. He hands me the newspaper from the city. He has folded it so that I can see a small paragraph, and it is bad enough. There is no dark headline or journalistic fuss, but it drives upwards from the page, like a double black domino. It tells of a young man in America who, thinking he had been given a dollar wrong in his change, in a small restaurant, throws a heavy weight from the counter scales at the woman behind the counter and kills her for a dollar. The man's name is given and in carelessness, nothing else, not wickedness, the man is said to be a native of the seaport town. I show the paper to

Bowsie, and he, in an instant, realises that the landlord knows well that this name is only of this seaport. There is no one bearing it there now, but, a few years ago, there were, perhaps, two people. They are dead, but earlier some of this family had gone to America.

The weather will break when it will, and no colloguing talkers will be walking in the streets of the seaport, as they were the night before last. The winter will have come. The slayer for a dollar is in a jail. The people of New Garden Street don't understand the others of the town. They would be ready, if they got a single helping hand to take a small steamer—a coal boat, now lying at the quay undischarged, and sail to America in her, march on the jail and take the man out, and let him have justice. So that by no loophole, of law tricks, could he still live on—no lynching ideas in their heads, just take him to Justice—Justice that they would be sure of. Two women above Look-Out Lane have a plan to make a bonfire and burn an effigy of the young man, who took a woman's life for a dollar. They have got an old coat, and hat, from an old age pensioner. But no bonfire will flare to these wives' satisfaction. Their husbands have seen to it, that all their plan comes to nothing. It all comes to nothing and that's the best after all.

In the afternoon, there is a ring at the telephone bell, silent all the day. The landlord is across to it, across the stone passage, and into the small back room where the telephone hangs on the wall, among old coats. " Yes, yes, yes, yes." Why do people answer telephones so noncommittally when other people, knowing they will know soon, are twisting their fingers at waiting. Bowsie and I are standing behind the landlord in the room of old dried-out frieze and homespun and tweed, and tarpaulins. Like faithful spaniels, our questing eyes and noses are tilted expectantly. They sound good "Yesses", but we don't know the man's voice so well as to be sure. If his wife would come and stand here with us, she would be able to read his tic-tac tongue. But she, Noble Roman wife, is waving her distaff in the bow window. Where the pale skirted fuschia looks out at her wild red sisters, when they are in flower, and she hanging demure, and spiritual, inside the glass wall. The landlord's wife thinks backing horses foolishness, though she plays a little bridge.

The landlord at last reaches his " yes " and " goodbye ", and we know now that we are each a few pounds richer. Bowsie is six pounds better than he was yesterday, and I have my four. The landlord pays us himself, at once. In half-notes—it looks so much more. He must dream some more good horses. We give him our blessings in this matter. And soon again we are arranging that a passing car takes our baggage on before us.

Now we are on the road again—the land ahead is flatter than yesterday's land. But in the distance we can see the green rise where just hidden by a fold is the Pride. The sky circling over us in every colour that is, and silky, a tinker twisted withy tent. The old tunnel shape and we two, like tinker fleas, skipping on the tent floor. Great energy in our thighs. Three large flat-shored bland bays lie on our southerly hand. Short green grass, or sand, is all about our way, and the road is built on stones brought from a distance. It is a road that waves up and down, too short the rise and fall to give it the name of undulating. It is a dancing road, a singing road, and Bowsie sings, just a " lal, lal, lal, lal, lal, lal, lallity ". And I don't feel in any way irritated by his voice, any more than I feel irritated with a bird which tells me the same fine thing over and over again.

A thin stooped man comes up a little green path on our right, and falls into step by us. He nods his head in time to Bowsie's lal, lalling. Then he says " It's a pleasant, and a natural day to be walking this road." He joins us, of course, from the land side, and at first he stayed by me. I was in the middle of the road, and Bowsie on the left by the sea. But after a few paces, this new passenger moves round behind us, and comes up on Bowsie's left, between him and the sea. Observing these bays : " The sea never did me any harm," he says " and I don't believe I ever did it any harm unless it was an insult to throw a bucket of potato peelings on the surface of it. You would notice that potatoes are peeled at sea. There was a time when there were darn few potatoes going on the long voyages, but that's neither here nor there. I am the man that never misses anything on this shore. If it was an empty box, it makes its presence known to me. A wild bird of the ocean laid an egg just above high water spring, among the stones that were like eggs on the point beyond. I walked straight to it, here from where we were standing. I never touched the egg. But she never came back. I think it was a foolish egg to make me look foolish. But if that was her idea she failed on me for a man that is so much by the brink of the sea as I am. I could never be made look foolish by its brink. It was a bird that was long on the wind, and swift, and had no very important knowledge of shores. There are places along those bays where there are little farms of shells that would delight your heart to look down on, and to lie

among, very sweet and clean. There is no contamina-
tion on these three bays. The draining from Hayden's
Hotel sink into the ground. I spoke to Hayden and him
building the place. He agreed, as soon as I moved the
word from my lips, that no house of his would con-
taminate the whiteness of the strands. Wasn't it a grand
thing that a man would have so much respect for the
sea's lips that he would not annoy them. He's full of
songs sometimes. Like our friend here. He thinks it
does the air good to ventilate it here and there, with
the voice of man, singing praises on himself. You'll
forgive me speaking so openly and 'foolishly', you
might say, if you didn't understand the respect I have
for you both. Of the two of you, our songster here has
the more understanding ". Bowsie goes on with his
" lallity ", either from toughness of hide, which makes
him not notice a personal appraisement, or from the oil
on his old ducks back of individuality, or just general and
panelled vaguenesses produced into perspective until
they meet in a point.

Sea-gulls are flying about us far more than we noticed
along our ways yesterday. Sea-gulls have the gift of
changing their shape, and size, at will. One type of
gull will in an hour look as all types. And a herring gull
can hang in the air close to your face, his jeering cry still,
and be for a time an albatross. In mist he can draw
the grey gauze round him and disappear behind its
curtain, and he comes back a pierrot of the first melancholy type, cringing at Pierrette's door. Then with a
flirt of his tail, he can stand up into the sky a white-
washed tabernacle. I look over at the passenger on
Bowsie's left, and he looks to me like a white-washed
tabernacle. He is so cleanly shaved—so sea clean.
Clean in his blood; he looks as if he lived on spring

water, and the leaves of the ground. His whitewash is of that pure variety that hides nothing, but whitewash beneath. I suspect him for an instant of being a martyr of some kind. But then, I know he is not. He has a springing defiant walk, as a man carrying no other man's load ; but bringing his own along, held up by the end of his finger, with a conjuring trick, which has taught that finger to lift, and convey, a heavy package, by pressing its tip against the packages' upper side. As I think about him, wondering, he turns his face towards me, and a smile beginning on the forehead, and sweeping down to the chin, shows me he eavesdropped on my thought. He looks to me, this moment, as small as wood sorrel. But this one, he looks to me like Downpatrick Head in a gale of wind. We are walking in step, at about three miles an hour ; a nice pace, the legs swinging steadily on, while the body, from the hips, can twist about as it likes. Three gyroscopes nicely balancing, in that better society, where three are company, and none compromises. Nobody passes us by. If they did, they would just see three benign looking men, who must, they'd say, have lately fed well. As a matter of fact, all of us are hard set. Bowsie and I forgot to eat, even a biscuit of lunch. And the passenger eats when he rises at dawn, and again immediately after the sun has set. He allows the sun to rise him up, but he, in return, tucks him into the hay at night, and often, at this time of year, the sun does go down under a fiery bunch of hay clouds. In the early days of magic lantern, an exhibitor would simulate a dissolving view with a wisp of hay, moved up and down, between the slides. But the passenger thinks nothing of magic lanterns. He is old enough to remember when they were a novelty in far-away valleys, and he has sat in little halls, in distant lands, watching

the bright, and gloomy, pictures on their white sheet.
If he was in a position, at the time, that gave him a right
to be close to the engine, then he would stand behind the
lantern, and view the slides in his hand, before they
were pushed into the lantern, to be enlarged into jellyness.
Especially he liked the bright-coloured ones, he liked to
see them in his hand, and to hold them up against the
small back light of the lantern.   Then he could be ready
to hand the wanted one to the exhibitor, the lanternist.
Once as a young sailor he got a full night of entertainment,
when, because the sheet was set up clear of the walls,
he was able to get to the back of it away from the
spectators, and so see the other side of the picture that
they saw.   He knew there was little difference between
the two pictures to the ordinary gross eye.   But with him,
and his eye, the people and the houses, and the trees,
were in a world, a third world, in a ciotogact world.
There was first the event, then the slide made from the
photograph of it and shown to those in front.   Then the
inner side of the second world, and that belonged to
him—all that evening.   He was the last out.   Indeed,
the caretaker, who smelt of cedar, was in the roadway
pulling the door to after him.   When, out of the dark
building stept our young sailor-man tripping on his toes,
but too wrapt up in himself to give away his soft breaths
in talking to the caretaker.   He just said " farewell ".
He is like a man, to me, now, that is constantly saying
farewell—tipping a past over the side.   As he walks
with us, I have a sense that he is making a prolonged
farewell with us, because it happens that his freakish
plans take him along our way.   He has only a blow-
away interest in us, and why should he have more.
We are unable to see the grain of the material of his
memories as he is hoisting them into the deep blue sea.

We neither get the pictures of his old mind in the detail, or in the broad swing. We get something, and before we pass it along the wooden cash holder, and the stringy wires, to our own cashier's perch of the brain, we try to make out a bill for it, in some striking little language of our own, flippant when it ought to be prancing, and buoyant when it ought to be sunk.

But this man is a great man ; I can tell it by his way of walking and his leaning on the greatness about him ; for whatever way our values have moved, up and down, and round about, one side for correspondence, the other for address and stamp, like a foreign-going post-card, everyone alive allows the sky is great and this man knows that.

If I let my imagination pull me about, I will be seeing wild things, wilder than I ever saw them. Just now this man steps off the roadway to walk by its side, where a long strip of emerald grass, short as the fur on a young seal's back, lies by the road. And I could think that before each footfall the little blades of grass made themselves into a little pattern, to take the tread of his foot. Just now he is silent, his arms hanging lightly by his side, except when he lifts one hand, or the other, to, with his finger tips, move back a lock of his brown hair, which hangs before an ear. It is as though he likes to let his ears think they can listen to all he hears.

But now he is talking to me directly, his chin on his right shoulder, as he paces along, and he does not seem to look on the path he treads, even with a glance through his fringed eyes. There are white stones here and there along it, but he never stubs his toe on them.

I listen to him talking, but my eyes are watching his feet—their careful " rise and fall ". I would say only that I know they are not under the governance of the eyes in the head above them. They are very neat feet in boots of thin leather, old boots, but well cut and sewn together, long ago. Handsome boots and handsome is that handsome goes, they walk handsomely. We are moving along slowly, but I know by these swinging steps that these feet would eat a road before them as fast as any man, short of a champion, very short of a champion, could cover the ground.

This man tells me of birds he has seen in foreign lands. So small that one perched on a high swells necktie. " People standing about, at the edge of the wood, on a summer evening, shaking the sweat out of their hats, thought the bird was a stick-pin head. Like a jewel, you'd say—yes, a jewel on a finger, finger ring perching, a jewelled ring. They said, some of the ladies, fine ladies, stylish, would put a bit of honey on the tip of the ear. So the bird would perch, ornamental ear-ring, jewel hanging, one on each ear, ruby you'd say, this side, sapphire that side, biting the lady's ear—all in the dusk of evening. Darting out of the trees, to throw themselves around in the last bit of sun, when it was sinking very strong, long strokes of it maybe split round a rock point on the horizon, and coming up to you, where you stood, like a gold corridor. Some say the shine of snow is very fine. I have never seen snow. I was never on a winter day in the land when snow was on the ground. Snow doesn't like me. It melts before I come. I was in a seaport, where the town streets were torn up with the melted snow. But the last lump was carried down a gutter to the sea before I landed, a day before I landed. I don't mind thinking of it—I'm not afraid of it. There are few men who move about but have seen snow, if it was only on the top of one of the great high mountains, where it never melts. But I never saw one of these mountains. I was off a coast where there was a high scattering of mountains just within the coast.

We came round a headland, and the men got me up out of the bunk to see snow. I was in my stockinged feet, but there was a roll of mist all along the mountain-tops, and the boys said to me 'There's where it is anyway, behind that curtain hanging down'. That night we were blown off the coast, and I never saw my snow that was waiting for me behind the curtain. Now, I don't care about it—I didn't care then, but the crew they wanted me to see it. They were always talking about it, snowballing when they were children 'nothing like it. Makes you laugh. And snow-balling girls and it goes down their necks.' There was one man, he was the oldest of the lot, he said he got cross because a girl said there was too much snow down her neck, and this man, just a child then—Joe was the name I knew him by—'Joe Boots' because he had a fine new pair of sea boots, very big for him, but padded with old rags when he had time. This man, then man-child, hit the boy that threw most snow at the girl, and the boy, when he got the blow, he caught it in the chest. He went down into the snow, into a soft drift, and all the little boys and girls ran away, and there was Joe digging at the drift with his hands, to get the boy he hit, out. The drift was deep enough, but by the sides of it, there were two pieces of drift, like little cliffs, and they fell down. Only one child stayed with Joe, and that was the girl that complained that she got too much snow. She stood behind Joe, just the two there, and the darkness falling down. And Joe scratching at the heap. He did get the boy out. He didn't seem to be breathing. The girl she kissed the boy's face, and then, Joe said, she kissed him. And then the two, Joe and the girl, dragged the snowbound boy away about a mile, and they got him into a little house, where a shoemaker lived, he and his old wife, and they got hot cloths on the boy, and kept taking him out of one hot blanket, and putting him in another. They had all his own clothes off him. And, Joe said, when that snowed boy, quivered an eyelid, and came up alive, he felt grand, and he sat down flat on the hearth, by the old woman, with his back against her knee, and went asleep like that. But the girl when the boy came alive ran out of the house and cried loud. Joe heard her going away towards her own house getting farther and farther away as he fell off asleep. Joe said he'd seen all the snow he wanted that night, and though he'd often seen it since, he didn't want to, and what's more, he didn't want me to be looking at snow."

As this passenger along the roads by my side talks of the past, he loses his stoop and comes upright. But in a little while he stoops again, and then for a little he is silent. His eyes are now looking straight forward along the road, and presently, far away over a hillock, I see a figure of a man riding a bicycle. I know it must be a postman for I can see a bag hanging about the man's side. He comes very slowly nearer, for his way of riding is to pedal quick, and hard, up any little hillock, and take his feet off, going down. On the level he plods so slowly as to be little better than under steerage way. Come abreast of us, he salutes the passenger, by beating his left hand to his breast. To Bowsie, and myself, he gives a quizzical nod, and, by way of delaying the time in its flight, he rummages his bag as if he expected to find letters for us.

By the aloof smile of the passenger, I know he expects

no letters, and neither Bowsie, nor myself, left any address for forwarding of letters to. So it is not within the fence of possibility, post office possibility, that there should be anything for us. The postman is a middle-sized man with sandy and grey side whiskers, clipped close to the cheeks, and covering them to the line of the mouth, below which the face was close shaven, three days ago. The man has grey-blue unquenchable eyes, and it is not by the laws of chance he became mercury to this flat hand of country laid down on the Atlantic edge. He is a man who knows everything that is written on any post-card, and in every sealed envelope, and parcel he carries, not because he reads with these eyes of his, the post-cards, nor by experiences and deduction, makes the covers of the rest translucent. It is simply, that he doesn't care, and so the messages inside screech to him to give them the importance of a habitation in his mind. Now he empties, out on the grass, the contents of his bag, about a dozen letters, and post-cards, half a dozen circulars and newspapers, and one, badly tied, parcel. He shakes the bag well holding it upside down. He goes a little way from us to do this. I think it is to remember the secrecy of the post. But, in a moment, I see that it wasn't. Starlings have come from, God knows, the old ruin inland. They settle with commotions on the shakings of the bag, and the postman, coming back to us, explains —the parings and sweatings of wedding cake coming out of the little boxes last night. A flat stone or so has kept the letters and papers from any sudden blast of wind. Now, the postman picks them up, and drops them back in his bag. He stands with us watching the audacious starlings lunching on the sod. They are quite fearless before our feet. The postman's voice speaking to us has given us a proper standing with the starlings. The postman sighs, re-mounts his bicycle, and goes slowly pedalling away in the direction from which we have come. It was on a dead level piece of road we met. So he must pedal, as demurely as he is capable of, until he meets a little rise and makes his scuttling effort for the fall beyond. The man walking with us spreads his hand out over the horizon from sou'-west to nor'-east and he says : " That man goes through this country every day, and will so continue until he goes out on his pension, and yet he doesn't know the first thing about it, and he is as well off. His friends are just over it, those birds and the like, if he had wings on his feet; he would just stay hovering, and perhaps, by the time he's out of his time, you'll be able to get wing seed and grow wings on your heels, good luck to him anyway. And you two men look jaded. You can see the winning post now." He is pointing to the far huddle of houses where the Pride Hotel stands up against a yellow sun. He turns short to the right, and passes behind us down a little dell among the bushes on the land side, and on a rabbit path, he passes on inland. " We meet again," he calls, and, with our faces set on a course, we plough along our way. " Jaded," he said. Bowsie's untidy clothes, now look jaded. Am I jaded ? I didn't think I was until that man spoke. Do I look jaded ? But isn't that a permanent look on many of us ? Bowsie does not turn his face towards me to appraise my appearance. That might mean politeness, or it might mean that my appearance has been obviously jaded for several miles past. I wish a bird would sing, a lark climbing up his song into the sky, would cheer us both up. But some more sugary song than a lark's, would be better just now. The lark is so clear, and so full of joy unattainable to me on an ordinary day, at this hour unattainable to Bowsie too, I believe. Squelch, squelch, squelch, squelch. Neither of us had noticed that a little stream, dammed up on the sea side of the road, had spread over the road for a space of five or six feet. Half an inch to an inch deep. However, our boots were water-tight to that, at any rate, and we escape to the higher grass by the roadside. Bowsie says, " It's a good road anyway, and that flash wasn't the road's fault, but the fault of some careless-in-honour contractor who scamped the dab of cement which should have given the entrance to the pipe below the road, a smooth curve, which would have made the stopping up of the pipes' mouth, with floating sticks and sods, not so easy." So Bowsie stooping down and prodding here and kicking his heel there, is beginning a breaking up of the dam. Now, I am helping, I have a beautiful lump of a sod—just under my foot, and am just going to move it on one side, and exult myself, as the exulting water rushes forward—unbound. But something in Bowsie's eyes is so wistful, I turn away and move to some meanly secondary, obstruction of short twigs and straw, and a wisp of sheeps wool. I know Bowsie breathes thanks to me for my generous holding back. And now, his work on the pipes' mouth finished, he comes up to my fine sod, and, waiting a second or two so that the flood may be held up as high as possible, to the very top of the sod, Bowsie pushes the sod away and the flood curled, like a dolphin's forehead, plunges to the pipe head, and gurgling in its pride, rushes under the road to spread on the land side, a little kite-shaped patch of sand, sticks, and straws.

I think to myself, if Bowsie would only listen intelligently to me I would say—now we gather the skirts of our togas about us, and leave the highway of utility for the highway of romance. Some link is rattling in my brain between Romans making aqueducts and ourselves directing the gutter flow. And it comes to me, in a flash, that those voluminous long and baggy double kilts, one time called plus fours, appeal to so many men, because they flop about them like toga ends, and I believe that those, to whom these flappings appeal most, are those who do not feel within themselves that noble pride, which remembers that " The noblest Roman of all " is dead. Anyway, I am not going to say any of these nonsensical mistings of words to Bowsie. for I am not sure, whether he is for the wide, and ankle long floppings or against, and as we go wandering on jaded, " jaded," he said, we are not either of us in the humour to stand an argument in pure asthetics ; for neither of us, I know, would, even at the last pinch, and cornered, introduce any material values in such a case. Jaded we may be, but at least we are of a kind fit to meet on a field of honour, no matter how long, how short, or how shivery we make our stay there. On we go—plod. I think if I turned my head and looked back, it might make the way we have yet to go seem a mere bagatelle—to gaze away in comparison to the long distance behind us, to our sleeping-place last night. A huddle of specks just breaking the edge of the green grass, a grey sand line of distance, only faintly silhouetted, against a pale blue, pencil scratch of the day before's starting hill. But I'm not turning my head ; I am facing the last lap, breasting the storm of fatigue that seems to press down towards us, loth to let us win our way gaily up the road, down the road, over the bridge, running water very trying on frayed tempers, up the rise to the glass house door of the Pride.

This bit of road is sacred to fatigue. On it when Bianconi was in his prime, ahead, where the Pride now stands, was a long stone cottage with stables for tired horses, and a space in front where the fresh team waited. The fatigued legs of horses came along this last bit of road. But, ah, they were brave legs, and they made an effort—where? here? No, not yet. Now? No, a little further, Bowsie. Ah, it's you, Bowsie, who have ever the bolder heart, and the wish to jump into your collar. But now, my boy, you have your chance. Down this short dip. Scatter the gravel. Up the hill—we're carried under on our steam down again. Up over the ridge of the bridge. The rhyming bridge. Now, stride more handsomely, up, up, up. Three ups. Three efforts. Now, down into a sloping stroll, to bring the battering hearts to quietness, and we are in the Pride's mouth. Successful wanderers from no prosaic shore.

Before us shines the owner, at the inner door, where the tall planking of pitch-pine is broken. The second time, the first was the little hatch, battery hatch, or bar hatch, that was on the left. I never have got any but a mournful feeling from looking on pitch-pine walls, except in this house, in this hall. It is a pleasantly shaped room, the whole width of the building and the pitch-pine has never been varnished. Then the pictures that hang, all crooked, as the wind has wished them, have dabs of colour that beat down the blatant self-consciousness of the pitch. Self-complacent in the satisfaction that it gave, once too easily, long ago. Iron tabernacles lined with it long ago, kept many a soul from its true heaven, a while. Too long, is the purgatory of sloughing old skins. But here is a picture by a Neapolitan artist, of the early days, of the Mediterranean trade, when this island and the adjacent one, returned the Phœnician compliments, by coursing up the landlocked sea with schooners and blunt brigs and the tall brigantines, that magnificent woman of the sea, with her little mizen husband. It is a picture of Vesuvius in full blow. The vermilion high in the air and spilling down the side, and out on the bay. Now, here's a picture, a lithograph of New York Harbour, and the City. No skyscrapers when the artist made this picture, but round it, entwined, are two flags, the bright blue, and the vermilion again, of the Stars and Stripes. Then the green of the Irish harp. There is a drawing by a Westernised, Chinese artist, showing the front of a laundry on the Pacific Slope. It is in the same shade of red and blue, as the American flag, with the addition of a bright canary yellow lettering over the shop front, where the name appears in Western style. While down the side, on a claret red ground, Chinese characters in black give the trade a boost. Here the door intervenes, and now stands forth shining, Robert Emmet, the green coat bordered with spangles shining bright. On the end wall, the easterly wall, I know it well, there is the pink blotting-paper shade of the old Police Gazette, and two pugilists, one with a heavy moustache, are standing face to face, in a ring. It is a large illustration, and among the spectators we see torsos of dignity, some covered in evening dress, resplendent. One or two sportsmen have long beards. An intellectual has pince-nez and is looking amused. But it's nothing to laugh at these great heavy men, stepping in the ring, are quick compared to the ordinary man, and when an express fist hits a cheek it is never the same cheek again. But the owner of the house, for fear this exhibition of manhood in mimic anger, should be too much for the stomach of delicate lady visitors, has seen to it that on either side of the fighting picture hang two European oleographs of the days of the bustle, and the little parasol, they show a picnic party, by a lake. And a picnic party by a sea. The green of leaves, and the gentlemen's coats are strong and heavy in the lake picnic. And the yellow sunset sky at the back, and the massed, and embossed chignons of the ladies in the front in the sea picnic, have the power of flame. At the westerly end of the room there hangs a reproduction of a Christmas number of years gone. It is

CHERRY RIPE.

The owner of the Pride is salaaming to us, with his hat, which is a high-crowned, battered light fawn, pressed against his heart. What so sweet as the welcome at the inn. Our bags have arrived, our rooms are prepared. The owner has an enormous lot to tell us. He talks fast and slow, in fits and starts, a slow drawl from one of the States, and quick-firing yep, yep, yap, from some two-horse city. I listen to him, for I must, I am not able to get the thin edge of my tongue in. And Bowsie wouldn't try to. He isn't even in his humour when he doesn't want to talk, or let anyone else talk. I listen, and I cannot make up my mind whether it is the quick talk, or the slow that comes with the most interesting waves of the story. I come, now, to the conclusion that it is a lacing accompaniment, and that every conversation of the landlord's of more than a quarter of an hour's duration, is paired by the rising, and falling, of this man's life, from the cradle until this moment. The speed, the rise, and fall, is a running water to the news of to-day which he is telling us. He has had a most interesting season. American visitors from a quarter of the States, all living here, side by side, like birds on one bush, and artists, two of them, and an elocutionist, dumb, resting, a conjurer, everything of private property nailed down. But the Boss, free and open, let the conjurer conjure his fill. Notwithstanding, the nailing down, gold watches, lost a moment, chain hanging down, swinging, widowed; move a picture,—tucked in the back of the frame, the watch pinned to the edge with a diamond tie-pin. The ex-railway man put his hand to his black plaister necktie. His pin! He hadn't missed it—— The gold watch ticking with the pin through the ring. Bridge players beaten to the ropes, to the open air, walked about under the stars—counting them for pips. You can't play flitter decks with a wizard in the place, what are aces to him. Bridge players, grumpy at first, the wizard took each of them apart and showed them just how to make a certainty. They lit the lamp early, all sat down, full of opportunity. All did the same stacking. What's a good thing among too many. I should worry. Oh, singers, a quartette—a strong banjo, " Grandfather kept slaves " passionate brown in the white of the eye. Melodeons no class. But, still if you laugh, " Grandfather kept slaves ". Everybody loves a melodeon deep down, and a tuxedo and long cuffs. White wings they never grow weary. " All swinging to it in the dusk, same with me, the old man. If you took away the melodeon, and the worker, we'd all go on working our hands, in and out, swaying. So, Micky's head on Juno's shoulder, and Juno's head on the Judge's shoulder. We had a new Judge this time—Grover Cleveland— come again. Say, but we had a summer and this is the end of it."

The landlord has everything ready for the ball to-night. The band has arrived. They have gone for a walk along the straight miles of sands.

On the flat space of the roof above the kitchen, Hayden, the proud hotel man, takes even the far sands to be, by right of community, the hand-maidens of his hotel. He points to specks wavering about, beyond the dark stain of two small rivers. The band has gone a long way. It is to be hoped the sea air won't make them sleep up against their drums and cymbals to-night. Nor let the bones fall from languid hands, nor let the nutmeg grater noise maker be forgotten by the side of the watchman's rattle. For this band is middle-fashioned noise, unashamed. Hayden is genuinely glad to see us both down to his boots. He has put the finishing touch, as far as his own hands could, to everything several times, and he's spoken on the telephone with everyone who could possibly want to hear him.

Miss Julia Starrett the lady who looked out of the window has come. She also is walking on the far strand. After a time, with Hayden's glasses, we make her out. She is wearing a claret red dress, and is homeward bound. She has gone farther away than the band ; they have turned, and faced for home a few minutes earlier than her turning. We are wondering how she crossed the dark spread estuaries of the streams. But while we are watching her, we see she takes a sweep up to the edge of the bank, where, we know, there are stepping-stones. We suppose she will do the same when she reaches the next stream. We are watching her. She likes to be near the sea's edge. She makes her way, at an angle down the sand's face, but before she reaches the sea, she turns to look straight before her, and then moves quickly inland. I feel a moist puff in my ear, as if some cold heavy breather was trying to wheeze some secret in my ear. I turn my head, and as I turn it, Bowsie and Hayden, turn theirs. What do we see now, but blackness all before us to the east and south. The wind has backed and up comes darkness and rain in sheets and spillings, accompanied by balloons of grey spongy fog, in barrel shape, all one drench of all the spare moisture of the sea to come on us. Near us, we see the band ; their jacket collars turned up, absurdly, to keep their necks dry, while we know, and if they weren't so busy running, they would know, their backs and right sides, and legs and arms, will be sopped in rain water before they reach the hotel. Though they run gamely, they take time to look back, to see how Miss Starrett is making her way. They see her reach the bank just by the far side of the nearer stream, and they know she will skirt the edge of the sandhills for a while. To cross the stream by the stones, and come inside, the sandhills, and struggle along getting little shelter, but some comfort, from those small hills, she will not see so much of the dark sky. That would be a comfort to most of us ; but she would sooner look it in the face as it frowns. But in this common-sense idea of keeping yourself from getting wetter than you can help, she must, she supposes acquiesce, for the sake of conformity and come inside the sand-hills. We know, Bowsie, and I, that even by this, she must be wet to the skin. Hayden has gone below, and we are wet enough as we follow him, to take a towel a maid hands us and to lightly rub the heavier drops from the surface of our coats. Hayden has run into the hotel yard. He is hoping to find a car there, but his hotel guests, who have between them, three or four cars, are away to the railway to meet dancing friends from a distance. His own car is down at the seaport to bring two guests—old friends who have never sat in a dance-house for twenty years. But there is a car. A boy, of ingenious fingers, said he took it to the bog for turf yesterday, and it brought him back. We have heavy waterproofs on ; we took them from the hall, as we passed through it, and we give Hayden all the help we can in getting this old resurrected machine on the road. There is a hood. We lash it well down, and away goes Hayden to save Julia Starrett, struggling heavily along.

We can see what goes on by standing by what little shelter the westermost corner of the glass veranda can give. A cement pillar stands here, and we look round the edge of it. Myself, at my natural height, Bowsie stooping to shelter by my chest and to squint round it.

We see Hayden splashing his way down the track ; the water looks blue by contrast with the green of the grass, and the dark wet sand on the road, and, when the water rises in spray from the motor wheels, it shines white. I know, and Bowsie knows, that Hayden is going to make an error in judgement. He is going to turn the motor in over the grass, and race it towards Miss Starrett. We know it's the wrong thing to do. The car is jadey, and has run down the road because a resolute hand was controlling it. But turned into the grass, Hayden has lost his determination of control. There are two deep ruts in the sod, and the car bumps in and out of them, and when Hayden turns it, sharp and short, to the left, and straight for where Miss Starrett stands, in a little shelter of high grey bent grass, and black sand, it goes poorly. It has done enough for the present time. It slides over the wet grass, ten or twenty yards and stops. Now, Hayden is doing what he knows he should have done from the roadway ; he is signalling to Miss Starrett to come to the car. She struggles forward and trots, when some lull in the wind, releases her from the weather's grip. Hayden is out in front dragging at the engine. He turns quickly, and helps Miss Starrett into the car, and throws a rug over her, so that it is covering her from her chest to her feet.

And then he gets back to the engine—five minutes all in sweat—his hands are twitching with energy. While the right hand works the left moves with it. If, by the pupils of his eyes, he could turn the engine into life, he would push them down into it. In a sudden short gasp the engine is alive. It stops again, but only for a couple of minutes. Now, it's churning on. Hayden is back at the steering-wheel. They are turning in a wide sweep before the wind, taking, at first, the hummocky grass tenderly. But we can see a fury has caught Hayden ; the car is coming towards us fast. It looks, for anyone else but us, who sees it, that it can never keep going, so shaky is it, over grass like that, and it will be finished for good before it reaches the road. But we smile, because we know it'll make the road, and come on towards us, and into the yard, passing in front of the hotel—going game and well. And so it comes to pass. And we, like two comical cats watching a clockwork mouse, turn our heads as the car passes. And, as it darts the corner for the yard, we still keep our stupid faces gazing at the bit of road where we saw the car's tail disappear.

We are going back across the front hall, the lounge hall, into the back hall, and we meet Hayden supporting Miss Starrett, and two maids come with them from the yard. The one who gave us the towel to dry our clothes, and a younger maid—small with naturally crimpy hair, ruddy brown, and a grave look. I can see the maids' heads are sparkling with raindrops, so they must have run out into the yard to help Hayden with Miss Starrett. I expect, queerly enough, that Miss Starrett will be making some cheering remark, and I expect it to be in a deep voice. I expect her to be so glad to be safe in port, that she will be talking all the way up the stairs. But she is silent ; so is Hayden, and the maids seem to have left away all their professional bustling. They are quite silent, and soft-footed. Indeed, the younger maid must be soft-footed, for she is barefoot. It isn't that she is always without shoes, there are no barefoot people working in this hotel. No, she had her stockings and shoes off in the kitchen, and was paring her toe-nails for the night. She thinks the dancing, that will be in the air, for the hotel guests, may spread to the kitchens. When many doors are open a strong band carries far.

The stairs they take the invalid up are the back stairs, narrow and twisty. There is one picture hanging on the wall—a German oleograph of a scene among mountains, with peasants, standing up to dance to a tinker band. The stairs are so narrow, that, squeezing his way up them, Hayden pushes the picture so that, when the four people have passed it, it's hanging as crooked as can be without being upside down, and off the nail. A man comes along the passage ; I have not seen him before. He is, I suppose a gardener, or outdoor servant of some kind. Though he is dressed like a fisherman in a blue jersey. He has a wiry brown beard, and a soft felt hat, quite dry, so he must have been sitting indoors by the fire. This man is carrying a great heap of blankets. They are new blankets, and

the heat of the man's body, and his bother trying to
do his best, bring away the heavy oily smell of the
wool, sickly to many people, but not to me and Bowsie.
The man follows up the stairs, meeting the younger
maid pattering down again. She disappears into the
kitchen, and we hear shouts of encouragement from
the cook. We know it is the cook. And now, out
into the passage comes the small maid, with two great
cans of hot and steaming water ; some splashes over
and falls on her foot. It must be very nearly boiling
water, for she winces. As she reaches us, Bowsie, letting the glum mask he has worn as he watched all
these preparations, fall from him, steps out firmly, and
takes the cans from the girl and carries them up the
stairs. The girl stops for a moment, for she has not
noticed us standing in the gloomy shadow. She could
have, and must have done so, with the fronts of her
eyes. But it shows how out of herself and bothered
she is, that we, our images, did not reach her brain.
She only stands still a moment, and then with the soft
flap of her feet in the air, where she ran, she gets back
to the kitchen and soon is out again, with two more
cans, for me to carry. They are just ordinary tin
milk-cans. Then she herself goes once more to the
kitchen, and very soon after, I reach the landing above
she is after me with more hot water. The idea is, I
can see, that Miss Starrett must have the hot bath in
some way in her room. Or perhaps constant cloths
rung out of hot water. It is all in the plans of the
elder maid, and Hayden has agreed. We leave the
row of cans by the door, and Hayden, who is standing there, says : " Hot water all up " and taps at the
door. Then we three men come down the front stairs
of the hotel, as the little maid slips into the bedroom,

sidling round the side of the door, as if she was a bookmarker, inserting herself in a book.

Hayden goes towards his office, which is in one side of the middle hall. He is going to telephone for the doctor. He says he's sure to be out. " But I'll hail him on the road. If this was the kind of wind that'd bring down the wires we'd be done. But it isn't, thanks be to God." For a quarter of an hour Hayden called up people everywhere to the east, within say, twenty miles. In every case, where he got an answer, he got some word of the doctor's passage. He had gone by twenty minutes ago, or two hours, or an hour. At last he has him between two views, hardly five minutes between them. But there was a rough mountain boreen —he would likely now be up on it, and no telephone there. At neither of these five-minute spots was he certain of an intelligent, and trustworthy, messenger. But two miles farther away, across a ridge, near a post office, he knew a black-haired boy, sometimes used as a telegraph messenger. The post-mistress, she ought to have been filmed, for she'll die some time—specks and deafness, but understanding. The village post-mistress off a Christmas card. She—never deafer, yet can hear Hayden's voice, and he can hear her, out in the road, in front of her shop, ringing her heavy bell. In a moment, he is talking to the well-found dark-haired, messenger. Hayden comes out into the big front hall, and sits with us. He lights a heavy, sooty black cigar and waits for a call.

His messenger, pale at first, his face soaked with the heavy rain, so that only the freckles show, but soon flushed and ardent, his cheeks giving out a radiance that mounts to his eyes. He breasts a hill. Then, on a level, he patters along with his middle wind standing up to his young bellows well. He knows the house where the doctor must be, if he isn't too late. But he knows, though the house is hidden from him by a rise ahead, that the doctor is still in it. His car on the roadside, sheltered by a thorn, a hundred yards down the farther hill, from the cottage door. There is the last steep piece of road to make. This will be where he makes his strong effort. And forty years from now, this effort will pinch his heart just when the heart is unaware. But he comes up the hill like a gallant pony. He tops it, and the doctor is out of the cottage, and moving quickly to his car through the rain. The messenger, with the saturated hair against his forehead, has no spare beats for a hullo, so still he must run for it. And he does; he gets, not all the way, to the doctor before the man turns his head, fifty yards from the car. The stout flushed face of the doctor is holding his small eyes steadily towards the running boy. After a few seconds, he realizes that the boy is coming towards him and him only. He goes to his car and starts the engine—the boy comes up, gives his message, in a quick short sentence, and then gets into the car beside the doctor. Over the way, the boy had run his young heart so fiercely, the car goes carefully down into the village and to the post office.

The bell rings in the Pride, and Hayden puts the stub of his cigar down on the side of his small desk, as he quickly gives the doctor some rough idea of the case, he'll find waiting upstairs here for him.

The doctor will be coming on as fast as it is possible. But it must be some time yet before he can be here, he has two desperate cases on his way. He has no other doctor he can hail for them.

It is getting dark now, and the rain and wind are muffled by the falling of evening. But the weather is as bad as it has been all day. In the front of the house there are the rows made by arriving people. The guests, and their friends from the station, are arriving. They begin filing in ; they are unexpectedly trim and dry. We forget, Bowsie and I, that they have been in a comfortable train all day and brought on here in cosy cars. We thought they should be dripping, weather tired. Instead, here they are as fresh as paint, and full of hotel lounge yellings. The visitors vying with their guests. Up in arms, their spirits, to show that they aren't afraid of drowsy-looking soiled darlings sitting in the easy chairs. Sitting easy, by the radiator, before the picture of Cherry Ripe. I don't move ; I know Bowsie will. He gets up and his crumpled clothes look worse to the people, men and women, so full of themselves, and their touchy dignities, than they would have done before I had them ironed. These people think that Bowsie, and myself, God forgive us all, are pushing forward our travel-stained appearance, as a man might cut up his lunch on the mountain-side, amid the heather, with a jack-knife, just because he never lunched at home, without a sword dance, of at least five knives, by his plate. How it goes now, is that, Bowsie has all their want of confidence taken from them, when he explains that there is a good reason for quiet voices lying ill to a finish, upstairs. Without a thought, for the funny fellows and girls, founded on fiction, they had been trying to be, they are now falling quietly into the dusky mood of this hotel. The women move into the body of the house. I never knew that women could move so softly. That is soundlessly, not that softness that makes a loud purring noise. The men, with the help of two chauffeurs, move their luggage into the inner hall, and then come out again and join us near the westerly radiator. We are all now in almost a steady darkness, and I remember for the first time, that there is no glow to come from the radiator. The eyes of Bowsie, and myself, are so used, by now, to the slow coming on of the blackness, that we can just make out blurred figures—the bears in the nursery rhyme looking for somewhere to stretch themselves. But they cannot see us, nor each other, and soon we are not able to see them, because of the gathered darkness. There is a little talk, voices coming from here, and there, among the people—just about the dreadfulness of the day, or about when first the trains ran into the thick weather.

There is, after a long drowsy period, one break in the darkness—a slow voice says " I have studied medicine in my youth, I wonder should I offer to have a look at the sick lady." Another voice, a small quick voice says, " Go, Judge, it will be appreciated." So here we have another Judge, and a transatlantic one again, I know him by his intonation. They can't be all Judges of the Highest Courts ; perhaps they are something like J.P.s. Perhaps they have just " studied law in their youths ". It must be grand to have had a long youth and to have studied many things concurrently :

    Dancing,
    Fours-in-hand driving,
    Skating,
    Marbles,
    Art,
    Lace,

Embroidery,
Law (I nearly forgot you),
And War,
And Love,
And Medicine (like the Judge gone above),
Hearts,
Palmistry,
Engineering,
Conveyancing,
Poetry,
Salesmanship,
Photography,
Cooking,
And the Management of Lamps.

Bowsie controls the air of this hotel by some unseen power, it would be from some glint of his eye, if he had cat's eyes. The maids will make no move that is not already scheduled for. The hour for bringing the lamps into the hall depends on the will of the guests, as some love to sit in the dark, while others love the blazing lights. It depends on the ringing of a bell—a bell is near Bowsie, and he does not choose to ring it. There are other bells, but none of the figures about us, buried in the shadows, even those who already know the situation of those other bells, will dare ring.

As the Judge opens the door, on the corner, to move into the inner hall, a flash of light juts into the room, and lights up two profiles, one a handsome haggard superior eminent—mum, mum, mum, member of one of the more earnest professions or to be considered so. The other, a fussed, woolly-faced man, thirsty-looking, unsatisfied, short-breathed. Then the door moved gently to close itself again on the Judge's heels. Bowsie says to me : " Nice and quiet the house." I say, Yes, did the band come in ? " Yes, you've forgotten. They came in at the back a long while ago, and peeled off their soaked clothes, and got into blankets, and fussed about themselves, and now they're all dressed up in their little chopped-off coats with violet and green facings, that used to be the suffragette colours one time in England. And they've got their clean shirts on, and silk handkerchiefs pinned over them, to preserve them for to-night's ball. And there'll be none now ; they're drinking rum and milk in the little back room that hangs on the side of the yard. You've forgotten all that." Yes, of course I have.

Haggard face, or woolly face, though the words seem to come from where I'd seen haggard—still the voice is woolly, hearing about rum and milk, says to his end of the room : " A little drink perhaps would do nobody any harm." And now three pairs of feet go slithering out of the door into the inner hall, and to the bar hatch beyond the office. The hatch opens into what is hardly a room. It is narrow ; it has no door ; there is a step up to it, but it has a thick, old, worn, Turkey carpet on it, which is unsuitable for a bar, but it's restful. There is a narrow plain wooden bench along the side wall, opposite the bar hatch, and broken topers have slept on that narrow plank bed, with one hand hanging down to touch the comforting carpet. The place isn't five feet wide, so there is hardly room for a sleeper to be on the plank and more than a single line of drinkers standing towards the bar hatch.

Our three deserters from the dark are soon back

again. They don't even—not one of them—say " That was good " or " I needed that ". I suppose their drink has livened something in them. I never felt myself less longing for alcohol. I think it is the heavy sea air, full of salt, drifting, invisible, into us through the crack under the door, though there should be no crack there, for the heavy thick mat is drawn up close. I suppose down with Davy Jones, if he opened his locker and asked you what you'd have, you'd ask for something solid, without any excitement in it. Certainly, nothing to excite you while down with that old sea-lousy man. An emerald anchor studded with rubies, a bit of a rusty iron anchor fluke, or a miraculous preserved tarry inch of rope, mementoes for a museum for old tars. I think how successful I would be talking to old tars by some sea shelter, where pilots, retired, look pitying on fishermen fiddling about with nets. I would be showing them my keepsakes from Davy Jones. But I know, in a moment now, I wouldn't be a success at all—I don't feel I could make anyone listen to me. Bowsie, here, he could make me listen to him now without effort. I wonder he doesn't talk. He will sometimes, never for any good or pleasure to himself, except for the pleasure of doing his trick of legerdemain. For, when he had ever opened out in talk, because it was time for talk and he was the only one to come out with it, I have always seen him hold his right hand, palm upwards, slightly cupped, before him, and keep moving the fingers of the other hand towards the open palm, as if he was always dropping some little thing into it. And all the time, his eyes are on the palm. If he was to begin talking, now, I would be certain I'd hear a movement of the two hands, which I would know were following his old tradition. Perhaps he won't talk now because he will not have light, and he cannot see his palm without light.

The Judge's slow sliding steps are coming down the stairs ; he is in the room with us again. The back of his neck, and his delicately curved head, is illuminated for a moment, when he shuts the door behind him. He says to me, " The lady above looks to me as not long for this place. The attention she is getting is, I believe, as good as human aid could supply. That is, unprofessional aid. That is, until the doctor comes, I believe nothing can be done that is not being done. I do not believe that any trained nurse could do more than the devoted woman who is now with the lady. I hear that there is a maid or personal attendant long with this lady and with a thorough knowledge of her constitution. But she is many miles away. And I say on my own responsibility, if it is wanted, that she could not exceed, in any way, the careful attending which the domestic maid of the hotel is now giving the doctor's patient. The patient is, I may say, practically unconscious at this present moment." The Judge says, " Will you have a cigar, sir ? " to the place in the darkness near him, where breathing tells him a fellow human creature is sitting in an armchair. It might be the breathing of some lazy old sporting dog, he thinks, only it comes from too high up above even the seat of a chair. Gruff voice says, " Ah, no thanks—I seldom smoke a cigar in the dark." A thin acid voice, close beside me, a little back behind my chair, startles me. I didn't realise anyone was there. The voice says, " Allow me, sir." I hear a snap, and a tall spare young man with receding hindquarters is walking across the floor of the room, holding before him a petrol lighter

with a tiny flare on it. A doll's flambeau. He lights
the Judge's cigar. The Judge would have preferred a
large old-fashioned wooden match, for this is a very
good cigar. The Judge is down to one a day, and
while he lives they will cost him one hundred and
eighty-two dollars and fifty cents a year. I know that.
The young man, with the flame, walks back to his
place slowly, that we may see ourselves squatted in
our chairs. He is amused to illuminate us, and when
he smiles, he shows beautifully clean bright small teeth.
He is a very old-fashioned type of handsome young
man, or looks so now, walking across the floor, the back
of his short jacket hanging so straight behind him. I
know that once he has doused the gleam of his petrol
lighter, he will have made his last appearance as a
handsome young man of years long gone. It will be
just that I saw him, by some trick of the shadows, so.
But also he will have been within the part I had cast
him for, and if, by a lucky chance, I had been quick
enough to have accosted him with some speech of
those old days, he would have replied in perfect keeping
without knowing how or why he spoke so. But now
his petrol light is out, and he has creaked his basket
chair with his absurdly small weight ; his bones are
small. He is a very nice fellow, if you stroke him the
right way, but his protective fur, which he has imagined
about himself since youth, when his mother, a widow,
left him alone in the world with a slight income, is so
short, that any stroking must be just right. He is short
tempered like his fur, but you might never know it. He
walks away with his temper and lets it air itself away.
I don't want to know him any more than I do. He
knows himself far more than most men know themselves, and he wishes he was better worth knowing.

Every now and again, he gets a cold in his head, and he is glad to look at himself in the glass, and to see that he looks as repulsive as any other man with a cold. He feels then that his spiritual history must be the same as other men's. He does not long for a very long life—if he has to be conscious all the time. But, if he could live in a trance, for long periods, he believes he would like to live to an age so far on as to be in a day when no speech is necessary between friends, and so that when he thinks well of anyone, they should know it at once. He could not bear the idea of being dumb for he likes to call out, with an open throat, when he is far away from human beings. He likes to call to sea-gulls and all old birds, big or small, whose voices he can hear. He could not bear to be dumb for that reason. But, otherwise, he would be more successful, he believes, carrying a little pad of paper and writing messages on it, and watching people's faces as they read them. He has seen dummies watching faces that way. But then he remembers they were deaf also. And, under no circumstances, could he wish to be deaf. His ears are of a pleasant shape—not too big, nor too small. He knows that it is his little blue bright teeth which make his speech unrelenting in an insistence, on some light spitefulness.

A deep hound-like voice comes from directly opposite me. I saw the man it comes from—I saw him when He-would-be-a-dummy lit us all up. He was a broad man, middle-aged, sunk deep in a low chair. He says —" This gloom oppresses me. I quite understand that that is as it should be. I understand the feelings, but if circumstance were otherwise, I would think that a light would be better for us all, and indirectly, better for the lady who is so ill upstairs. Everyone who knows me, and I was ever an open book, knows that I have made it my business, all my life, to try and understand the feelings of others. My workers, I believe, understand my attitude, I believe, and hope so, with understanding. I have tried to draw aside the curtain, where permitted, and not only understand, but enter into, the feelings of my fellows. But in this case, I feel that I can only hope to understand from the outerside of the Threshold." I know quite well what he is thinking. He is thinking that Miss Starrett is some heroine of Irish barricades, or some last descendant of an Irish chieftain, or someone who remembers the old fairy tales of the raths, and round towers. Or perhaps some lady interested, and active, about creameries, and homespun, and lace-making.

Bowsie stretches his arms, and presses the electric bell plug. I know it, and immediately, as by magic, the door from the hall opens and the younger maid walks in, very upright, with two huge lamps held before her. They have very large globes and no shades. The globes are muffed slightly, so there is some slight subduing of the great light. From the tops of the globes, by the chimneys, where there is no muffing glass to intervene, two fierce shafts of light pour up towards the ceiling.

We all can now see ourselves focused high, greenblack shadows under our chins and behind our ears, making them seem to stick out.

When a fireball falls out of the sky, and lands in a forest, this is the way it lights up the foresters. But they have deep foliage behind them, and can step back into it, and let it close over them again, like a green dressing-gown lapped about the place where once they shone. We can recede into no soft forest. We have only the pitch-pine planks behind us, or the windows of the veranda, blue dark now, and streaming with the rain outside, and on the inside, the condensation of the moisture within the house. The maid puts the lamps down—one at each end of the room on a table with a glass top. Under the glass top of each is an ecru-coloured cloth with a lace edge, and in the centre of the cloth is a painting, deftly scrubbed in with water colours. Under one glass dimples an Irish lake, surrounded by mildly, down-gazing mountains, under the other glass is a wild and gushing mountain river under an indigo-streaked sky, buttressed by ginger-bread-tinted rocks tufted with green. When the lights are at rest, the maid seems an encouraging sight, and all in the room ask her to bring them their various drinks. In a little while, she is back. Just long enough delay to let every man stretch himself where he reclined, or walk a pace or two, or stand by the windows, and tap them, as if they were barometers.

Some of us make theatrical noises as we drink. Some of us smack our lips, and some do delight to spill a little. So it comes about that quiet lake and bounding river, are looking up from their tables, through wheel rings of spilt liquors.

Hayden walks in, his thin solid shoes very noiseless. The true hotel host. He seems lifted a little off the ground, as though he gently wafted himself all about his own country, welcoming guests, making them at home in their own inn, while his own home is on some invisible wire on which he walks. True innkeeping is not a prostitution of hospitality ; it is not an erecting, and a bolstering up, of a symbol of hospitality. It is the lively core of hospitality itself up to the moment, when, his bill paid, the guest passes over the step of the door.

The bill even is not the end, whatever size it may be, it is but the passing knell, and is just a sop to some uninspired, earthly science, invented by an idle-skulled group, long ago.

It would be well if hotel keepers all over the world, to crack the knell's note, should agree every fourteenth, or even twenty-fourth, or ninety-ninth guest should be presented for nothing, with his bill receipted,—a washed slate.

Hayden talks to everyone, but particularly to Bowsie, who is standing on the mat inside the door, looking out on the blowing rain. He says, " A young boy working in a bootshop in the port got into Shutters Town a while ago, on a lorry, and now he's coming on the rest of the way on a bicycle. You see, he's got a pair of shoes, a pair of little red shoes belonging to Miss Starrett, the lady lying ill, dying, I believe myself, upstairs. For her to dance in, little red shoes ; and this boy, Timmy, that's his name, Timmy, he's got an idea in his head he's a knight of the plains on a high-bred horse coming along, hand over fist, carrying a gift from the mountains for a lady, grand, of a dream. A señorita in a castle—and a God-damn queer old castle this house of Hayden's—that's him." And Hayden prepares to open the glass door quickly. He's not opening to Timmy, he knows the doctor's stamping walk.

The doctor comes—a stout man—looking stouter than he is, for he has two overcoats on, the outer one a stained waterproof with a thick belt. The doctor passes through the wraiths of foggy blowing rain, following him until the door is closed. He goes in to the inner hall. We do not hear him go upstairs. All his stamping steps were for his entrance. Those firm, resolute steps get the Devil sickness in the patient down in weight, and gives the doctor a chance to be wrestling him away—if that's the sort of devil he is. Now he moves softly. He is a little while in the room where the sick woman lies. She was a sick woman when he arrived, for she was breathing. He does all that is possible. The maid stands by his shoulder, gazing down on the sick woman, and raising the waves of her own breathing, as if she could, by some buoyancy, not understood by herself, keep this woman from sinking to death's sea.

Miss Julia Starrett has died. She has not regained consciousness.

The doctor stands by Hayden's desk in the little office and tells him that it was inevitable, Miss Starrett knew her own heart almost as well as he did, and she knew when she was finished.

Hayden comes into the hall, and says : " What you, most of you, expected, after hearing the Judge here speak, has come. Miss Starrett has passed away."

Bowsie says, turning his face towards me. It's a square face, and an angry face. " I'll go and have a look at the weather, I believe it's giving a bit." He goes alone to wash the anger from his face in the first strong buffet of the pouncing rain. He turns to the left, and blunders in the darkness, until his eyes become used to everything that envelops him. Now, he walks serenely, until he comes to the bridge over the river— now a racing brown flood, making a sucking noise loudly, every time a higher billow of brown rushes up against the arch. There is a rail of larch, with two strong posts of sea-cast timber, in a gap where the stone wall of the bridge was broken in the last flood.

Bowsie leans against this rail and gives it a shake. He finds one of the posts, the westermost one, is a little loose ; it moves in its socket.

Bowsie stands away from it cautiously, turns his head towards the east and watches the darkness. A little while and something makes a smudgy darker patch and is coming near. Tim on the bicycle coming along fast, against wind, and rain. Not dead against him, but on his left cheek. He stoops and digs away at the pedals coming up the curve of the bridge, and Bowsie steps before his wheel and stops him. He is saturated with rain, and his own sweat. He's black as some hunted thing moving fast with fear.

" That's too fast up a steep," Bowsie says, with his hand held tight on the middle of the handlebars. Timmy has to get down on the ground, and he is bent like an old man, so long has he been crouching in his ride. Bowsie says, " You have some little shoes there for a lady." Timmy says, " They're Miss Starrett's. She wants them. Let me on." " No," Bowsie says. " She don't want them. She gives you all the good thanks for bringing them. She says you're the finest of them all, and you're a good friend. But wait a moment, I must tell you—good boy now—Miss Starrett, that young woman, she is dead. Now, now a seizure of the heart, and died within the hour." Tim, with his jaw dropped, is fumbling at the string holding the box with the shoes to the handlebar, and unexpectedly the string comes away. Bowsie steps back instantly, to get room for his arm to swing, to catch the falling package, knowing well how the quick trick of catching it in the air would be a diversion. But, in stepping back, he pushed himself against the larch rail of the bridge. It carries away, and with it, into the river, goes

Bowsie, bold and clever. Timmy, the grown knight riding for a lady's pleasure, becomes, in that instant, a child, a child trapped. Up goes his small chin, the string of his neck stretches and he screams into the darkness.

Four hear the scream. The loud-voiced man, myself, a fisherman, a hanger about the hotel, a man in patched clothes, soft fed on what he gets sometimes at the kitchen door, but high hearted, and a tall, bony, quarryman who had started to face for home along the westerly road. As soon as we reach the bridge, we can make out Tim on the western bank of the river, looking down the river and moaning. Once, and twice, illuminated by the foam of the waters, we see Bowsie struggling, but pulled away, half sunk, and rolling. A twist in the river and ahead a low bridge, with no walls, but the water is up within three inches of the arch. On that arch Bowsie may be killed with a blow, or held imprisoned, to his drowning beneath the bridge. The quarryman is first by the bridge, and goes into the river, and Bowsie's no one to him. If, instead of a river of water, it had been a river of fire, that gaunt man was for it. When he first ran, from a stand before the front of the Pride, he ran, for all which came his way. Now, he's gone under, and through the bridge, and lifted his head wild, and his eyes greedy for danger. He's hunting now, and has forgotten his own bravery. He is sure that Bowsie went through the bridge, though he may have been deep below, and unconscious. The quarryman swept to the bank, climbs out and tries to search the darkness. Hound voice raises a shout. None of us had thought of that. If Bowsie is able he will answer back and we may hear him. Hound voice springs a petrol lighter, in the shelter of his cap, and

holds it up and we all shout. The fisherman moves
away from us back to the low bridge ; he crosses it ;
he is going to search that side of the river. Tim
has been sent back across the field to the hotel for a
lantern.

I follow the fisherman along the farther bank. The
ground is more marshy. Here and there are places
where the river overflows into branches bewildering.
The lantern has come and with it a crowd of men and
two or three women, visitors from the hotel. The
lantern shows us their movements. We know they are
searching everywhere on the banks that their lantern
light will reach. In a moment, some change is about
us, as in mockery of our lantern, there is a clear spot
appearing in the sky, a star, a bunch of stars. The
wind has shifted, the murk of the day is drifting down-
wind, and we see, as though we were in some cave lit
by a crack high in roof, the floor about us. The tawny
river, twisting about, has branches like a cat-o'-nine-
tails. Black rocks here and there, and tussocks, surrounded by water. But the main river is well defined,
as it pours its strength out to the sea. On the western
bank we see the crowd, with their dim lantern, reach
a point which must be the river mouth. But we get
no hail of discovery. Myself and the fisherman search
about for what we think would be a corpse, and poor
to look upon, draggled. But we find nothing, and we
go back and slowly, with no lantern to help us, come
up with the others.

The three women are glad to see us ; they have not
been able to get all the way with the others, for a very
dark-looking ditch of water has stopped them. The
men have got across it, some by a bold running jump,
some by a floundering plunge, taking them half in the

water and half up the bank. But the jumpers have hauled the others up. It was obvious that no woman —except an amazon—and clothed for it, could get across this obstacle.

I, and the fisherman, tell the women to take care of themselves. And get across the water clever enough. The group with the lantern have turned. They have searched the river mouth and waded in as far as they could, and are sure there is no sign of poor Bowsie wedged against any rock or sandbank.

And now, the tide has turned, they say, and they will wait till a lump of sand which is, as we stand, splitting the river mouth into two is exposed. And if the body of Bowsie is not there, then it's out on the wide ocean.

We are walking up and down on the grass ; it's very wet, and we are all chilled with the water we have been through, but I haven't the stomach for it. Even though Bowsie is alive.

He is still with a flicker of his love for living in his body. He is on his back, in a narrow gully, and the tide has ebbed away from him and he is well enough. If he was living in some old schoolboy story, the sun would now burst forth as it climbed over the palms, and dry him, and so he would come to full life, and be able to drink a bowl of warm coco-nut milk handed him by a Circassian belle, escaped into the brown country from her father's sheepfold in the hills, far away. But my Bowsie rises, or rolls slowly up, on one hip. Then turns round until he has his hands on the grass side of the gully. He is over on the east side of the river, nearer to the sea than the fisherman and I got. Bowsie is straightening his arms so that he is like a seal propped

up on its flippers, and like a seal, he begins to drag himself
along his gully a few feet at a time.

Bowsie drags himself along.

I turn with the group, Tim and the quarryman, and
the rest, with the lantern swinging. But the quarryman's wife in her small cottage, on the land side of the
western road, a couple of miles away, is standing in
the middle of her floor listening. She believes she could
hear her quarryman if he was moving anywhere on the
road home. She knows he hasn't taken heavy drink.
She knows he is coming along to her, unless something
with life and death in it stops him. The quarryman's
wife looks at her two little girls gazing from their boxed-in
bed, on the northern wall. The sun pours into that bed
all day. Her son, who is five years of age, is sitting on
a creepy stool by the fire, with a stick in his hand ; he
is guarding the house. The quarryman's wife takes,
from a box on the chimney shelf, a noggin bottle, three
parts full of whiskey. She cuts a long slice of soda bread
from the round cake, she puts some of it in her mouth,
the rest she wraps in a cloth and puts in her pocket.
In the other pocket she puts the whiskey. She opens
her door, and steps out on the road into the night, now
fine and clear. She had been listening from her floor,
only for the sound of her husband, and had not yet
heard the cessation of the sound of dripping rain, so the
clear night is on her like a miracle. And she walks fast,
and strong, along the road towards the Pride. She is
almost on it when she meets her quarryman homeward
bound, with a puckered brow, wondering how he could
come to miss Bowsie.

We, the rest of the rescue party, are back in the hotel,
cold, in comparison to what it should have been, with

its dancing and its bang, jangle and trickle, trickle, swoop, music.

We have a sort of hot mixum-gatherum supper, and all would launch out now our clothes are changed and we are in fair comfort. They would launch out with tales of successful rescues from drowning, of which they have some knowledge. But I am the wet blanket, I and Bowsie were friends. The funeral-baked meats are truly well baked, kept warm in the oven, for the rescue party.

The landlord of the Pride is not in sight, and the lady dead upstairs—well, the abandoned dance is her requiem. But, I am here, knocking about ; still, it's right that the Judge should see I get a good stiff whiskey into me early, before anyone else sips theirs. As though I was a royal toast, being respected, in another country, than the royalty's own.

Almost as though a republic drank to a monarchy's good health. I drink miserably in my throat, but the warm spirit warms me, below the neck, and my heart is dissolved with the heart of Bowsie, in life, or in memory.

And, Bowsie is on his feet, shaky, but upright, and he is making a meandering journey forward. He sees a lump of darkness on a little piece of higher ground, and in the middle of the darkness, standing upright, a red stick, a red stick of light, coming from a loosely fitting door. Bowsie walks now, very groggy, and very sour in the stomach. He has a hiccup ; he thinks he's like a drunken man, and now he vomits. That makes him feel marvellously restored. He puts out his left hand and tries to see it in the darkness. He thinks it should be greeny white. A merman's hand, for he knows he has been under water. He recalls falling backwards into the river—and then a crash of a star. His head's soreness tells him he must have hit it against something. The bridge it was. He puts his right hand up to his head, and feels the round, tender lump. It feels cool, or perhaps it is his fingers, which are cold enough to chill any old head. He thinks : If I'm cold, I'm not in a fever. The fever will perhaps come later." And then, all in a moment, Bowsie understands that he has only escaped drowning by a turn of a current, in the body of the river, turning its Bowsie aside, so that he lay in his gully, wedged safe, at high water, and so left by the falling tide. He is very thankful to have his life still with him. Though he does not immediately let his fancy run dancing, in a plan, for how he will spend the next day of his new life. If he had visualised this moment yesterday afternoon, he would have been certain that a snatching from death, so delicately exact as this, would have put him stuttering with happy plans of celebration. Now he thinks of me and letting me know that he is still alive and bothering, and he feels, for a moment, melancholy, as he makes my melancholy come before him. He thinks of the boy Timothy standing proudly by his package of foolish shoes. He thinks of the boy standing there until he can send him a message to desert his post by the bicycle, and the broken rail. Now he has reconstructed the accident—and he knows it was the pole of larch which had broken away from him into the flood. He goes dragging on towards the red stick of light. He will fall into the room behind that door and, now he's been sick, he feels he'll be able to make clear, to whoever is in the room, that he wants word of his living sent to the hotel. But he's not so sure about being able to talk very clearly when he gets to the room. Because he's finding himself very wobbly again below the knees. He wishes he could be sick again. But he thinks that first volu-

minous vomit was all. He likes the word voluminous, as he tries to make better going, by swinging his foot forward with an outward sweep, he thinks to himself " voluminous steps ". Now he is regretting the word " voluminous ". He thinks " that's what that old river looked like when it rolled along with me in it and down —that's it—down ; put the foot down, up, down, down. What's this so bright ? " He brings up unexpected straight against the door, and smacks his hands against the posts, and lets the long red split of light come and shine along the right of his forehead, down the side of the nose, down along his chest, down his right leg, to come out again along the toe of his right boot, and back in the dark wet door stone, and into the earth floor of the room. He stands there a long time. He will not try and peer into the room. He's too proud in his supporting unseen hands. He looks at his own, white and hairy, against the door-posts, and thinks that the hands which held him, and helped him to safety, in the flood were not like these.

He is too proud to take forethought. He pushes the door with his chest ; it opens gently inwards, and he steps, without a bother, into the large living-room of a cottage. A turf fire, heaped an hour ago, now a cone of rose light. Bowsie knows that there is no ceiling aloft, that the blacked rafters and the underside of the stout thatch is above him. Before him is a table with a lamp on it, and behind the table a bed built against the wall, a wooden box with a square opening, and in the opening, half-lies a man in a grey flannel shirt, among a heap of brown blankets, and the man has spectacles on, and has a book in his hand. It is a white-covered book, shining, and the stars and stripes are broad on the cover. The man has a long-featured, handsome, brown face, his hair is black, tufted with grey. The man in the bed has not heard Bowsie push in the door, which seems queer to Bowsie. It is perhaps the sound of the rain which has drowned the noise of his movements, and then he knows that the night is quite fine, and calm, and has been ever since he came to himself in the gully. Then he thinks the man is deaf, stone deaf. " I'm out of the frying-pan of the waves, into the fire of silence." But in a second, his eyes, and brain, now working more evenly in the old surroundings of a room, he hears the whistling of a jet of steam, coming from a log of log fir, at the base of the glowing turf. He cries out at once in a voice which he had never heard from his own lips before. " All hail, and God bless all here." The reading man, as he languidly lifts his chin, and his eyes, from his books, says, " And God bless you also," and then he says, " You are like a man that was in the sea." " I am lately from it, or from the river water amid the salt waters. I am now on my way back to my friends, at the hotel beyond. They might mourn me as dead." And the man in the bed says : " It is a strange twisted way from here to the hotel. You'd want a lantern, and a guide, to take you ; there's a lantern, I have that standing there by the dresser side. But though I'm willing, I'm not able to guide. I'm a cripple, and I'm tied here, until the day comes when I can harness the ass to the cart, and drive, if the tide is out, and the river not too floody, across the sands, and round through the sandhills, to the hotel, or back here to the eastward, taking a circle round where the ground is hard to the road. But let you take off them wet rags, throw them on the floor, and take that old frieze coat hanging on the back of the door and wrap that round you. And put that old suit-case, there by the window, put that under your head, and wait by the hearth, till the light comes. Peel off, now, hardy man, the coat is snug and dry, I warrant you. It was on the back of a chair by the fire a week. It takes a day's continuous rain to soak him—and then it takes a week to dry him. There's an old bathing towel in the dresser drawer—dry yourself down with that, and then hop into the coat. Bowsie follows dumbly these directions. He's beginning to shiver and he doesn't want to talk while there's danger of his teeth chattering on him. He has settled his pillow now on the floor, and stands upright in the dark grey frieze, his lazy body proud of its fat which so protected it in the river.

The man in the bed looks at him with steady eyes and says : " There is one other thing. Do you see that box of turf there ? well, take out the sods, throw them down. Now, have you got anything ? "

" There's a bottle down below."

" That's it, the poteen. The aged sort. Take a mug now from the dresser, take two mugs, one for the guest, and one for the Man of the House. Open the dresser door, and you'll find a lump of butter, take a bit out of that, as big as your thumb, put that in one mug—that's the mug for the traveller from the waters. The kettle is breathing all the time, but stick it on the hook and let it steam up a bit."

" Now, you have it, my boy, just a few spoonfuls on the butter to melt it, and now in with the poteen."

" How do you like it yourself ? " says Bowsie, coming towards the man in the bed with a mug in one hand and the bottle poised in the other. But the man takes the bottle from Bowsie and gives himself a helping, suitable for a man who is at home, but is in no special need of medical comfort. Then he calls out to Bowsie who is going back to where he left his own mug on the floor.

"Your hand's shaking, slide the little mug along the floor to me or you'll spill it." He had retained the poteen bottle in his hand—and so he is able to make certain that no false politeness of Bowsie's loads his mug light. Lasho—in goes the spirit ignis fatuus, softened from its folly, by the butter, from the cream, from the milk of the gentle daisy-munching cow.

"Now, a little hot water for yourself, just to raise a foam, and a harmless drop or two for me. Then sit down on your hunkers by the fire, sup that, and roll into your old coat for the night. I'll see you in the morning."

"Some sort of a short circuit," Bowsie says to himself, thinking it rather witty, as his eyes close. But as the lids fall he sees that the man in the bed is still reading. When he was close to the man with the poteen bottle, he was able to make out the title of the book, it was:

"THE FIREMAN

AND

THE FIRE BUG".

The frieze coat is deep chested, and wraps well round Bowsie, but the tails are not so long as they might be, and so Bowsie must double himself up with his knees to his chin. So, folded up, he sleeps.

I am half asleep now. I wonder as I pull off my clothes if the Judge put any sort of a settler in my last glass of grog. He had studied medicine in his youth. I shouldn't wonder.

Bowsie wakes by slow degrees. The cottage is light, but there is no blazing early sun, for the door and window face the west. The first thing lazy Bowsie thinks of is his clothes, thrown wet on the floor, in a heap,

last night—and forgotten. They are not on the floor,
where are they ? Hanging on nails. Spread to the heat
of the fire, they look dry, and Bowsie is sure they are,
and full of the blessed turf smoke now for ever. But
the host of the cottage, where is he ? Not in the bed
place, that is empty. The bed neatly made up. Bowsie
wonders what woke him, until a pinching feeling in his
belly tells him that it's hunger that has brought him back
to the world of cares. And he thinks a little of worried
friends, looking for him, or having given up the search,
mourning him with soapy words. He's morbid from
hunger ; he knows that, so he very discreetly, with his
frieze coat hanging over his back, reaches up to the nails,
and gets down his drawers and his trousers and puts
them on. He is discreet, for he does not know whether
the day is far advanced, or not, and there may be eyes
peering in at the window. Sparrows watching a canary
shaking into his feathers. However, the coat falls from
his shoulders as he pushes himself into his singlet, standing there so cosy before the fire. He has not often
during his life had this luxurious moment of dressing
before a fire, already he wishes for two fires, one at
his back, as well as the one he faces, for there is a strong
draught of air, even though the morning is not windy,
coming from the crack of the door. Then on, and up,
into his shirt, he pushes his old foolish head, and he
tucks in the skirts, and he takes his braces from their
nail, dry as a bone, and no less elastic than ever they
were. He buttons them on and adjusts them. On the
stool in the chimney corner is his money ; the two or
three notes kept down by the silver and copper. His
collar is improved by its rough adventures in the flood,
all starch spent, his tie, black, with small green spots,
is crinked, but it looks up from all its bright eyes at him

in a friendly twinkle as he holds it in his hand. And the collar-studs, the front one and, that wild pig of the world, that incorrigible fugitive of the funny men, the back one, are beside his money on the stool. If Bowsie had breakfasted, he would be saying to himself: " Surely some plump-armed, tender-fingered, fair girl of the clear shore, has taken all this care of me. No old tough in a box bed reading about fire-fighters would have the nattiness." " It must," he says now to himself, at this moment, dreaming he sees the woman before him, " be a woman of noble mien ; a woman who pities me, and she is tall, pale and calm looking, and is wearing a black shawl like a cloak, and in a second, started on her speech, by the falling of an ember in the fire, she will speak of serious things, in a cool, serious voice, pitched low, and Bowsie, his head bowed on his breast, will be most immeasurably thankful that his life is his own for a little longer, that he may do good deeds, and think good thoughts, and make his friends better, and proud of him, not letting him know their pride for him, but, as it were, veiling their eyes shining with the glamour of the brand-plucked." Now, Bowsie's head feels as empty as his belly and aches a little. He is glad to sit down on the creepy stool in the corner, and pull on his warm socks and his shoes. He has found the shoes full of oats, which he had emptied out in a neat heap behind his stool. He remembers now it was the old trick, to substitute oats for boot trees, to keep wet boots from shrinking, and losing shape, in the drying.

There comes, at this moment, a thumping outside the door. It opens boldly, and in comes the man of last night, his square shoulder and irrelevant face reaching to only a little more than half-way up the door jamb. The figure is shorn off above the knees, where the legs finish in round boots, blackened, and polished—the protectors of stumps—this man lost his legs, long ago, in the United States on a railway. A fast engine struck him to one side. It was a pilot engine, rushing on a track newly cleared of snow, to search out that all be clear, before a long train, with two engines, and crowded with passengers, some of great importance. The man fell, with his two broken legs, into the snow beside the track, and when they found him in a snow doze, it was too late to save his legs. He was pensioned handsomely enough. He was on the path of duty, waving a flag. But flying snow dust hid him and his flag ; the engine ran on, and might have killed her driver, and her fireman, but she ran into a slide of snow, and stopped, fifty yards this side of the broken track. The broken track for which the leg-broken man had waved his flag so gaily.

He lived in America, careful and moderate in all things, many years. He wrote articles for a small-town paper about woods, and streams, and ponds, and swimming in the ponds, and he signed his writing " Silvanus ". And the Editor touched the articles up, where he thought necessary, and added to each one crisp tag. Silvanus used to call round in the dark and get the Editor to translate the tags, and as the years rolled on, Silvanus had a fine collection of tags and their translations. He had a whimsical plan of some day collecting enough money to lock it away, and then have his executors see that his collection was engraved, and put down the back of his grave-stone. He thought it would be nice for a stranger, visiting the cemetery, to read the wisdom on the back, while another stranger read just his simple name and death and

" Better known as Silvanus ".

He thought also of the tame cemetery birds perching above the tags, which they found as little applicable as he did. Now, he felt called upon to say something about his want of legs. So he just smiled a morning smile at Bowsie, and said, " I lost them on the railroad in America a while ago—— Now for breakfast, my lad, unless you think you must tell your friends how you are. But still, I think, they have missed you so long, a little more will do them no lasting harm. You look to me a little herring gutted. And so it's breakfast for us, and then a little thought about the morrow, which is always here. Yesterday, to-day and to-morrow, my friend will pass the time away until the curtain falls. The day is a pure gem—look at it." He waves to the door and Bowsie goes and looks out on a ready world for a lark to sing it. The inside of a cup of sky, belted, streaming, laced, and latticed with all the clear colours of the mind's eye, and in it, three parts of the way to the right hand, up above the flat green land behind the sandhill, is that lark. He is too far away to hear his song, but when he flitters his wings the sun sparkles there.

Bowsie swings his face slowly round, sun-way from the east of south, to the east of north. A specked band of the clear horizon, a low cliffy headland farther in, and then a beating wave. There is a little wood, almost, it seems, its roots in the sea, this side of the headland and then low billowy hills of yellow and green grass. Then distant pale blue mountains, and nearer darker blue, except in one place where the sun shines on a quarry scarf. The eye drops, and by the roadside a tiny cottage, by its door a woman stands, a toy figure. Bowsie cannot see her gesture so far off. But she has shaded her eyes, not with her hand, but with her whole arm. The sun is not fierce enough to bow down her strong eyes. But she respects the sun. She loves the sun. She loves her God, and thanks Him that her quarryman is well, with her, and her children, in her house. And when he cracks the rocks in the quarry, and heaps them for the horse carts, and the lorries, she thinks the rocks laugh to be split by such a man. Bowsie's eyes move round over two little flashes where the reeds are comfortable with small wild-fowl, and then an undulating huddle of small hills, with small enclosures, and between the hills, or on the very tops of them, cottages. A larger hill of bright green grass-land. Behind it lies the railway track. Straight down a roadway now brings Bowsie's eyes to the string of sheds and houses, where, standing in the middle, is Hayden's proud hotel ; the sun is on it. But only a thin exhala-tion of smoke comes from the kitchen chimney. " It's early for them," Bowsie thinks, " but it is my stomach's moment, and I eat."

Soon a short-legged table drawn up before the fire has Silvanus and himself on its sides eating well, and with thankfulness. The two sit back satisfied and Silvanus says, " You'd call that a lovely day, and so would I, and I have seen days so lovely that I ached in the heart to think that the stars were not in the sky, to be of it. You are a man washed up from the sea and you should know of these things. You weren't so long in the sea you'd say in your foolishness. I tell you now, you were long enough. You were in it, rolled in it, lost in it, found in it, and the tide left you, so you are a son of the sea. The Good God has rinsed you in it. You will never think of the sea again but as of a friend. If you were in a dismasted ship alone, rolling in the troughs of the waves, and hopeless in the minds of men, you would not hate the sea. The man who has never been handled fully by the tide of the sea is always in fear, not so much

of his body, but of his spirit. He thinks the sea will try
and get a piece of it anyway, though he believes perhaps
he can resist the sea, and get away with it. But a man
such as yourself knows that the spirit of the sea will never
touch your spirit—your spirit lives above the waters—
anymore. You have often, I have no doubt, bathed in
the sea on a summer day and enjoyed it. You will never
enjoy the sea in the same way again. The sea will never
be again to you an extravagant bath. It will be always
to you, from this on, a hail-old-fellow-well-met, and you
will always have your secret understanding. The other
bathers, standing about on the brink, and swimming,
and diving by your side, will not know anything about it,
nor could they understand if you tried to tell them. If
they looked in your face, as lovers look in each other's
faces, they would see there your sea companionship.
But nobody not a lover is able to see another's face like
that. They make a mask and look at it. I say if they
could look, as lovers look, they would see the true. But
I didn't say that lovers saw a face that wasn't a mask."
" Ah," Bowsie says, " what face do the lovers see then ? "
—" They see always the same mask—the lovers' mask.
Two masks back to back, and so always facing outward.
Both faces are the same ; they have never varied. Many
fancies have been written, and painted, and drawn,
about them. I've seen the backs of a deck of cards,
all with the lovers' faces. I saw a man shuffling them
and he was holding the bank, and he said, " These are
no good to me. They all look different to me, like as
though they was marked. He saw a different tilt in
every eye, and he thought someone had been manipulat-
ing the pack. And so he got a new deck and it had a log
cabin in the snow on the back of it. And he counted
the logs in the back wall, and when he found in half

a dozen cards the numbers corresponded, he was satisfied."

Bowsie cries out suddenly, " You are a terrible man for fancies in the morning with your masks and your decks of cards, but you can't make anything of me but an old goosey, goosey, gander, floating easy."

" No," says Silvanus, " I'm not a man of fancies. I tell you the truth, and I don't mind your yelling. You can yell as loud as you like, old son. No one will interfere with you here. If you go out on the grass and yell, the sea-gulls will yell back to you, and give you their idea of a royal welcome." And Bowsie answers slowly ; he's thinking as he speaks, which is unusual with him. His thinking, and his speech, with him are separate, both arranged carefully, as tableaux, on different stages. His thoughts lie about a dry dock, repairing, while his speech is afloat. Bowsie says, " You are a serious-minded man, and no doubt you are able to penetrate the ambiguosity of my shell, and know me better than I know myself, whatever that may be worth. I have no desire myself to know myself any better than I do, at this moment. To know which is the weak leg, and which is the weak shoulder, is useful to me—that's enough. But to watch the sun come pouring through your little easterly window and shine on your floor, and to know that all outside this house is belted, and circled above, and around, with the dazzle of the sky." " Yes, and the innumerable little birdkins are flittering, and skipping about their business, among the grasses, and the little bushes, and the small fishes in the shallows are rubbing their stomachs on the sands." " Yes, and the grasses are making music for the birds to imitate, as the breeze goes puffing by."

" Yes, and there are horizontal-eyed goats bringing

everything to the level of their own vision—a goats' world."

" Yes, and there are subtle-expressioned grey asses, wondering when we two will emerge from your house and take the air, and sun. The slightest hillock is drying nicely now, even after all the old rain of yesterday."

" You are right—that's what they are thinking. They want to see us out. We, the sheeted ghosts, galvanised for a time, they think, should take our place with the others, as soon as the lights come on, here, on this floor, that was under the sea, or under the ice, on a mountain-top, rubbing eyebrows with the moon. And other sheeted ghosts thinking as strange thoughts as you or I were ever capable of thinking, walking in the rocks and the heather."

" Well, if it is comfortable outside, it is comfortable here within, and strolling among the singing birds, lifts the heart to a scentless, sightless, deaf, unfelt ecstasy. But the gentle fall of the rose-burning turf, turning into grey, mousy dust, makes a small noise, and I think I can see, feel, and scent, the noise. But now it's gone. The word ' rose ' remains only with me, a description and translation, a man's attempt. Now it has gone. My friend, you have a pleasant smile." " Have I so ? Then it must be that I met in my life many pleasant smiles just going about streets, and lanes, and up and down hills."

The room, with its east and south windows, is full of light, yellow and cheerful. I am half awake. And now, almost, fully awake. I am wondering what could have woken me, not the sunlight, for that is so strong that it must have been in the room for a long time. Perhaps, all the same, some plastering of sun has fallen across my eyes and brought me up out of sleep. I rub my hand across my face, ridiculously, and look at my hand, as if I expected the sunlight to be smeared on my fingers. It must have been some artificial measure of sleep which came to an end, because its end was due. I think it may be that I have been giving thought to Dunne's *Experiment in Time.* Now, I should wake myself up into such a daytime energy, as to get a piece of paper from my coat, as it hangs, on its coat holder in the wardrobe, and write the particulars of my dream. But I had no dream, and, if I have to write down anything, I will have to get the pencil from my waistcoat pocket. My waistcoat is hanging on the foot of the bed. Wisely, I put it there. If I had put it near my head, the ticking of my watch in its pocket would have kept me awake. But Dunne said that, even if you could not recall a dream, what you were thinking of when you woke would do for experimental purposes. What was I thinking of? Of, now I know—what I should have been thinking of. Bowsie, I had forgotten you were among the lost of the world. What a trouble you are to me, and what time, in this day of irritation and worry, can it be? I have the watch. It's ten o'clock. No wonder the sun is strong. The Judge must have been heavy with his medical hand.

I must get into my clothes. I get my trousers on. Wash, bath? No. I'd be sure to meet a procession going, or coming, and perhaps the Judge. He wraps himself, I daresay, in a great bath towel. Shave? yes; unshaven, I will do Bowsie little credit. My boots are, I suppose, clean outside my door. This is a house of death, and of a lost man. I'll open the door and see if my boots have been moved. I go to the door, open it, and at the same moment the Judge steps into the hall from the stairs. He is not wrapped in a bath towel. He is full, and neatly, dressed in blue. He looks trim and well. He says, " A body has been sighted on the farther shore, perhaps you should come down." I pull up my braces and put on my waistcoat and coat over my pyjama jacket. I have on my feet a pair of hotel slippers. I follow the Judge down the stairs into the hall. He takes a hat from the rack and puts it on my head. We go out into the roadway in front of the hotel. I can see no sign of any attention being given by anyone to the moving of the light clouds slowly, or the flitting about of the birds—at first. But turning my head, in imitation of the Judge, to the right, I see a small group standing on the top of the nearest sandhill. They are not looking at clouds or birds, but in their centre is the figure of the watcher who walked by us yesterday. He has binoculars to his eyes and is looking with a stiff neck to the west. I shuffle across the road, and drag my way through the bent grass, with the Judge ahead of me, up to the top of the sandhill. The watcher hands me his glasses—I cannot get any clear image with them at first, but fumbling, in a little while, I get the true focus, and I have under my inspection a patch of whitening sand, ten or fifteen yards from the water's edge, half a mile away. And, on the sand, I see something rather whiter than the sand, and I am sure it is a naked body. The watcher takes the glasses from me ; he says—" That is not your friend. That, I am certain myself, is the body of a young banker, who was lost out fishing in the horns of the bay, better than a week ago. He was leaning over the side looking at a codling that he thought should be his, and he overbalanced himself and fell into the sea. He was well guarded, you would say. There were two young men with him, expert swimmers and divers, and though they saw him sinking under the water with the weight of his clothes, and they dived in turns, deep, they never got him. Though the first young man got a grip of his shirt collar, but it came away in his hand. He is naked, now ; the waves and the circles of the waters have taken the clothes from him." The watcher looks down at his own feet where a bundle of light canvas, the sail of a small boat, lies. I know it is with that he will cover the drowned man. We, all seven—the Judge, the watcher, myself, three visitors from the hotel, and a fisherman, walk back to the road where we meet another fisherman pushing a hand-cart. The watcher throws his bundle of canvas on the hand-cart, and helping the cart along with one hand, marches to the west. I go also. But the Judge, and the visitors, turn back to the hotel. I shuffle along beside the watcher for a couple of hundred yards, silent. The watcher has his thoughts about this weary drowning of men, and the two fishermen, the one pushing the hand-cart, the other lighting his pipe, are thinking that they are men living unfair lives, because they never more go out on the deep bay to trust its vixenish ways. Their safety gives them no comfort at this moment. The watcher turns his face round to me, and speaks. He says : " This young man is not for you —you don't want to bother about him. You can do him no good. He'll get a good inquest, a good burying ; his people have plenty of money. They have no need to be considering the cost. Here, to-morrow, you'll see the motor hearse ; it's new with us about here, for a distance it saves horses. It looks very decent. Now, I think you might go back. Now, we'll get along fine, the three of us." So I turn back towards the Pride Hotel. I stop and shake some of the small pebbles out of my slippers, each slipper in turn. Then I get on to the grass where the going is better.

Back in the hotel I dress myself in proper form for a

hotel guest, and I shave cleanly. A new blade gives parts of my chin the satiny feeling suggested by the advertisements of shaving soap. Those coloured glossy pictures where you can see the swath of pink flesh left behind in the razor's wake. The sweeps of the broad sword exercise done on the chops and there you are. Well, I am not quite so fair-faced as all that. When I am finished parts are stiff and stubbly.

Then here is breakfast, late breakfast. " Late breakfast " was always truly early lunch—hunter's appetite ; not because the meal was early, but because the boys were late the night before, and not able to face a strong-smelling breakfast, in the latter half of the first twelve. So, when the sun climbed over the main yard, they were ready for a collation. No appetite for the first few mouthfuls, just feeling their way, and then the appetites begin to grow. The most æsthetic of appetites is made on its own ground. Any tough mouth, and thirty-two good teeth, which have been breathing cold air, and doing nothing else, while their master rolled over hill, dale, and ditch can bring a raw appetite to a meal. There's nothing in that. Give such as them a joint and let them hack it. But a clear, pure-minded, void of a stomach, too lackadaisical to reach for the fruits or the crubeens. That puts a spread late breakfast table to its metal, and it calls " Eat me, eat me, eat me." I see it, that table, in my agéd eye ; it's long, and the cloth is blue white, and very thick, and has a picture on its centre and patterns, big, rolling, on the side. The picture, flossy shine and brown flat, is Italian, with pillars half in ruins, a harp with broken cords. There is water in the picture, with ducks upon it, and ladies in a boat like a crescent moon, with a tassel on the tips of bow and stern. And a blithe boy stands high on one

tip propelling the boat with one long oar. There's a
bacon grease stain on the lake, between the heads of the
ladies in the boat. There are six fair ones in all. The
artist didn't forget to be lavish with them. And round
the lake there are flowering bushes, making moping looks
at the waters, which are shown by very straight horizontal lines below the bushes, save where a leaf falls.
And on that table are all sorts of cold meats, and eggs,
a circus of eggs, in a silver stand with a cloth over them,
to keep them warm. There is a fire up in the far end of
the room, though I believe it is very early autumn time,
when I am seeing this room. In front of the fire are
dishes—old plated dishes with covers and full of rissoles
and bacon, and fish too. The table has plenty of silver
and silver plate on it, on the sideboard there is more,
and decanters also, and long-necked bottles. There is a
brace of soiled plates on the sideboard. Someone has
had fish, and meat too ; yes, and he has sat down by
the long bow window, where the sun shines in on the
old carpet, with its pattern of green and brown fern
leaves. I see a chair dragged up, and on it, a little old,
leather-bound book, of plays I believe. I say to myself :
" he sat there " for I know this is a breakfast-room for the
men. Why I know it, I cannot tell myself ; I know there
will be half a dozen to come down very soon to eat
this breakfast. No servant will appear. This wing of
this long house is without any servant moving about
at this time. Outside there is a billowy park with
clumps of trees, round clumps, in the old-fashioned style.
But I am day-dreaming, and the late breakfast I am now
chewing my way through, is unlike the one in my dream,
and the back room, where I eat it, is in no way like that
other breakfast room. And instead of waiting to see
those old six breakfast men come down into my mind,

I should remember Bowsie, a cold corpse, some would be sure, but I'm not so sure, anyway, I should be thinking about him, though what good just thinking about him is going to do the poor devil, I don't know.

However, now I'm out on the road, I must remember to worry about him. The visitors are talking to anyone who will listen to them. The Judge is resting indoors.

Now, the hearse for Julia Starrett comes out from the yard. Entering the stage of the road, as though it followed a stage direction. There are only two horses. I had hoped for four. Though I knew that it was very unlikely an undertaker, in this part of the country, could turn out four horses as a successful team. The hearse looks very well washed and clean, and the horses if not so very deep a black and with a white speckle or two, are better-looking roadsters than some you might see in the cities. They have a long road before them even for their first stage. The undertaker might have thought of hiring any coloured horses, and so with changes, made a quick passage home for Miss Starrett. But it isn't so easy to get horses now in these days of motors. And then, he wanted to carry her along with the blacks all the way. And his old hearse-man would tackle himself to the pole before he'd drive bays, chestnuts, grey roans, or piebalds, in a hearse with a body in it. There is a carriage also, and yoked to that, there is a pair—one a red bay, the other a black. There is dying ember thought about the bay, that is in keeping. Who will ride in the carriage? I know, I think I do. Miss Starrett's maid will ride alone in there. She will get tea, and an egg, and tea and currant bread, several times on her long ride, and she will be encouraged to talk a great deal about her dead mistress. In that way she will forget for a little, the dead body that was once a living, blushing, laughing, crying, aching body. Forget it in being herself, for a little, a somebody. I don't care whether I am right, or not, even if the maid isn't sitting in the carriage when it trundles away, she should be, to make my story complete. Perhaps Hayden will sit there, but why should he, when he has his car. Perhaps there's a lawyer, a lawyer's clerk, sitting somewhere inside the hotel, and perhaps he will be inside the carriage smoking too many cigarettes. The old hearse driver is talking a little to the hound-voiced visitor, very politely—his voice low. Hearse drivers never know when they may be talking to their next customers. The coachman of the carriage is young to be in a black coachman's coat with old-crested plated buttons, and a tall hat down on his head. No, down on his ears ; nothing ugly or comic about it, but screwed down to his head, and when he gets the hat off at night, his head will be marked across with a red purple sabre-cut-looking ragged stripe. Now, we are all falling back, softly, towards the front of the hotel. The coffin is coming out. There are flowers on it already, white and stylish, got from some good made garden, and there's a tiny wreath of wild things from the hillside. I don't know who made it, and who thought of it, but it sits there above the coffin, like a bright little field mouse spirit among the great lions of a garden tame.

As the coffin comes out we take off our hats, the last act of decency to go from people on a public way. We are all a little self-conscious about it, and those that are not wearing hats, head free, are sorry about it, and will, for a time, manage to carry a little cap, at least, in a pocket, so that should another incident of this kind come their way, they may be able to act the part of men of good human behaviour.

I was right, I was right, I was right. It is the maid. Hayden goes with her to the carriage door, opens it, and sees her in it. She would like the window open, so he gets it down for her, and away trundles the hearse and its following mourning brougham, first walking, then in a steady trot.

We stand about in the roadway filling up pipes, and lighting them, and watching the black spots on the bone-coloured road, under the flaming white and blue sky move away into the distance. Simple little foolish shadows passing through the land. Shadow and Sunshine. There was a painting, and a print of it, selling largely long ago, and something like that was the name of it.

Here comes our second excitement. Out from a boreen on the right, beyond the bridge from among the hillocks, comes a donkey and cart. It comes this way on the road. There is a square stocky figure filling the small cart, and by the donkey's side walks a rolling figure ; I know it well—Bowsie in the flesh ! The equipage ; that's a word I seldom use. It's a very nice word now, comes nearer. The sweet little grey donkey is planting his neat hooves very carefully, walking with ease and discretion. The Judge comes out of the hotel, and looks along the road. He recognises Bowsie, now much nearer. He looks at him bitterly, for the Judge has a kind heart, and it has been much moved at the untimely burying in the sea, of Bowsie. The rest of the visitors on the road, heart-whole, are more in the mood for welcoming the saved from the waves hilariously. They would burst into some familiar song. One of them, the one with the suitable voice, thinks of Auld Lang Syne. One of them, a member of some Presbyterian Truth Society, thinks of " Will ye no' come Back Again ", but in the end there is nothing in familiar song to meet the moment. Of course, no-stern-acid-voice though he thinks of " When Johnnie comes Marching Home Again " keeps it to himself, as he doesn't know the tune. If he did, our Johnnie isn't marching, he's just slipping along with his feet turning lazily outward, the way he always strolls when he is in easy circumstances of the mind. The lateral pointing of his toes keeps back any eager rushing forward of the hour. I know him well ; he's fatter than he was yesterday, and his clothes cling about him greasily. If he knew that he had wrung a Judge's heart it would lie no heavier than a feather of the ceannbán lies on the bog. That's the very sort of simile he'd like himself. This bog and mountain lake, river, and tumbling sea background suits him well—the snail of fashion but the mould of form.

The donkey cart has arrived in front of the hotel on the swept hard ground. The lion-faced man, with his stumps before him, turns his donkey to drive into the hotel yard, and as he does so, he waves his hand towards Bowsie, who has stopped, stock still, in the roadway. And Silvanus in the cart seems to say " There's your middle weight cupid for you, washed up by the tide, and Silvanus." Bowsie gives a short enough, account of the miracles of his being alive and on the road with us, very terse, not even enough for the shortest paragraph. But the local correspondent of a Dublin paper is already stirring in his sleep, by a widow's fireside, and he'll be down by the shore soon, and if he can't get a paying story out of Bowsie, he'll get it from someone.

Bowsie speaks nicely about the funeral procession that passed across the asses head, as he turned towards the roadway along the boreen. He gives in quiet, gentle words, a short oration that, could it be repeated there, would satisfy those that will stand about Miss Starrett's grave, when the handful of clay rattles down. He must have himself well timed for a grave-side, for he booms out two or three words, loudly and defiantly, just where the first of the grassy clods should fall on the coffin's roof when the men of the shovel seem to come into their own old graveyard pasturage. If men could be buried alive, suffer no harm, and finish their death at their own chosen minute, then some of these old graveyard shovels would like to be alive, facing up under the roof, hear the first clod fall, give a knock with the knuckles back—and then pass on.

Bowsie having ended his oration, waddles into the Hotel. The Judge looks after him, and thinks to himself : " I would like to have had him before me in a dock when I was in my prime, or myself there before him, and he on the bench—the ruffian's full of dirt— track dirt—dust in summer, clábar deep in winter. In mud, as in snow, you would require a sled to pass over him. Well rest his soul—when it's required of him."

A little while, and Bowsie comes out on the sunny road again. He looks certainly sprucer than he did. His clothes are as shapeless in themselves as before, just gripping and dragging about him. But he has had his boots cleaned and he has put on a clean collar, and he has found a bright blue new necktie, tucked away in a long envelope for a time like this—when he should try and better himself. I see he has made an effort. His hair is well brushed, and sleeked, where it is not bristling. He thanks the group in the road for all the trouble they took about him last night. They were waiting for those thanks. He speaks directly to them, but he looks at me. While he is talking his wandering eyes turn away to the west. He sees a hand-cart coming, and pretty soon, it is obvious that the long shape lying out under the sail, is a dead body. Bowsie says " What another of them " any harshness in the words is taken from them, when I know he thinks of himself as one of the corpses. He is so sensitive to other people's imaginings, though careless about them, that he knows to all of us standing about him, he is still just half a corpse. Curiously enough, he hasn't smoked yet. I will offer him a cigarette. Oh, I have only an empty packet. I fumble at it, and one of the visitors, takes my hint, and produced a spanking fine case with gold corners. Bowsie lights the cigarette, a second visitor being quick with the match in his arched hand.

As soon as the smoke begins to puff away from Bowsie's mouth, he stops being a half corpse, and it is natural that he should fall back with the rest of us, with the heaped sandhill behind us, and let the hand-cart, the watcher and his helpers, pass by and on into the hotel yard. I suppose, in an outhouse there, the inquest will be held, the Coroner will be along pretty soon. He likes inquests.

Already men, who know they may be called on to build up a jury, are slipping away into the corners of the land. If it was the heat of summer, and a great many inquests holding, it would be pleasant to lie hid in narrow places, smoking in little puffs, no big pillars rising over the banks to give away your hide. But at this time of year lying out of doors is poor comfort. It's the same in most sparsely inhabited places. The men will take the greatest care in keeping away from a Juryman's work on a body. But when they are rounded up these same men will give the same great care to arrive at a true verdict between the body on the table and the world.

We are all restless, Hound Voice, Woolly Face, and the Judge pace about together. I stand by Bowsie, who, grudging, is giving some idea of the sort of man Silvanus may be. As Woolly Face passes by us with the other, he is talking, and the potato-in-the-mouth voice makes it impossible for me to know what, on the earthly world, he is talking about. I am supposing it's something in the earthly world, for Hound Voice has not that fretted irritated hit-under-the-belt-with-a-mean-advantage mask with which he would shutter his face, listening to talk of higher things. And the Judge has the expression which seems usual to him—not the bland furiousness of face, which he lifts, as a protection to his dignity, when a criminal in the dock comes back at him with a prayer, up from the pit of his stomach, for the enlightenment of the Judge, and a leading of him, to the Heavenly Lands, when the poor grovellers on earth can spare him.

There comes a relief—" Lunch is on the table." These others are hungry, and so am I, though it's only lately I had my late breakfast. In we go to the dining-room. There are three ladies to grace our board. They look as if they'd missed something. They feel that the men have been having emotional excitements which have been denied to them. Two are young women, nice fresh and clear looking, in real silk blouses and rough tweed skirts. The third is a middle-aged woman, stout, red-faced, and managing with nothing to manage.

If she tried to manage either of the young women, at this moment, the young women would be capable of rapping on the round back of her hand with the spoon with which the tinned mixed fruit salad is lifted out of its glass dish.

The two young ladies have already met Bowsie since his return to our life. They came on him, as he was dodging his way to his room, to clean himself up. They wouldn't have chosen to see him returned differently. In the half light of the hall he did indeed look like spindrift settling, for a moment, on a craggy rock. Hayden was looking out at his office door, and so was able to welcome Bowsie home, but he left him to the quick questioning of the ladies. They had some idea that he must have come up to the surface three times. It wasn't a very good place for hearing. The dark hall made it impossible to see the expression of Bowsie's curling lips and the ladies were most anxious not to have their romantic pictures of the Bowsie in the sea destroyed, as so many romantic pictures had been destroyed before the spiritual eyes of both of them. Even the youngest had given up all hope of the romantic being presented before her—she thought she knew, that she must always, down to the long years of her life, construct her own romantic bouquets for herself, using paper flowers.

The elder of the two girls believed in one more romantic figuration. She was only a little older than her friend. They were no relation. They had met, for the first time, in the train coming here. She looked forward to see once a romantic figure of a man passing, a silhouette against a pale grey sky.

Now in the dining-room none of the three women could be bothered any more about Bowsie eating so near them. The meal was taken with hardly any conversation to sauce it down. But passing pepper, and salt, and castor sugar and cream, yes, cream, not just unskimmed milk, keeps us all from relapsing into grumpiness. We are all dissatisfied even with our appetites, which are not so good as we thought they would be. In my case it's natural that I should feel apathetic about the meal, after the first half-dozen mouths full. But the rest are a good many hours away from their breakfast. It isn't just that the untimely death of Bowsie has been followed by his untimely plucking back to life. It isn't that we died with him, and came back with him, in a go-day, come-day, God send Sunday spirit. The day is bright enough and should be exhilarating. When lunch is over, and we are out again on the road, we wait about, each thinking that the arrival of the Coroner will be a break in the day, which has become a burden to us. But the Coroner is already here. He came into the yard in his very new car, and is now in Hayden's office, talking very slowly. Everyone expects a Coroner to be a man to arrive with a rush, and hustle about. But why should they. The dead can wait a little longer, and nowadays when amateur revenge is frowned down, there should be no great hurry on the relatives of the dead. Death may have come quickly, but even under the very chariot wheels the victim may see the shadow first, and at that moment, he is not, in his mind, clear about the measurements of time. There on his back in the road—on a cliff edge where time ceases and the endless, boundless looking-glass back of no time begins. So, even now, about the poor dead body, there is the veil of the eternal floating above face, and body, and listless hands. Contradicting, even now, the time when decay will be obvious to the clods, that nestle about the body under the ground. Bowsie is fidgeting from one person to another, and now he announces that he will go to his room, and " write some letters ". That feeble hotel resters " not at home to anyone " excuse. I turn away towards the east, the road on which we came in yesterday, and the road on which Miss Starrett's hearse travelled home. I am walking slowly. Someone overtakes me—it is the man with the low small voice. He addresses me as " sir ". I don't suppose he's any younger than myself. I'll see him far enough before I'll " sir " him. He is going to walk alongside of me. Can I not be alone, where a bird can rise above the land and sing to the sun so that he flutters in the centre of a space of air reserved to himself. If I let my fancy trip above, I could fancy that I saw him held up by his whirling wings, in a great egg-shaped clearness, where his music had drawn out of the common air some grossness that it had, before he began to sing it clear. But Small Voice, if he doesn't seem very significant, has a kind thought. He wishes to interest me. I do believe he is as free of egotism as any man might be, but he is sure that to talk about himself will be the way to interest me to being alive. He doesn't pretend to be a wild one. He doesn't break into song. He doesn't quote poetry. He doesn't tell me about funny books he's read in the railway carriages. He doesn't tell me about his wife and family ; he hasn't got any. He has no near relatives, though he has a distant one, whose money he expects to inherit. But there is no certainty about it. He has no plans for keeping himself before the relative, and the man can leave his money where he likes. He has a small clerkship in an old-fashioned brown office, in a city, built on an island. Of course, there are bridges. The office makes most people think of Dickens, but Small Voice never thinks about Dickens. He drags the heavy account book from desk to table, and back again. He looks at the point of his pen before making an entry, and he writes, always, very slowly, his figures are made in an old style and confuse people who are too young to remember the time when those figures were made that way only, by the spry, and dashing, young cits. He takes a long while sliding his pen along. There have been days when his work consisted in making no more than twenty entries. But since that day he has always arranged to have a dozen new envelopes ready, so that he could address them slowly to different customers of the firm ; getting them all ready should they be wanted. His employer is a gambler, and requires excitement, so, as if gambler's excitement wasn't enough, for his over-worked heart, he gets drunk once a month, and lets himself into his own room at the back of the house, and then falls on the floor. Then Little Voice, goes into the inner office and lifts his employer from the floor, and arranges his body in the armchair, and his legs on another. Then he searches the lower shelf of the cupboard, on the right of the fireplace, until he finds a small saucepan. He fills it with water, from the tap outside the yard door, and makes preparations for making coffee, as soon as the Boss shows any sign of being about to awake from his stupor. Small Voice brings forward a black tin deed box and sits down on it, and watches his employer sleep. It is then his thoughts about death come to him. He would like to co-ordinate everything

he has ever heard, or read, about this important subject.
But when he tries to do so, he finds he is unable to
keep any order in his thoughts. They refuse to put
two, and two, together, and just go wandering up
tracks that end in a tangled wood beyond which lies
a Promised Land. He says each time to himself
" Promised Land " and satisfies himself, and is for the
time, content. Then there comes a sudden start as
though he'd heard a sharp noise, though he knows
that he has heard nothing, and his employer is lying
just breathing a little short, as yet. He has not jumped
up and thrown an inkstand through the grey dark
window, with the whitewashed yard wall only a few
feet from it. With the sudden start Small Voice raises
his chin and looks straight before him, and always
then he is looking straight up a slight hill. A village
street, on each side there are beautiful cottages, some
thatched, some with red tiles, and all have flowery
gardens in front and little green wooden gates, and the
whole thing, in shape and colouring, is like a picture
post-card enlarged to life size. And out of each cottage
come men and women, most realistic and all smiling,
with apple cheeks. They are all grown people, no very
young ones, and they all shake hands with each other
in the middle of the village street, and he thinks,
somehow, that they have all walked into these idyllistic
cottages, through the back doors, coming in from some
purple heathery downland, with little clumps of fairy
trees. And he thinks these people are foolishly kind
to each other, and delighted to meet. He thinks they
have never met before. Each time he sees this village
street, when his employer's monthly overtaking comes
to him, is always the same, except perhaps for some
changing in the flowers, with the seasons. He's not

absolutely sure about that. He doesn't know anything about gardening. He's never seen the street look like winter ; it's always summer. But the people are never the same twice. He doesn't know how long he is looking at the village each time, because he thinks he dozes off into real sleep, and wakes again with the people still wishing each other pleasant times. He never hears any words that he remembers ; just several good wishes. He, not at the time, but after one of these viewings of the village street, tried to imagine that the people were like a pageant of Auld Lang Syne. But then he remembered that the people had never met before they came through the houses, through the gardens, into the middle of the street. What made him think of Auld Lang Syne, he doesn't know, for he has no ear for music. He wouldn't know people were singing Auld Lang Syne, unless he heard the words, or saw the people hold each other's hands. The next month after that as soon as he found himself looking into the village street and watching the people,— they happened to be a thin, tall, people, all of them ; this time high yellow complexion, not bilious, but like a faint sun tan. He tried to remember the words of Auld Lang Syne. He thought he'd call them out and then perhaps the people on the post-card village street, would begin to take up the words. But he couldn't remember one word, and then in a flash, he'd forgotten the title of the song, so he just watched the people turning about and passing the news, or the good will, and sometimes they looked outwards towards himself, but looked over his shoulder like the tigers and the lions in the zoo.

When the light in the yard had fallen away, and it was after the time for the office to close, and the sleepy man on the chair came to himself, and Small Voice got up stiffly to get the coffee, then his employer began to sing with a husky drone—" Should Auld acquaintance be forgot, and never brought to mind ". And Small Voice was very put out about it for he thought that his idea about his village street had just come, a thought transferred from his sleeping employer, who had perhaps always associated deep drink with " Auld Lang Syne ". He was so disgusted that he sat down again on the deed box. And before him again came the village street, and the people had all little pieces of paper in their hands, and pencils, and were holding the pieces of paper against gateposts and into coping of low walls, and writing on them, and he thought— " They don't talk, perhaps they are unable to talk any more ; perhaps they are dummies for evermore." And he felt as if he was to blame in some way. He looked over at his employer but he was back again huddled in the armchair asleep. The pieces of paper were floating in the air, like Chinese butterflies over the village street and the people were greeting each other, all over again, as if they had just met and were as glad as the first time. Immediately, Small Voice got up and made the coffee, and when, in a few minutes, his employer staggered to his feet, he was glad to drink his bowl of strong coffee. And when he started for home, he gave Small Voice a queer look. But he said " You're a good man to me ; coffee is very good for me."

Once in the heart of the summer, the employer was told by a doctor that he must have a long change. So he went away and was away nearly two months. So Small Voice missed his village of flowers that time. " Now, sir," says he, " as soon as he came back and was at work only a few days, what happens, but he goes on another buster and comes into the place on all fours. I puts him up on the chairs, and sits down on the tin box and starts to watch my village come to life with people. Very nice gentle people are just coming out of the cottage doors ; there is a kind of yellow light in the sky, very nice and pleasant. The people, they were all new to me the same as always, only just a sort of family resemblance, something in the expression. I was waiting to get the sensation of goodness, and good-heartedness, when I heard my old man give a gurgle and a little cough. I didn't want to bother him, but there, you know the way it is, inclination draws you one way, and duty the other. Which wins just depends on your training. Not that I had ever much training. Still I was with some respectable boys and girls at school, and then the master had always dinned into my head, duty first, the rest follows. I don't know about that, but when I got up and went over to my employer he was slid to one side and when I put my fingers on his shoulder he slipped down on to the floor, between the two chairs. Silly things you think of at this time. I thought of : ' Between two stools you fall to the ground.' The old man was dead. I was in a pretty to do. I was sorry too, we'd never given each other much trouble, and if I wasn't grateful, he was. But I was bothered and flustered to think there I was, a friendless man, as you might say, alone with a man just died, a sudden death. I began going about very carefully. You know, ' Signs of a struggle ' stuff. I'd often read that in the papers. ' No motive ' I said, but suppose, he's left me all his money. He'd very likely got his life insured. He might have done it years ago when he was young, and before the liquor had begun to make him a bad life for a company. If he'd been to an insurance company since I knew him to take out a policy, I thought to myself, the company's medical man would give him such a bad report, that I'd know, by his look, he was after receiving a slap in the face. But he never went about like a man in fear of death, and when he went for that change it might have been a change of air, but it was no change of drink I thought. Well, I don't know what you would think I should do. I might tell you now that I needn't have bothered about him leaving me his fortune. He, we found out, had only just, only just, enough to pay off what he owed, including my salary to date, and nothing over. His friends buried him—we saved on that. I don't know what you would say I should have done, but what I did was, I ran out into the street. I shut the doors behind me, and locked them. I know that, so I wasn't beside myself. I went up the street until I met a customer of ours—a Mister West—a very respectable man. Well, he didn't know my late employer outside business, but he knew the name of a crony of his, and he got his number in the telephone book, and he told him, and then he came back to the office, and had a look at the Boss. He was just saying to me : ' We must get a doctor at once ', when in blew the crony. I didn't remember ever seeing him before, and there were five others with him. I never saw such people. I'd been in the City a long while, and yet I'd never seen them walking about, perhaps they didn't walk. They all had a black look about them as if they were in mourning and yet they weren't—some had blue suits, and some grey, and some brown. They were black about the visage, perhaps it was the drink. They had a boy with them. He was different from them ; he had red round cheeks. He was a sort of messenger boy. I think wherever they

got the drink they must have sent the boy to keep an
eye to them, and run for more drink when they wanted
it. One of them was a medical man. He pronounced
that life was extinct, and the rest said it after him :
' Life is extinct.' They talked a bit about the de-
ceased ; they said he was without fault as a friend ;
they said of course he was too generous in taking different
kinds of drink. They got an idea then that they should
take a last drink round the body. They were a strange
nasty lot of men, and I heard them tell the boy to go
and get some glasses, and a bottle of whiskey and bring
them round they said, in one of those little despatch
cases that they use at Christmas for Christmas presents.
But that boy wouldn't go, he had a sense of decency.
But he led them away. He went before looking—it'd
make you laugh, like a goat leading a lot of big sheep.
I thought of that at the time—black sheep I thought.
Mister West left me, and he went away, and telephoned
and got another doctor—felt it his duty.

Then more of this death business—we weren't finished
yet. There was the funeral, and a certain number of
people, business people, and the six friends were right
up by the grave-side. They looked different. They
had no drink smell off them that I could catch, and
they looked cleaned up for the day—perhaps it was the
contrast of their black clothes. They looked, sir, quite
like statues in ebony. They were putting back the earth,
when, one of them broke up at the knees and went down
by the grave-side. He was dead in a few moments.
He had a clergyman and doctors there at hand. He
looked to me, lying there, like an old horse, dead in the
traces, all flattened out, except where his hip stood up.
He fell with his tall hat on, but one of his friends took
the hat off before the breath left his body. Funny thing,

this death. I was observing everything. I was out of it, to one side. I went away not very long after that. I lived for a time in Clonmel and over in Bolton. I had to come back one time to get a trunk of clothes I'd left, and I met a funeral, a walking funeral. I stood in an office door to let it pass. It was a child's funeral, you could see the little coffin, and walking along, side by side, were two of my late master's boozing friends. They looked older, but about the same. I knew them at once, though I don't remember the names of any of them. I saw a list in the paper after the funeral, and I made a guess and which were the governor's old friends, but I was never certain. Then I left Bolton and came back over here again, and another firm was in my old office. They took a fancy to my looks, and I'm back in my old place. But I never have occasion to sit on a tin box in the inner office, any more."

Small Voice looks up at me now, and yet I don't feel he wants me to say anything more than just " strange how these things come ". So I say that. He seems satisfied. We have got a good way from the hotel, along the road to the east, and I rake about in my thoughts, to think of some subject of conversation, that wouldn't seem too much like a flippant changing from this death and life experience. Some rattling of a stone on the roadway, in my ears sounds very hard. I suppose, after listening to a quiet miniature voice so long. I look back over my shoulder and lo ! I see coming towards me—Bowsie, waving a green telegraph envelope in his hand. I am nervous of Bowsie now, he may burst in too extravagantly on Small Voice's memories. I look down at the man by my side. Bowsie must have seen some timidity in my look, for, when he joins us, he does not flash the telegram about, though I can see he has it crumpled up, palmed, in his left hand. Bowsie says nothing, but falls into slow step between us. I feel tongue-tied. But there is something amusing looking, about the nearest to me, of Bowsie's eyebrows, and, of course, I knew from the first waving gesture, that the green envelope contained no terrible news. It is Small Voice who speaks first. He says " We were discussing the bagatelle of life—how the balls go rolling round, getting in each others ways, until in a moment, they come to rest, and those in the holes, look as if it was the only place for them."

" Bagatelle " is the word says Bowsie and " rolling round ". You've said it and " Life " and " Ending up in a hole ". I have a telegram here. I have no secrets before you, sir, either of you. I have received the offer. I have feared it for some time—of a post in a semi-Government office. Well, so nearly attached to a Government Board as to be hardly distinguished from the real thing, answers to any test, including a pension, of sorts. There were several chances, my friend who sends the telegram, had his eye on, and he believed, he was holding somebody else's finger on. They all had a pension at the end ; I insisted on that, also a position of headman, no one above me ; I insisted on that. I used to see a boot black, one time. He was a man, even though he knelt at your feet and polished, and breathed his breath on the toe for the final shine. But I once had my shoes cleaned by his helper, his understudy, his employé. I could have wept on his bent head, or perhaps my tears would have fallen on his neck, to see a human being so lowly, bowed before me. The gestures were the same but there came some little tinkling spirit of pride, like an aura, from the crouched figure of the Chief, which this man had not got. My friend's telegram gives no details; it just says " You have it if you come at once ". " At once means to-morrow morning at nine o'clock—O very early. That means I must get the evening train up. What a life it is my friends, we lead. I do not know whether from to-morrow I will be with a saddled, and bridled, fish, fowl, or good red herring, under me and a waving ornamental cosh in my hand. Or perhaps, nothing more than a Nurse to some, as yet undiscovered, Zoological Member of the comity of creation.

With my post there will be holidays. Real earned holidays. A change from being a toiler. These unreal holidays, I have been taking for years, without pay, in my own time, are no good except for the companionship of friends. But the earned holiday with the relaxed brow, the tired eyes resting, resting themselves on objects of beauty away from the dust and grumbliness of office life. And at one o'clock on Saturday, springing down the office stairs, with a memory song on my lips, and springing into my neat little car ; I will get a new car every year, and the makers will charge me only the price of the first one, because my sitting at the wheel of a car, will be such an advertisement, such a showing of how well a middle-aged beau can look in one of their natty little cars. I will always be in the office in time in the morning. I'll show them how, when the burrs are out of the hair of the mountain goat, it can look all the same as a stay-at-home tame one. I'll join a golf club. I'll play golf—I can play golf. I have done so. I'll very likely get drawn into bridge. I have missed it so far. But I will be a yachtsman. I'll join a club at once. I'll get myself put up for the highest one first, and if they blackball me, there, I'll go to the next, and so on, and each time they don't have me, I'll see that anyone, in any regular office, within the reach of my influence, leaves their smelly old club, and goes down the road with me. And if the lowest rung won't have us, we'll buy a large cruiser yacht, and we'll go cruising to all the regattas round the coasts. I'll form a club myself. If I don't form a regular yacht club with a building and all, I'll form a club which just goes in for a one design class of little skipabouts. I'll soon get into the way of sailing the little things. The great thing is courage, and to remember the names of the parts. I'll go to the theatre a great deal. I'll be great at first nights and amateur productions. Of course, I mean the intellectual drama. I may give up tobacco, and I may start wearing an eyeglass, and I may take to wearing stays—I don't suppose I'd have to wear them all the time. I'll go to public dinners and I'll make speeches. I won't care a damn' thing what I say, because I'll be unshiftable in my job. I have seen to that. I go in on my own terms. You should see the letters I would have written to them if they hadn't agreed to everything."

Bowsie is very much above himself, but he is also timid within himself, as he raises this monster, which he believes he may become, which he believes, he hopes, to become. He is afraid that some uneasy plank is his bridge, the bridge that takes him from his old self to his new, may tip over, and bring down the whole concern into the depths. I look up into the sky, and about me to left and right, and we three seem like three little moving pegs of wood shaped to be equal, but lifeless, while all about us is the great ocean of air, with singing birds, who throw their sweet shrill cries, cries sounding to me as if they were manufactured out of the murmurings from myriads of shells. They throw them up, up, into sky tunnels which carry them, it seems to me, into the infinite. Beyond the blue of the particles of sky matter, sky dust, sky powder, there is, they say cavernous ether, where, should you be catapulted into it, in a cylinder, and step out, you would stay where you stept, all in your uniform with your helmets and your atmospheric systems, all self-contained, making no difference to the emptiness. There propt up on it, you stay. The inside of an echo that's too proud to repeat itself.

I am very glad I have a definition of Eternity, and the endless, for my own use. An echo always outward bound, and never coming back. Later on, I may get a better one. But here is Bowsie weaving himself about on the road, between the two of us. He is trying to think of anecdotes about the people he expects to meet in his new life. He fails to think out anything good enough to offer. His head is confused and so he suggests that we turn round and go back to Headquarters, the hotel which ceases to be his headquarters this evening. His headquarters, in future, will be a hearth-rug before a hot turf fire, in the winter, or an empty grate with cigarette ends, in the summer, or his office may be heated with a radiator, in which case, he will stand facing the pipes in the winter. If the radiator is by the window, he will have to stand back in the room ; otherwise, the passers-by will see him standing doing nothing. If the building is central heated the cigarette stub business, he knows, will be settled by each office having a large, indestructible, bowl placed in a good position on the table.

As we get nearer the hotel, we can see a shining, large motor, on the road in front of it. We know it means that the relatives of the drowned young man are here, and we are sure the quick inquest is over. And sure enough, not directly in front of the hotel, but a little way off to the west, discreetly stands the motor-hearse, all ready to take away the last of our dead. Unless Bowsie blows up, or the Judge drops dead. We think, together, that if we delay a while, the hearse with the drowned young clerk, and his friends, in their motor, may leave us alone. So we turn to the right in on the grass, and, threading our way round some clumps of low bushes we arrive on the shores of a small lake—a flash of water in a hollow. Deep enough, the hollow is, to leave the water glassy calm. On the lake's further edge, thirty yards away, a couple of moor-hens are darting, in and out, among the short reeds. On our side we find three, out-cropping rocks, to sit on, or lean against, at a convenient height. The lake just now has above it a clear patch of sky, except for two or three small clouds in it.

The scene before us composes itself into a Japanese print, and earlier still, it comes from an idea for a Chinese painting, thought of, never executed, just thought of, by a Chinese painter long years ago, who painted the ornaments on the ends of pagoda timber, or down below in the mouse house of a junk. He knew that some Chinese rats once deserted a sinking ship, or a ship that was due to sink—" for it " he knew there were some shore mice, busy-burning-the-candle-at-both-ends mice. The kind who live in wall villages, where no man bothers about them, and where they live short, merry lives, eating their candles at both ends, and never sleeping, except for short mouse naps. These shore mice tight-roped their merry way into this junk, and, bringing most of their building stuff with them, and picking the rest from cracks in boards, they built neat nests for themselves everywhere, always stopping up draughty corners. And the draughty corners being

the places where the coloured seas were to come squirt-
ing in, to sink the doomed ship ; of course, when they
were filled with mouse apartments the ship floated on.
There was a one-mouse position on that ship. One
mouse working at a time, short scratches. He got under
a very heavy ringbolt, and scratched, very enticing.
And, lo, above the ringbolt, the ship's cat watched,
without food, until it was thin and weak and left the
junk, by the last shore rope, only just in time. And,
from the perished way of walking he had, the news
went round all the ports that that old junk was a sour
ship for cats. I see at once why this painter painted
the lake—just to amuse himself. And, for the same
reason, he took two of his admirers, hand in hand, and
walked down into the painted lake, in his picture,
until he and they were gone completely below. And
a young Chinese maiden came and sang over them a
dirge, so sad that she cried as she composed it. She sat
on the rock, as it might be the rock I am sitting on.
She sang so beautifully so long, that when she rubbed
her eyes, and stretched herself, and spat on the ground,
for fortune, it was too long a time since the painter, and
his trustful admirers, went below to think about dragging
them up, except for funeral purposes. And I remember
that we have had enough of woe's paraphernalia to-day,
and so I don't go on with any showy fishing up of the
old Chinese painter and his mates. I wonder what
would Bowsie and Small Voice say, if I took a strong
grip of their hands, and, one on either side, walked them
down the slope into the brown lake water. Small
Voice, a retired man, done with his picture post-card
adventures for ever, living on the accumulated fat of
them, like a bear, in the winter-time, and Bowsie, just
at the opening of a new day, with his yachting cap,

and his one design class, and his bag of golf clubs, and his new plays, and his old newspapers. Their points of hope would be quite different, yet they would, I expect, both struggle a good deal and splutter. I could take these two as my theme. Their points of sinking—so different, yet the same, and make quite a lake-side oration. But neither of these boys would listen to me once they realised that I wasn't actually dangerous, and suddenly daft. Bowsie would begin talking about the refreshment-room at Mallow. Humbugs of the type that Bowsie is, love rolling " Mallow " round in their mouths. It is because, if ever the Rakes of Mallow were revived, they believe, then they are the ones cut out, in all the world, to be the pattern, or the mould, for all the others. And Small Voice, he wouldn't listen to me, because he has a stiff-hinged working memory, and having associated death with graves and cemeteries, he cannot be thinking now of locating it in a bog-water lake, with unconsidering moorhens zig-zagging about the edge of it. Midges ! midges in the neck ! Who'd have thought of midges just at the time of the almanac. But here they are. It'll be a pouring wet day to-morrow. Well, Bowsie will be in his office high, wrapped in his brand-new dignity, watching the rain wash the pavements clean and brown. But perhaps the rain will be only here in the south-west. It's a grand thought, that you have your particular weather, and haven't got to share it with all your lonesome friends, and half friends, all over the country. Perhaps Bowsie will be able to stroll out to his first lunch as a permanent official in a crisp dry air. My gaiters ! He'll be a success, from the first, at the first restaurant he patronises. If he isn't he'll try another, until he finds the exact place, where his

personality will best tell. He will, I know, choose a
place where he can sit on a high stool, and wipe his
paws on a hanging napkin fastened to the counter front.
And where, thin-waisted, constant, half-one lovers can
lean over him, and apologise for discommoding him in
getting his mashed potatoes and cutlets into his mouth.
And he will accept the apology, as man to man, with
a crouch of the shoulders. And he will think it no harm,
as he is in a way, in the position of a man of magnani-
mity, to listen to the conversation behind him. A
certain winner is of very little interest to him, if he's
heard the name before, but if he's never heard it, he's
sure to fall at once for its hooves. Bowsie is the long-
shot man of all the world. Always something to beat
the ring. Five hundred thousand to one wouldn't be
too long odds for the Bowsie sportsman. He lives by
such things. One good win wipes out all the previous
wanderings in the moping vale. What does time mean
to the man drawing his winnings, if they are big enough.
Time gone—what is it ? Time to come—very nice too.
Time here—put my winnings in my hat, if my hands
won't hold them ; winnings to spill. I am sure Bowsie
would like to talk to me, he is making muttering noises
inside his throat. But I cannot suffer him, just at the
moment. He thinks I am working at some deep
problem, watching the Absolute float, watching it to
see if it bobs. But it'll only be a nibbler at the bait,
Bowsie believes. Bowsie would like to give Small
Voice a large helping of his own oily voice, with the new
brogue thick on it. But that talk about life being a
bagatelle made Bowsie feel cold. It's all very well, he
thinks ; but to keep up a conversation on that level,
at this time in the afternoon, you'd want to be a professional. Bowsie sinks into himself picturing his office.

He thinks that it would be rather sensational if he got some very odd-looking old sporting prints, horse-races, and hung them, at regular intervals, round the office walls. Especially if his appointment had nothing at all to do with grass in any form. He thinks every other official who came to call, and see how he was getting on, would run away to tell his brother, and sister, officials all about what a funny man Bowsie was. But it wouldn't be any funnier than if he was discovered, sitting sideways, at his desk, while a middle-aged Anglo-Irish, Irish-Anglo writer read a review he'd written about a half-friend's book of short stories, about a rebellion in a far, far land. Especially if the writer's clothes were in a festoonery about him, as though they were hooked, and eyed, here and yon, instead of being buttoned like Christian clothes, for a purpose, and an example. Small Voice thinks that for two obvious Angelic men, who live on flittering like the midges, myself and Bowsie, have very poor parlour manners. But he always had suspected it was so. He has known, he thinks, for a long while that manners were invented to curtain a void. He believes that the thoughts of Bowsie and myself, at this moment, transcend anything you could read in a daily newspaper ; even a cross-channel one. He believes that our thoughts are smooth and round in the girth, but long and torpedo shaped in the length, the better to dash through the grey matters of our brains. He believes that he himself has grey matter in his skull but no torpedoes. Curiously enough, for a man living a life such as his, he is not proud of not having any torpedoes. That's because, in the matter of grey matter, and torpedoes, he never has had to justify himself. Now he comes to think of it, he has never justified himself since his employer died, that evening long ago, so suddenly. Then he discovered that should there have been motive strong enough, and a Coroner vague enough, to suggest that it was possible that his employer might have met his death by a sudden blow, or even push, and a too conscientious Coroner's jury, he might have found himself later on in a dock. Why didn't he get a doctor himself? Why was he sitting on a tin box, anyway? He escaped that, and came to the conclusion at the ripe age of forty-five that justification should be kept on ice—in the hope that it may never be required. He thinks I am wiser than Bowsie, but he thinks Bowsie has more experience. He thinks I have a musical face. The midges have ceased to bother us. They are floating in a wad over a piece of clear water opposite us among the reeds. It seems quite chilly, so I get up, and stamp my feet on the short hard grass, and I see, what I had not noticed before, a cigarette carton. I know the cigarette, you get coupons, and you collect them, and you get a share in, maybe, thirty thousand pounds. " Macra, Macree," " Don't Forget Me Nurse This Time."

I had thought that this lake shore belonged to me and my two dismal companions only. But now I know there has been another here before us. I am disappointed, and I turn away to begin the picking of our way back to the road. But I look over my shoulder and I catch the twinkle of the moorhen's tail. And I don't believe, on God's earth, any cigarette chuck-about-carton smoker ever had a moorhen's tail twinkle so well. On the road, all clear at the hotel ; the glittering car has gone, and the motor-hearse. We have the place to ourselves, except for the dross of visitors, and the Judge, but he is in a class by himself. A class, I believe, I know something about. Bowsie, and Small Voice, are out of it. I think I know something about the Plains, Saratoga Trunks, White Tigers' milk, and " Don't You Remember Sweet Alice Ben Bolt ", and I fancy I might dig the Judge in the ribs, and call him " ole hoss ". But I know that I have lapped the Judge about with old-time fancies, which it would hurt him to be put with. Still if Bowsie, or Small Voice, chatted with the Judge about the time of day, they would have the back of their minds full of Miss Mae West, and skyscrapers and Coney Island, and High Gun Play, and Stockbrokers waving Million Dollar Bills, while I could just let my mind make the pictures of the old timers, while my words were of this day, and of this hour, and so the Judge and myself would meet on a level. Two men in two barber's chairs, side by side, all creamed with soap, making our faces look pink as pink velvet.

Bowsie goes into the hotel to pack, not write letters this time. He will have all the long, long days, from this on, to write his letters in. I suspect that after he has crammed his clothes and shaving-wallet into his suit-case, that he will idle, with his hands hanging, until he is actually in the chair of this appointment of his. I think I will tell him to try and get his clothes ironed again. If he wraps himself up in the eiderdown I will take the clothes away, and try and get someone in the kitchen to improve them. I hammer on Bowsie's door. He says, " Come in," and I come in. He is stooping, red in the face, in the centre of the gale, as the crest of the waves of crumpled newspapers lie all about. They have been used for wrapping round spare shoes and hairbrushes. Bowsie has brought up to his room a last Sunday's paper, and he is plucking sheets from it, I know, newly to rewrap his property in. In a less-trusting hotel than this, should servants see him now, so bothered, and yet so ruthless in his expression, they would creep away for the manager to come up, and watch to see that the visitor did not pack up the vases from the mantelpiece, and the pictures from the walls. He refuses to give up the clothes from his back to me now for improving. He agrees, he says, that he would like to feel smart, and brushed up, but there is a question about it. If he looks too clean and comfortable he may be shelved, and the post be given to someone who looks more as if he wanted it. " The worst of you is," Bowsie says, " that you believe so much in appearances for other people. It is possible to overdo neatness— sameness, all as if we were dropped out of bandboxes, or were a lot of little old-fashioned tailors' dummies. The world asks now for character."

Yes, Bowsie, but it doesn't want character appearances that they know nothing about. They like of course the Greek God classical, and after that, the advertised faces, above the striped shirts. Neither of us . . . " Speak for yourself, Alexander. I daresay if we saw an original Greek God, here this minute, not in the cold marble, but in the colour, he wouldn't be so damn different from me. It's these tiresome sleeves and leg stuff that make us so wretched." As he is talking Bowsie is throwing his jacket, which is certainly loose, and easy, as jackets go, across the room. And it slides along the oilcloth into a space of water, where Bowsie is emptying the basin into the slop-pail, slopped over. Bowsie takes up the jacket, and shakes it, and rubs it with a towel, and hangs it out of the window to dry in the wind. He pulls the window down on it to keep it from blowing away. He stands now by the window sideways, looking out and away towards the nor'-west. The sun is not very far above the sea and the light from it along the woodwork of the window, and on Bowsie's old jacket, is a cold yellow. Bowsie stands a long while looking out and he does not speak to me at all. He thinks that this is the most ridiculous moment in his life, since he grew to manhood, and became, in the world's eyes, the master of his own fate. He thinks it is ridiculous that he should leave this pleasant place of sun, and sea, and air, and hurry, hurry, birds. And he makes a doleful thought for himself—— Stiff, and seeking a position, at a railway journey's end. Sitting in a railway carriage, with the axles beneath him repeating some dull refrain, while we, he thinks, will be dining, happily, listening, perhaps, to the sweet round tones of the Judge calling up some scene of the Golden West. Bowsie is not cross with me. But he is cross with almost every other thing near his hand. He takes his waistcoat from the bed, where he had thrown it when he first had eased himself for his packing. He takes it up now, one hand holding one shoulder—the other thrust through the armhole. " Look at it ! Look, four pockets, and old wool dust, and fluff, packed inside the lining in the corners," and he presses his finger where the lump of neglected refuse lies, hard. " Look at all the buttons, and the stitching, and look at the back strap and buckle, and linings. I declare, sometimes, I believe I was invented to hold up harness ! Is it a life for a man with a heart in his breast ? Is it a life ? I don't know what to make of it. I suppose when I'm older I'll get used to it. Is there any warmth in tattooing ? I suppose not. I never have cared for the improved toga wrap-the-rascal light costumes, any that I ever saw illustrations of, or on the stage. A nation's beggars, street beggars, should wear the toga. It would mark them out from others and so you would get your halfpence ready for them, and the folds would hold the coppers well. The toga is a one-piece garment, isn't it ? They could be easily washed. One vat of soap for the beggars and another for the togas. And every wash day, at evening, there would be a fine, healthy soap smell all through the streets. The beggars would sometimes be fresher than their patrons." But would you dress the female beggars in the toga ? It's for the males only I believe, and what about the bath. You wouldn't stand for mixed bathing, Bowsie ? " I would not, sir. In the first place, there are, as far as I am concerned, no women beggars. Before they can beg, I give them their share of my donation to the needy. Even if they sing melancholy and low, I do not give them money for their song. No, sir, I give them what I give them, because they are amateurs, though I would not take it on myself to tell a woman who stood by the kerb wailing that she was an amateur wailer. But if I ever encountered a woman pickpocket, face to face as she took my watch, I would wring her wrist as little as possible, in getting my watch back, and I would, by the direction of my glance, suggest to her some other stout man's easier-got watch. But if she had a man friend who, as I was taking back my watch, hit me on the back of the head with something in a stocking and all went black for me. Then, when I woke up in the St. John Ambulance Hut, I don't know that I would bother myself about placing these eternal females in togas of their own. But they would wear classical flowing robes of some sort. I won't be long packing now. And I'll be down in the road, for a while, before I have to be off to the station." I go downstairs a few steps. Bowsie's door opens, and he comes on to the landing with his damp waistcoat in his hands.

"Like a decent man get them to put that before the kitchen fire for a few minutes. The sun has lost its strength, and I'm afraid of getting lumbago." He tosses me the waistcoat. It flies through the dusk of the landing and the stairs, leisurely. Something curious in its shape, the armholes perhaps, causes a rush of air to hold it up, so that it planes towards me. I spear it dexterously, with two first fingers stiff, through an armhole.

The kitchen door is ajar; I push it in, and walk towards the middle of the floor with the waistcoat held before me. A kitchen-maid, very striking looking—the type for a St. Patrick's Day post-card for export, takes the waistcoat from me and props it up against the back legs of a chair before the glowing fire. I say to her, "Ten minutes like that ought to grill it, and will you please send it up when it's done to Mr. Bowsie." "Which is he?" says she, and I answer her—"That medium-sized man, he's not so young, getting on, middling stout; he wears a light brown kind of suit, and he's got a blue tie with green stripes, diagonal. I don't know the number of his room. He's going away this afternoon. He's packing his things now."

"Oh, the gentleman that's going in the car. The poor fella; he'll never do any good in Dublin—he's too delicate to be in a rough place like that. Work wouldn't be good for him."

I cannot make out how Bowsie can win sympathy so easily. I suppose it is that there is nothing which he can do in a first-class way. When he begins to talk, before he has gone very far, his tongue begins to fumble the words, and he has to laboriously straighten them.

And he walks like a swan. He can only eat, tidily, by taking very little for a mouthful. He has never learnt to breathe through his nose, and when he drinks, he is quite likely to spill some of the liquor about him. If he was down on all fours, he couldn't be less important looking.

I am waiting in the road for him. I will turn down into the shelter of the cutting in the banks which communicates with the path to the sea.

I can pace up and down and smoke and see him when he comes out of the hotel.

He has come out on to the veranda. He looks about there. I might have been dodging with a doze. There is a chair away from the light. He comes out in the roadway and looks about for me. He takes up a few beach pebbles in his hand, tosses one up the road and then the other, trying to hit the first one. With some sudden precision of his tossing muscles, he lands three pebbles running within an inch or two of the first pebble. He is delighted with himself. It's a good sign. He is master of something. He throws the rest of the pebbles away to one side. He will rest on his first throws. He swells out as though his chest would tear the top waistcoat buttons away. He is feeling quite cool. He believes that this new job he is going to is itself just a symbol of a splendour for himself, which nothing can dim. Himself, and he stands outside himself. I know he expects me to appear from somewhere now on the instant, so I come out of the cutting and begin walking towards him, and I wish, in my heart, that no homely sign in my look, or in the action of my pacing will give him, for even an instant, a poor feeling about himself. I hope his elation may last, as long as his life, at any rate, until that last hurry, scurry moment before the slow curtain falls.

He sees me coming towards him, and he runs towards me. He says, " The car will be ready in a moment. Time I was making off. I want you to stay on here and have a good time. String the Judge along and get fun out of him. And sing out off your chest whenever you feel like it. And when you want to play with the idea of having some sort of a Happy-go-Lucky-Job in my department, or adjacent to it, just send me a line by the mail, so's I can get it in the morning, first thing, and call you up on the telephone as soon as I get into the office. When I come down here for my holidays, I'll get some colours and bring them along, and paint some little pictures of the sky and sea. I'll give them to Hayden and he can put them up in the public-rooms. Many a night, late in the year, people will stay on here if they have something to look at when they are sheltering indoors, when it's one of those nights when you couldn't keep a pipe alight even with a tin crown on it. But here's the car, and I must be away. They can't hold the train for me many minutes ; it has a long way to go." I shake his hand. I would have used both of mine to have his, childlike, between mine. But he is quickest, and it is my one limp hand which is squeezed between his two powerful maulers. The boy in the car is holding the door open for him, and dragging the luggage over so as to give him room to place his back and hips, his broad chest, his shoulders and his strong neck with his head set square above, except for, ever such a little, tilt to the left. He has thrown his hat on the floor between his feet. His scanty hair is stretched. And as he sails away, for the fortune that he keeps waiting, he is Leander, who scorns to tame himself to swimming a second-hand art. He has plucked, from history, the Red Sea Miracle, and he walks the depths of his Hellespont. But no Hero looks out of any window for him.

I turn my back on the road Bowsie has taken, and I stroll slowly along the dry, sandy, cream-coloured road to the west. I am walking very slowly, almost meandering, as I stop from time to time, looking ahead, because I believe that somewhere on the road, a lift of a few feet, should give me the view of a distant low headland pushing out into the farther bay, where an Elizabethan tower stands, a spot of middling, historical interest. You look at these things and try and pump up some excitement about them. And, very likely, those square towers kept within them some fine fellows of the fighting type, away from their own homes—tourists. These square towers are a little more exciting than the cigarette cartons by the flash of water. This thought makes me feel superior to the tower, and the carton, and the people who had the lease of them. I hear a step behind me, a brisk, sliding step. I look round and here's the Judge. I know now he must have been walking in full view along the road behind me for a long time. Had I looked round, I would have seen his dark, respectable clothes against the light road. We are a long way from the hotel which looks very squat and small in the east. We walk along, side by side, the Judge pulling down his pace to mine. We top the rise with the view. But we do not observe the castle, as we are looking towards the sea at the moment it should be in view. And, in a few seconds, we are too low down in the land to be able to see even the broken battlements.

The whole place is our own, but for wheeling birds

racing the clouds and beating them, both moving slow, masters of themselves. Strong winds, coming round the world, will drive the clouds before them, and the birds will be tossed by them about, against their wills. If they have not hidden themselves in sheltered places. There are plenty such for them. And should a great gale spring up, and roam about, there is easy bird shelter to be found, green swards among the sandhills where the Judge, and I, could rest from our labours of living up to our effort's strength. The Judge gives me a quizzical look and says, " Apropos of nothing whatever. Nothing to do with the happenings of the last few hours. My father used to like to sing the old American songs. He, and my mother, remembered when they were apropos, and here's a song you might like to hear. It was once one of old Christy's songs—Christy's Minstrels. Without your permission, kind friend :

Let us pause in Life's pleasures, and count its many tears,
   While we all sup sorrow with the poor.
There's a song that will linger for ever in our ears,
   Oh, hard times come again no more.
'Tis the song, the sigh of the weary hard times,
   Hard times come again no more ;
Many days you have lingered round my cabin door,
   Oh, hard times come again no more."

The Judge has, to me, a lovely voice. He sings neither too loud, nor too low, but it is a private song. And :

" There's a pale drooping maiden who works her life away.
   A warm heart a-sighing all the day."

" Oh, hard times ". " 'Tis a sigh ". " Across the troubled wave ". " Oh, hard times ". " 'Tis a wail ". " Heard across the shore ". " 'Tis a dirge ". " A lowly grave ". " Oh, hard times come again no more ". " 'Tis the song ". " Weary hard times ". " Hard times ".

> " Many days have you lingered round my cabin door,
>   Oh, hard times come again no more."

I picture for myself, soft and miserable, and sweet, and heavy, tree stumps and trailing vines, a tumbled cabin on the back-cloth. And among the trees, far, faint and blue, away, great Pappa of the Waters. And in front, with his sad black hands clasped, and then unclasped, a tall black-faced minstrel singing for every ounce. I can even picture the audience huddled on the benches to hear him singing something with the truth in it. The Judge steps along more briskly now. After all, those hard times are a long way off, and those tha sang of them, and those who endured them, are a space of time under the sod. May the wild rose blow gently over their graves. The Christy Minstrel singer was likely buried, in a city cemetery, under two tons of white stone, and had white-faced mutes walking at his funeral, with a glass hearse. And none of his old-time companions who came was blacked up. I don't believe they were. When he sang he wore striped cotton trousers, striped pink and white, and a pale eau de nil shirt with a wide collar. The Judge, by his brisk walking, has cleared the cobwebs of melancholy from his sweet throat. I have had to exert myself to keep up with him. Now he half-faces towards me and says : " You know I'm not a judge at all. Some of the people here started the notion I looked like a judge—a retired judge from the U.S.A., and I dropped in with the idea, and kept it up when new people came along, and the thought was happy with the wish. Because I always had a liking for the position of a retired judge, home from America, on pension. I've always had a grád for the Land of the Free, and the people there, though I was never in it. Still, I'm faithful whether they are up, or down. Playing the judge comes natural to me, for I never was in any trouble with the law. And another thing, I spent a great deal of my days, that might be better spent, perhaps, with books, in sitting around in a lodging house, belonging to a connection of my mother's. And it was always full of the returned Americans. For forty·years, I've been in touch, more or less, with these old boyos. What is your name?" "Hector." I say quickly, "Well, I'll call you Hector, and let you continue to call me Judge." "Judge." I begin at once before I forget it. "Tell me, did you ever in all the ramifications of your imagination come across an old goldminer? I mean the remains of an actual old forty-niner."

"Well, Hector, I could not swear to anything I was told. Well, anyway, it wouldn't be evidence. But I have met, long ago, a couple of old hawks, who said they were through the lot, but I guess they were in their second childhood, and they had a general mix-up of the golden past, and anyway, most anything they wanted, they could have got out of books. The only thing in the favour of their veracity, I'll say, was that they were poor hands at reading when I knew them. They had pretty poor sight for anything close up, and they didn't understand above ten per cent of the words they came on. Another thing they couldn't understand was the want of blaspheming and cursing in the printed page. For two-thirds of their lives, I should say, they'd never heard the shortest sentence without words in it that no one would print. And they thought, when they took up reading, that the reading matter was true, or it wouldn't be printed. So they told me they couldn't

' take any pleasure in the conversation of these very good
men in these books '. They didn't expect the ladies to
use bad language, except when they were startled. They
liked them to be stiff, and starched, and polite. But
perhaps they'd never been near the diggings even. One
of them could open oysters the quickest I ever saw. A
flush man, with plenty of money, in from sea, brought
a barrel of oysters into the lodgings one afternoon. I
was sitting up on the top landing chatting to a cousin
of mine, who was trying to wash the petticoats of a fancy
fuchsia. She always expected that fuchsia to look better
than any other in the street. They'd got speckled when
the window was left open, or the rain came in and beat
up the earth in the flower-pot. I saw the man from
sea coming up the street, and a quayside labourer walking behind him carrying the barrel on his shoulder,
and he was smoking a new clay pipe. He looked like
a show pirate, with a barrel of rum, or gunpowder, on
his shoulder. This quayside labourer left the barrel
down on a chair in the front room. Then the man
from the sea sent the labourer through the house, knocking at the doors until he found the two old goldminers.
They came down into the front room, and one of them
began opening the oysters. I was called, and I had
a few, and the labourer had a dozen. But he was going,
and coming, with porter in a jug. The blind was pulled
down, a yellow blind, and the whole place was in a
yellow light. I was in, and out, several times ; they
were always at it, though they must have rested sometimes. They didn't talk much, or sing. They were a
small kind of oyster we used to get then—very beautiful
flavour. I offered to get some bread and butter and
a couple of lemons, but they wouldn't have them.
There was some seaweed inside the top of the barrel,

and it was under their feet, and there were broken shells crunched on the floor everywhere. There was a round mahogany table in the room. One of those that tip up, and it was cocked up at a slant. And the seaman had got a couple of chairs, with their backs stood against the low side of the slope, so that the jug wouldn't slide off. They took the porter out of mugs, and they put them down always on some straight place close to them, on the mantelpiece, on the floor, or on top of a little what-not, that was in the alcove by the fireplace. They never splashed the walls. They were papered in a light blue pattern, and any spots of porter would have shown up badly. They seemed to me to be always behaving them-selves as they thought right. And when they were finished, and the barrel was empty, one of the old boys went down to the kitchen, and got a broom where it was kept just inside the door, and he went back to the room, and swept all the broken shell, and rubbish, into a newspaper, and tied it up, and gave it to the quayside man to drop off the bridge on his way home. It was a carouse with a happy ending. The seafaring man, he went back aboard his ship that night, and she was gone, got her orders, in the morning. The old men, I don't suppose they ever saw that sailor again, but they were good little oysters ! "

This conversation between Hector and the Judge becomes a secret affair—a mist which dissolves into frag-ments and then goes up into the sky, straight, like a leap-ing curtain of lace, to melt in the sun. A mist made in a green, tree-filled valley with a stream in it, and bristling, unclimbable brown cliffs rising out of it. But in the bend of it, in the very cleft, a waterfall, falling straight, a sword pointing to the earth, and the branches and leaves of the trees turn lazily, as a light breeze comes up from the lake to curl about where the first of the leaves are ready to meet the lake's breath. In a short time, in an hour's time, the sun will be up in the heart of the valley, and then gone, leaving the shadow of the southerly cliff across the tree-tops. But, while the sun is in the valley, all the brown leaves and the green leaves will perfume the full air.

Judge, in your observation of the returned American lodgers, did you ever meet a man who had a real passion for any one thing. Or were they all just wide citizens, ready to form a vigilance committee, or move on before one out into the wide spaces?

" I met several, in the old days, who had what you are looking for perhaps, a passion for those wide spaces. They would go out into my cousins' yard and saw wood for them. They always wanted to saw wood. I suppose they had been those men who cut down virgin timbers with a bunch of others, or more likely single-handed. They were adapting themselves to the best they could get, sawing timber in a yard, into logs for a winter fire. Left to themselves they would, I daresay, if we were all dead, and nobody about, begin building log cabins. Then, some of them would sing to themselves a low whispering sort of singing. So that anyone passing near them would hardly hear them. But that showed making belief, and clearing the primeval forest, wasn't deceiving themselves. Because, if they were properly far away they would be bawling out loud at times, and then low at times. But these old timers always kept it soft and low, interfering with nobody. These old boyos always had a second line of defence. A drunken man threw something out of a window on one of these old boyos one time, and the old slimkin's stooped, and took a knife out the side of his boot, and a girl in the kitchen shoved the door to, and bolted it. And then they took the drunken man and put him away on the train. And little boys looked from the top of the high wall, between the lodging-house yard and a meal store. And they looked at the old boyo as if he was a mad dog. But, when they let him into the house, he'd forgotten all about it. And he gave up his knife to my cousins. He didn't have to have anything explained to him."

You, during your life, have never found time hang on your hands.

" Never, since I left off going to school. I was a clock watcher then. But I'm thinking, just thinking quietly, of going to some places where we won't be bothering about the clock anywhere. And it would be very pleasant if you could come with me. I have money put away for the purpose. I'm proposing, some time, to visit America. I'll just pass through the big cities. What I want to be about is finding my way along some winding roadway through the depths of a great canyon, with trees and ferns, as tall as one another. I think it'll have to be a place with only a pack-horse road. I don't want to have any motor-cars full of sightseers tearing by. Maybe a nice pony might carry me along. I want to see great rivers flow quickly, full of yellow water, in the spring time, and rafts on them. I want to walk down a dusty road, with trees on each side, and over-hanging, and I want to see broad light at the end of the road, and I want the river, a mile wide, moving along there, across the end of the road. Just an old timber jetty, the finish up of the road, and if there wasn't an old man, sitting there, fishing, I'd have to hire one. And I believe in a place like that I would be able to hire an old man, with a piece of cord hanging from his hand ; the fishing could be imaginary. I have always

noticed I can always get what I want in a place where the place wants it too. I think that atmosphere has never been properly understood."

I agree to this. What else can I do? So we go strolling on into the country where low hills begin, hillocks, not sandhills, but rock covered with sandy soil. Just the back of the butt of a peninsula. Hillocks are at every angle, tumbled, and soon we will be following a looping path, over the grass, through them. I don't think it will make any difference to the Judge. He puts his neat feet down without looking where he is putting them. But he never stumbles ; his feet know how to look after themselves. Among the hillocks, we will be in a dusk, though there is plenty of light with us on this road. The Judge says he doesn't want to be a dog in the manger absolutely about what he sees on our travels. " Our travels," he says. He doesn't mind if other people have seen before what he sees. He won't mind names cut in the rocks, if the dates after the names are of a generation ago. He isn't jealous of the dead ; he lives with them in the past. " Without the bother of a body. And that makes me forget my body that is with me now. Not that I have such a very troublesome body. I must touch wood." And he looks about him for wood. The rarest thing to look for on this road—sand, a patch of coral in the sand we passed some time ago, grass, earth, rushes, a feather. But wood, a very rare find. I hand my pencil to the Judge ; he has a pencil, but it is a metal one, gold, spectacular but not for this emergency.

He touches my wood ; I touch his heart, because I am ready with my wood. He calls me " Boy " ; the flatterer ! He will call me " Boy " again when we walk through those tall ferns, down the canyons, on the way,

by a roundabout route, to those rolling rivers. He says
—" My body is as good as most's and I don't show much
signs of wearing out. I know I am considered a good-
looking man. I know it, I have overheard, I have been
the accidental eavesdropper who heard good of himself.
It does not turn my head because I understand them ;
they recognise my appearance and the appearance of
what is accepted as a good-looking man, of the just off
prime type. I know my own face in a looking-glass,
because there is a lot of it to shave, and when my hair
was black my stubble grew strong and now, though my
hair is streaked, it still bristles around my chops pretty
hard. So I'm a good long time every morning going
over the hills, and hollows, and round the corners. I
have time to observe my features. I have a small foot.
I know by the size the bootshops sell me. People don't
admire a small foot for a man any more ; that is, for a
young man. But with me, it's admired. The man in
the bootshop I go to, the manager, wears boots himself
like a brace of barges. But when he has got my feet in
a pair of new boots he strokes my toes between his fingers
and thumb, and he thinks me a visitor from another
world. He'd nearly give me my boots for nothing,
Boy." He has called me " Boy " a second time, and
now I know that he will never call me " Boy " down
those canyons, for we will not be walking them together.
He will, he knows well, walk them alone. We are moving in among the hillocks now, a twisting way, but all
in a shade. The Judge is not affected in his spirit by
the twilight. That is, his spirit is not lowered, only
quieted. He speaks clearly and cheerfully of death.
" Children are afraid, and also curious, about dead
things lying on a road. But some softening of the wind
to them gives them no great opportunity of seeing death

coming suddenly in the middle of the movements of life, unless they are much with sportsmen. People with guns. I am not so very curious myself as I ought to be perhaps. But I have the experience, constantly now, as I grow old, of viewing the moment of disappearance. I view the living. I wink my eyes and I view the place where they moved in life. I pass a man at the same time, in the street, near my lodgings, every day. Perhaps I know him to speak to, perhaps I only know him by name. But one day I don't see him ; he's dead. Stept away back out of this place. The next day I pass the piece of street where I used to meet him. He isn't walking there. One time that would have made me uncomfortable and mopy. Not now, I just take my walk in future where I meet younger-looking passers-by. I calculate they'll last longer. There's plenty of room beyond the curtain. That's a poor word for it. ' Curtain '—fusty. The point about these disappearances, I am viewing, is just that there is not a curtain. And the people I get this hey-presto-gone touch about are the ones I meet in the bright light. If they were greys I met in the dusk of the streets, it wouldn't be one-half so final, their departure. ' Departure ' isn't a good word for it. Have you noticed how difficult it is to get a good word that gives just the right shade for any particular death. I suppose if I was a poet I would be able to put up a row of words, and choose the one I liked best. Like a young girl playing ' I wrote my Lover a Letter."

Ah, yes, Judge, I suppose you could.

" Well, what is the use of talking, here among these little heaps of green that were standing steady in the light, and the darkness, before we, or any of our name, perhaps, were thought of. They weren't standing steady, but vibrating the way they seem to be vibrating now. If there was no vibration in them they would notice us, and begin to chatter about us, and to us. And at first, you and I would be very flattered at their noticing us, until we discovered that they were only talking to pass the long time. That they were made aware of the loss of their vibrations. If you could stop the vibrating of the hills and vales, they'd all begin chattering for us. That's a discovery. Isn't that ·a peculiar thought for an old man, who pretended to be a Judge, to have. Isn't it now, Hector ? " It is, Judge, it is peculiar, but it pleases me.

" Ah, it's you that's the boy for smoothing the surface of the stream, with your hand, so that it goes rolling on. But you know, and I know, that the broad high people, who were here among these green hummocks, though it may be that, in their time, they were just rocks, with the sun on them. Well, we know that those people, the people of what they call the Heroic Age, didn't have the same discomfort about death that I have, and I'm not so very bad about it. We know they had the way of being here, and there. God bless us all and them also. They were grand people to look at. All bright like hawks, like actors that you would see with their faces made up early, on a summer evening, looking out of the dressing-room window over a river. Their conversation was on a great scale, about everything. Nothing they were afraid to speak of—well, very little. Though it's very likely they conversed without the speech we have to use, they were able to pass their ideas from mind to mind, by cracking their joints or twitching their ears, or smiling, or wrinkling their noses." Interested, I am on the watch, with ear, and eye. And, instantly, the Judge, not using his joints,—he isn't of the type who has joints that crack at ease, twitches an ear, smiles with that whimsical, drawn-down, upper-lip smile, and certainly he twitches his nose well.

The light is very weak, but I do read that the Judge, at this moment, is fonder of me than he is of any living being on earth. It is just because we are in a place where the grass, the soil, the rocks, and the salt still air are in a fondness for each other. If the swung swords and the thrown spears whistled through the air here, they fled to the hearts they pierced, with love. And they were never blunted with the smallest roughening of hate. And when the bodies of what we would call " the dead "—though they would not have spoken of them so, were piled high, some struggler would climb up the heap, until he could see over the rocks, or green hillocks, and view the sea and distant lands. And then come down quickly again into the shadows. For always in those days, they were lands surrounded by lands without relation to each other ; a place, a space of earth, a valley, a nest of hills, a lake, a gathering of lakes, where the shadow people met and played their games of here, and there. A place where the strong light fell always on a people knotted into arguments of all kinds, always afraid to be left with the argument against them. Those who were argued out, came in, one at a time, drifting down a hillside, to be among these others.

If we walked fast through the peninsula, and came out on the shore of the bay ahead of us, we would see the square tower before it melts its grey stone into the grey evening air. But the drowsy half-darkness about us fits still with the Judge's mood. He still wants to talk of his departing spirit. " There must be an immense gathering of spirits always in a World of Spirits. And yet my idea is not that I will be hobnobbing with them all, and how is that ? I have no great sin on my conscience. Don't be afraid—I'm not going to begin a general tell-out to smear it into your ears, with a lot of extra sins invented, just to make you think I was a worthwhile sinner. My idea is that there must be an enormous mass of spirits like my own, since the world began, crowding the shores in every place, beyond the dancing floor. Did you ever watch by a roadside dancing floor at night, and if you did, did you notice the way a girl or a young man would pass from the light into night for a moment, in the dance, and then come into the light again. Well, that is the way the dead die on me. Those I meet passing in the street and then meet no more. But that's where they are different from the roadside dancers. When they are gone, they are gone from me. This is queer talk, and what is it to do with me more than anyone else. This is a restless place where we are passing along at this moment. Some man fell out of life here, with his restlessness on him, perhaps his sword was half in, half out, the scabbard. Perhaps he'd thought a fight finished, and came in this far to sleep it away from him, and perhaps he had to make an offer at drawing and defending again. Oh, laziness, did I ever offend you ? I believe now, if I had found myself in this man's shape, in here, and called on to begin the dust again, I believe I'd remember my duty to Let Lie Lazy, and so, you, and myself, walking here to-day, instead of being fretful in our steps, might be in a quiet."

But we are rising a little on a slightly higher path, and are catching some small speckle of the last of the sky's light, where in the west a long streak on the sea horizon shows where the sun left us. " If you would listen to the talk some have, you would have to believe that where any event once happened it was photographed, for ever, on the elemental air. They thought of that when they had only the still photographs. Now, I suppose, they have pushed it further to an elemental moving film. Now, do you see how I am trying to disgust myself away from those long gone, with these raw words 'photographed' and 'film'. I have taken a fancy to you, Hector. A suddenly sprouting-up affection, you might call it, and I have an affection for the gay, bright people who were about where we are now, and though there's a great difference between the feelings I have for a fellow-man, and for these old ones, still, as far as having very little fear of yourself, or them, my feelings are the same. I would imagine, at any other time, that I would be uncomfortable talking so freely about them here in this place. Away from here, I'd think of these others with a soft sadness in the empty end of my skull. I feel here that we are all more on a level. But there's a great difference ; you ate a breakfast of bacon and eggs this morning, and we'll both eat a breakfast, please God, to-morrow, while these heroes are turning heedlessly night into day and day into night, in abysmal depths, travelling from good hollow to good hollow. It is they who are the globe-trotters—of all the globes. But getting about is nothing to them. That's how they differ from you, or me. You know a wise, intelligent man of arms explained to me once why an aeroplane couldn't drive itself through the ether. He said there was nothing in the vast coldness for the pro-peller to cut, and that's what its like to these Great Ones —when they pass from scenes of old life, old valour. Then they come to themselves fully. They are here on achievement, not on hope. It's as with them, the arrival, not the journey. Or the movement is so telescoped together with the stroke's end, that they are one. The sword in the air, the grin of the wound, the smile of the lip, the caress of welcome, are on an instant together —simultaneous. But look at our interruption "—I look as he looks, out over the last, low fold of the small mounds, and on the point just make out, dark grey, against a paler grey sky : The Square Tower.

" Look at her Castle or Square House. The Castle that belonged to Tin Lizzie. The spacious days. They have a good press ; she knew where to pick the man she wanted for the turn. They made too much of her ; they painted her portrait too often. Now, how do we best get back ? Inland, and turn by the lane that's there, or out towards the sea, and across the rocks. We'll be able to find our way over the rocks without the light. It's not very rough, as well as I remember it." Have you been there lately, Judge ? " I was there in the summer, but there were two beautiful young American girls, with ribbons in their hats, and they were talking so much that I never noticed the way. But I daresay we'll manage it fine, slow, and careful, using the hands. And it will be pleasant walking a while on the smooth sand across the rocks."

On the smooth flat sand we walk away home, or haven, bound. Certainly, the Pride Hotel is not the Judge's home, for he has no home. He walks in a style to the surface on which he walks. On the road he sprang from the ball of the foot, and on the grass path, he pressed down his shoes daintily, and moved with short steps. But here on the sands, he hardly lifts the foot from the ground. He walks like a barefoot man. The sands give up a pearly light from themselves, and when we look away towards the sea on our right hand, it looks very dark, except for the light crest of foam still left on the small waves as they come in, so slowly and steadily.

We are not walking very close to the edge of the water, but near to the sandhills, above all tide marks but the extraordinary ones. Sometimes, our feet touch a hardened, black sprig of old seaweed, blacker than my boots, not licked by the salt water for a year or more. When a man first dragged his canoe up these sands, did they look as they do now, to-night ? Yes, the sands looked the same and, if it was this season of the year, the old black seaweed looked the same. And the sandhills were something like this. But they were more changing, because the bent grass was imported here, and planted here, in the memory of living man. And I know that all about the very bay giant fir trees grew, and down all this centre of it, where now the sands are flat, or in heaps. The first man here didn't ground his canoe ; he moved here, among the trunks of the trees, at the top of a spring tide. Not using his paddle, but easying her along, pulling her, from tree to tree, with his bare hands, while his Princess sat aft under the canopy, and thought " What a man I have. The trees make a path for us, at his command." And when he came clear through the tall trees into a round cove within the farther shore of it, a stream falling, fresh, and lovely, water falling over rocks into the salt, and that was a sight, the best they'd ever seen, to a couple like these old friends. A long tide on the wide ocean, coming away before the strong wind of the west. Always coming away before it, not able to stand, with light provisions and very little water, any detainment, no heaving to, for that boy and girl. And the price of youth was, that when he was steering, and she was curled on bundles of grass in the stern-sheets, taking her watch below, his waist was too narrow to keep the high waves from coming in to them. A broad-backed, old fat man would have been a protection.

But this young split the wave could not help but let the cabin in the hay get afloat with white water. And so, a Princess would be bailing, bailing, all the time under the canopy, if the canopy was holding. Old fat back would be a protection in this regard of a wave only. He wouldn't have had the quickness and the push along of Split the Wave, and he would get soft in his body in a moment and get his hands on the tough toddy bottle, and think it time to let every cord and paddle go and sink in the large green ocean, taking the slim young with him. But this narrow waist is wide in the heart, and all for rush away, rush away, rush away. And that's how the little bays with the throbbing fresh waters are made. It is odd to me, used as I am by now to walking along the sand here with the Judge, that use has not made my eyes clearer, but, as it is, I lose the Judge if he moves a few paces farther away towards his right hand. I suppose the western sky has thickened up and overlaid the sun deep below the horizon. I hear a voice, shrill, and a deep voice. But though I know they cannot be far away, and that they are coming nearer, only now, when we almost walk on to their toes, come blurred and dark images of two from the hotel. Now another pair of them. They come talking also, and their talk comes through the talk of those right face to face with us. All four are talking at once. They've been whistling in the dark. They've been frightened ; the place and the hour have been unsuited to them. " Hello, Hello, Hello, out for a stroll ? So were we." " So were we." They were out hunting for the Judge and me. They've got deaths and drowning on their minds. They are a search-party, two search-parties—for each pair came away independently of the other. Hayden never knew they started on their expeditions. I am sure of that. But here comes another whistling. One whistling only, and, as I live, I know the tune I think. I think it's " Lilluberlara ". I wonder have I got his situation truly tagged up. I want to think it quickly before he comes in among us. I am betting he's alone, because no one would have the pluck, if he was like this one, whichever of them it is, to whistle an old tune like that, with someone walking beside him ; anyway, not if he was a man, and his companion a man. If they were men and women, I'm not so sure about it. But this is a man, and he is alone. His blurred figure is near enough for me to be certain, and now he stops whistling and speaks, and it is the voice of Small Voice. I wish now I'd had more time to work out my prophecy of who comes this way. I believe, in my pride, that I would have got my man, Lilluberlara. Old Heavy Cloaks of War, Burnt Brandy, Camp Fire doused, but a good thick sword trailing on the ground, and a broad sash tight round the waist to keep the entrails pressed tight together for company. That would be just the association of song which would appeal to Little Voice, coming out alone, a blessing on his brave heart, with only a stick in his hand. He has one, it has a duck's head carved on it ; it isn't his own. It belongs to the hotel, I know it. I've seen it in the hall there, waiting for an escort. With only a stick in his hand he has come out to bring home the Judge, and Alexander. Now we are seven, seven men on the sands of the south-west, all talking at the same time, and all talking nonsense, except the Judge. He is " Sunk in the Silence of a Wig ". I would like to say to him only American judges don't wear wigs. I wonder though does he think of himself in a wig, as an American judge so original that he can use imported elegancy. But no, I don't think he cares about the wig. He was never impressed by those he saw. No, whatever period he likes to fancy himself an impostor in, he is always wearing his own hair. Even now, when it is scanty, he would not add to it, if the blast blew ever so cold, and he wouldn't even wear a black skull-cap, as though he was an egg with the top taken away, before it was time to put the spoon in. I wouldn't say but in some of his imaginings he is carrying another man's hair at the belt—an enemy scalp.

We face along for home. Two of our rescuing friends make a pretence of going farther and then, deciding to change their minds, both their minds, they turn for home.

We string out, abreast, walking evenly, almost touching, sleeve to sleeve, and talk our nonsense, up and down the line, the Judge even taking his turn beginning on my left.

" And so we found you."

" Yes, you found us far away, our minds in strange tropic places."

" It's wonderful how the half-light, well hardly half-light, just no light at all, the dying embers of a day that is gone, takes our minds involving them in far-away lands."

" Yes, and it is just and right that it should be so."

" We enjoy ourselves best in little things. In the darkness we become like children when the candle's blown out."

" Where ? Like Moses perhaps."

" Like Moses crossing the Alps in an open boat. No, that's not it."

" No, that's not the sort of thing Moses would have been associated with. The Nile was a softly flowing river, except where there were natural weirs formed of the debris of the banks, that is below the cataracts."

" Did Moses know aught of yon cataracts ? "

" Moses was a man of the people. His canoe must have looked very fresh and green, with the giant bulrushes waving overhead."

" And bulrushes were bulrushes then. No ornaments to stand in a jar, in the corner of a seedy drawing-room. I have seen them. I am as old as that."

" Or to ornament a summer grate. I have heard of their being used so."

" Before that, I have heard that they filled the cold black place with strange cuttings of papers in several colours, very inflammable. It must have been before the cigarette age—a tossed cigarette—and away goes the home."

" The insurance companies should have forbade them."

" They would have, if they had dared."

" There are people who believe that the world should be made safe for the shareholders of insurance companies to live in."

" And so they yet will make it."

" Not while death walks in the form of delectable alcohol."

" Alcohol is a good thing they say, in moderation. I hardly credit it. I think that is rather begging the question, when we are trying to discover what it is that draws many to inebriating liquors, while others have no difficulty in abstaining."

" It causes a certain kind of laughter."

" Then you think laughter is for the general good. Perhaps our friend on your right here would list laughter as food."

" Not he, Judge, he's quite capable of knowing the difference between the solids and the liquids."

" A solid laugh from a solid man."

" The young have oftenest what is called a liquid laugh. I suppose it is not being suggested that laughter comes from pump water, so where are we ? "

" A liquid laugh suggested a rippling laugh."

" That would suggest a brook tumbling over shallows—— Poetic idea ! "

" But it also suggests continuousness, a going on for ever."

" I wouldn't like to laugh and laugh and not be able to stop."

" And I doubt if you'd be very popular."

" The laughter of the Gods, what was it ? Has any composer attempted to reproduce it in musical form ? "

" Hark ye, hark ye ; he is suggesting the laughter of the Gods on a gramophone record."

" Ah, no ; not that."

" And yet, my friend on my left spoke of laughter like a brook. He, I have no doubt, has heard a phonographic record of the tumbling of a brook, with birds singing in the leaves overhead."

" Strangely enough, I never heard it and I've heard so many things. At the same time, I think cinemas should show more pictures of nature studies."

" And yet, when they do show them, I wonder do the public crowd to see them. I mean absolutely tumble over each other."

" They would if they showed the right things. A string knot picker at work ; I wouldn't like to see it. But I would go, I am a string knot picker. I can't keep from it."

" I think it's mixed up with a moral urge."

" You don't think it's anything to do with unravelling a mystery."

" There is no mystery about a knot. At least there should be none. For a few pence you can buy a book containing all the basic knots used by man."

" I only truly know one. An employer of mine taught it to me. It's hardly a knot ; it's so simple. He liked to see it used to tie up bundles of papers. It would even tie up a bundle of fire-sticks. The great idea about it was that it required no finger placed on the knot before finishing it off. I remember, quite well, the day my employer first learnt it. He spent quite a while, all told, during the afternoon practising it. Then he taught it to me, and in the morning he examined me, and I came through with flying colours. I think, now, almost my continuous employment depended on my remembering the knot."

" I know a number of different knots—perhaps twenty. I learnt them for the purpose of teaching them to others. I never use them. The other day at home, I was tying together two broken ends of a blind cord and I found myself tying a granny."

" But still, to know you know, gives a feeling of magnificence. Your tying a granny, just that once, in a way, is as if a millionaire gourmand shared the bread and cheese of some wayside wayfarer."

" Yes, I suppose I have eaten bread and cheese at the Spaniard's, in the old days, or in some shepherd's inn on the Cotswolds."

" Cheese has been eaten a great deal more of late years in Ireland."

" Will it have, do you think, any ultimate effect on the national character ? Will there be less poetry and more realism ? "

" That's getting very near politics."

" I used to enjoy elections. I used to take an extra

half-hour at luncheon-time, so as to record my vote. Once I got as tight as a lord before I got back to my office."

" Did it come on before or after voting ? "

" Oh, after voting."

" Once, when I lived in Lewisham, I lent some bean-poles I had, to my neighbour, who tied bunches of primroses to them. It was a long while ago, and he was a conservative. But my father-in-law, who belonged to the other persuasion, was annoyed with me."

" Rightly so. You should always be certain in matters of a political nature. It's better to be sure than sorry—after the election."

" But he doesn't seem to have been in the least sorry, and his father-in-law must have forgiven him long ago."

" Yes, yes, but fathers-in-law they are for forgiving, and rosemary, that's for remembrance."

" And there is pansy. That is for thoughts. This man's father-in-law was, it is likely, an admirable man."

" I bet he was, sir."

" Often they are, it seems."

" He'd be delighted to hear. He's alive ; very lively and strong in the voice. The other day he introduced us, suddenly, to a stepmother-in-law, younger than my youngest daughter, and she hasn't matriculated yet."

" This citizen needs, from us, no defence. He is well able to take care of himself, let us hope he is as well able to take care of his son-in-law's stepmother-in-law."

" I picture a man of a vivid and abiding personality."

" Yes, and a man whose political opinions would vary very little with the passing of the years."

" I haven't got enough documentary evidence before me to be able to picture the man, at all clearly, myself, but he must be a worthy man."

" Worthy, you mean, of the young lady's affections. There, I'm with you when the young admire the, well —elderly. There you'll find there's always something to admire, even if it doesn't appeal to ourselves. Youth is unerring, in some respects. Young birds, especially young sparrows, seem to be hatched with some hidden sense of the proper values of food, you may notice. Heredity experience, I suppose. How seldom a fledgling sparrow will pick up anything that looks like a crumb, but isn't a crumb at all."

" Yes, I've observed birds a good deal, in my time, and I've noticed that, especially about the town sparrows. On a day after a Bank Holiday, when all sorts of unexpected trifles are lying about, unused food, the sparrows go for what they want. And it isn't that they are simply simple livers, they have a varied diet at all times. But after a Bank Holiday they have to use caution. I would say, intelligence, of a high order, seeds of piccalilli for instance."

" I shouldn't wonder. You make me think."

" Ah, well, a sparrow's a sparrow for a' that."

" The question isn't between a sparrow and a sparrow, but between a sparrow and this gentleman's father-in-law."

" I don't think there is any question at all. It seems to me, we have been giving our opinions, always a foolish thing to do, without sufficient data, on a matter that does not concern us."

" That's perfectly true. But the poor man's father-in-law may concern him very much. What was the general idea ? For a moment there I wasn't listening."

" There was no general idea, Judge. Only one of us, I, perhaps, began comparing sparrows with humanity."

" And I carried the thing on, because I am really interested in birds, more so perhaps than in humanity. Perhaps we were a little heartless talking like this before you."

" Not a bit. I shall tell my father-in-law, no, my stepmother-in-law, that we have been talking about her and a sparrow."

" God forbid. She mightn't like it. I know very few ladies whom I would care to liken to a sparrow, to their faces. A nightingale, or a canary even, under certain circumstances, but no sparrows."

" It depends on how it's said, and who says it, and also it depends whether there is a sparrow hopping about for comparison at the moment you are telling her she's like one. If there is a sparrow actually before the eyes, the comparison is dangerous. But if the sparrow has to be imagined, it's all right, and the lady imagines the sort of bird she likes, as she sees the love-light in her swain's eyes."

" It's a good thing we thought of a sparrow instead of a robin. Because a robin that isn't a robin red-breast, looks like a bank messenger in mufti."

" Yes, with money chained to him. Money, and not his own. It's he that's chained to it. Yet there are some who would sooner be chained to somebody else's money, than not be near any at all. I used to say I wouldn't care to be too rich. But now, I know I couldn't have too much. You want such a lot for contingencies. Investments stop paying."

" Contingencies, the employer said to the traveller— 'What do you want another fifteen shillings for?'

And the traveller said, 'That's for contingencies.' And the employer, he was a very ignorant man, said, 'What do you want with contingencies? I never wear 'em.'"

" Quite so, quite so."

" I wish I'd never left off mine. This summer's been too chilly for me. I know I'll be glad when I get into my good thick winter ones, and I will, at the first sign of frost. It's no use putting off these comforts too long I find. Don't wait until some fixed date to light the fires. Have a fire whenever it gets nippy. That's my motto in future."

" I believe you're right. It's very well for these young fellows. They're always on the move, dashing about, playing tennis. Then dashing somewhere else on a motor-cycle. I play a good deal of tennis, and badminton in the winter, but I must have the shower, and watch out afterwards, or I'll get a chill, and that's a loss to me if I'm laid up, even for a day or two. I haven't got exactly to keep my nose to the grindstone, but if my nose isn't near by, the grindstone doesn't turn very well, and I lose something worth while, while I'm at home."

" Ah, yes, that's the way. It's a lie and a deception to say ' The watched pot doesn't boil '. Nowadays we've altered most of those Æsop's fables. The pot, if it is to boil ever, requires constant watching."

" I'll say it does, sir. I've seen pots on the fire, watched, and unwatched, and I've known it happen that not only did the unwatched pot not boil, but, when they came to take the lid off it, I'm blessed if some clever cook hadn't taken all the bones out."

" And not enough left for a post mortem."

" Post mortem ! Not enough left to make a back

button to button your braces to, to keep your trousers on, and that's in the City of London."

" I don't know, but it's very hard to look cheerful under those circumstances."

" Still, there have been watched pots, in history, which never boiled."

" I shouldn't wonder. Then there's the saying ' Don't put your eggs in too many baskets '. But I think, and maintain, that if a man has his capital spread through a number of sound investments he's in a better position than if he had all in one investment, even if it was, apparently, equally sound. The law of averages must prevail."

" In this most extraordinary country, well, perhaps I should not say extraordinary country ; I should say absorbingly interesting country, to an outsider, proverbs seem to run ' by contrary ' as you say. I think I remember when I visited Ireland, as a boy, with my father, who was in the habit of coming over every year for fishing. And, just once, he brought me with him, though I am not, and never was, a fisherman. But I recall a little picture for sale in a shop window ; there were several little pictures. They seemed to me very funny, at the time, but, now, they would hardly appeal, would they ? There was, as well as I remember, a figure of a Paddy in a dress coat, and knee breeches. They were supposed to be worn generally some years earlier than my visit, my first visit. Indeed, this is only my second. But I promise myself to come again. I never saw any Irishmen in the costume myself. In the picture there was a pig, and a milestone, that read ' ten miles ' to, I think, ' Cork '. And there was another funny Irishman, talking to the first. I forgot to say the pig was placed so that he could see the legend on the milestone. The story under the picture was something like this :—

Tim : " Ten miles from Cork, are we ? "
Pat : " Hush, hush, don't let the pig hear you ; he thinks it's nearer."
Tim : " But sure he can see what's on the milestone."
Pat : " Yes, but he can't read."

" Paddy, and the little pig, they were always to the fore."

" Yes, and I was in the habit of telling the story to friends at home. I had to remember it. I didn't have the picture, and it was very curious, the effect on people. I don't think it induced anyone to visit Ireland. It made them doubtful, in some way, doubtful of themselves. That pleased my father, when he noticed it, because he never encouraged people going to Ireland, coming over here. He didn't want his favourite spots overrun. What would he think now to see motor-cars along in a whirl, perhaps beside the very river where he used to fish, with no living thing to bother him but the midges. He was an inveterate smoker ; he said the midges liked it. He said he wished before he died that someone would discover something new to smoke instead of tobacco. He said the midges, wherever he smoked here, had become tobacco saturated. He said they had tobacco hearts ; he could hear their throbbing about him."

" Did your father live to a great age ? "

" In spite of the tobacco."

" He died comparatively young. About the same age as I am now we buried him, but his death had nothing to do with tobacco."

" The case for, or against, tobacco is unproved. I did not smoke a single cigarette, not a whiff, for one year once, and I cannot say now whether it was my loss, or my gain. I certainly saved some money, but in the New Year, I transferred some little money I had into a tobacco company, for augmentation of capital. But when I sold out, in June, I was down, very curiously, to almost the exact amount I had saved, the previous year, by not smoking. I felt it was curious."

" It was an omen."

" I have no doubt we are surrounded by omens, but omens of what ? "

" I am not superstitious, but certainly one hears of very curious things."

" Ghosts and such-like."

" Stories, stories, ghost stories. In the stories one hears, from one's friends, the details are meagre and unsatisfying compared to the thrillers of fiction."

" I enjoy those extraordinary stories about marvellous inventions capable of laying waste the world. With the inventor, some multi-millionaire, inside the machine, working it, until something blows up, and the sky is full of falling debris, and shoots of crimson flame. I'm going by cover designs as a matter of fact. A multi-millionaire now can hardly get a shave without paying the barber a percentage on his income. And disguising himself in rags, and pretending to be poor, has only had the result of making every poor tramp on the roads suspected of being a hidden millionaire. So the millionaire, without doing himself any good, has harmed others. 'Twas ever so."

" And still I'd risk it. I'd be a multi-millionaire to-morrow, if I got the chance."

" I wouldn't, I'd sooner have peace and voluptuosity beside some purling stream."

" Health comes first of all. I'd be content to always be as well as I feel this moment."

" It is the air of this place. It certainly is feeding."

" It fills me with exuberance. But still, I suppose, it would wear off if one lived here continuously. The natives are not so remarkably robust looking, some of them, many of them, look worried. In fact, the Merry Irish don't seem to me to be as merry as they are painted."

" If you had been at the dance we looked in at last week, out in a country cottage—we were sheltering from a short, heavy shower—you could say they were merry enough."

" Ah, merry faces mean nothing one way, or the other ; all the faces are masks. It's right, they call the fox's face a mask, and when his sharp face is grinning into the face of the hounds that will eat him, it's all ' tally-ho's ', and red coats, and horns, and ' yoicks ', and ' worry ', ' worry ', worries. It's walloping noises, and blue skies, and clouds, flying overhead. But in the red fox's face there is hard beauty."

" ' The foxes have holes, and the fowls of the air '— how is it ? "

" I forget it myself."

" There is no time like the present. Perhaps it is all we have the right to call time. This young lady, whom we lost yesterday, and this drowned young fellow, and in a way, your friend there, Mr. Bowsie, was, as far as we were concerned, drowned too. Well, they had a present time, perhaps not at their last moment ; they were hardly conscious then, but there was a time when they felt, with every fibre, that they were here present, balanced on their toes, I believe. And Mr. Bowsie was in that position faintly, to us, for a moment of time."

" Yes, I feel what you feel."

" Yes, it must come to all and yet so few are ever prepared."

" Some are always."

" Yes, no doubt they are. They are to be admired, and very much admired, and it is for others to only hope that they may arrive somehow, at the same condition."

" In the midst of life, we are in death. That I think is misunderstood. Death is there to tap our shoulder, but we are not in it till we get the tap."

" Yes, and then there is the reprieve."

" Yes, a fright, nothing more. Forgotten again, a shiver ; someone walking over my tombstone."

" Not so much a warning."

" Warnings can be taken in different ways."

" I know what you mean. You mean time is short —make the most of it."

" Well, that might be."

As we walk along we are going more slowly always, and yet we must be nearing home now. On the sea side of the sandhills it is difficult to know how far we have gone on our way. The sandhills, as much as we can make out of them, are much alike. But what have I here—an opening, a series of openings, through the sandhills, where some heavy seas once worked their way. I get a glimpse of the country within. I must be looking right away up the road for I see a sparkle of lights, some way off and magnified, and a glisten put on them by the moisture in the air. The glistening means more rain to-morrow. A still day with a soak of rain. The lights I see are from the windows, and the glass doors, of the Pride. My right-hand marcher has seen it too, I know, for he quickens his pace to take us along with him, past that opening in the sand-hills. Three minutes, walking all silent we are, with our heads down.

And, now, before us, sticking up out of the sands, are dark objects. Bleached timbers, looking dark at first against the dove-coloured sand. These pieces are the ends of the timbers of a small coasting vessel, wrecked long ago. They stand around, like a cromlech, a few feet up in the sea air, and we, by their position, can trace the length and beam of the old ship. These timber ends are a comfortable height for sitting men. We are all sitting down except the Judge who keeps on his feet, and moves slowly up and down, fore and aft, aft and fore, along the clean sand, high over the lost ship's keelson. I see two or three faces, when men light cigarettes, or a pipe. I see one smoker holding his flaming match artfully towards his neighbour on a post. He wants to see his face, though he thought he knew all the six of us, by our voices. Still voices, where men move slowly along sands, in the dark, not far from a sea, are sometimes disguised in their sur-roundings. I know now, the voice he thought belonged to Hound Voice, belonged to Haggard Face. He is surprised and wonders if anything he said was taken wrongly. Because, even though as we walked our remarks were thrown out generally, still very often one man was spoken at.

A rolling voice begins, though the first words step short, and briskly. " This death is episodic, when we read our newspapers quickly, and see our friends falling like flies, it is so, to us. But what of our friends shoul-dered out of the way, out of the highway, off the road. But the road seems just as congested as before. I am speaking, as a man arrived at an age, when he must expect to lose his contemporaries. After all, there is the psalmist's three score years and ten. Cut down like a flower—— No, mown like ripe old hay, to be saved, in a good hour, we hope. Perhaps the tossing on the hay fork, the raking with the hay rake, and the stacking, finally, are like the latter days of an old man. You say, I'm sure, as the old humorist had it. ' Air you a preacher, sir ? ' Indeed, I am nothing of the kind, nor am I yet among the three score and tenners. But it's just there. I hear soft feet sometimes walking. ' In the midst of life ' as you said a while back—' In the midst of death ' ; we are as men on a raft, surrounded by a sea, into which the dead fall. But, in a real sea, there would be a bobbing about of heads. We are spared that, and to me, it seems, the Mercy of God. To others, no. The seeming final, they cannot bear."

" They cannot bear a break in continuity of any kind, as if time, and eternity, were drawn along by one engine, for which they prefer to have no name. And should a coupling break, they are afraid of a catastrophe to themselves."

" I had a young friend and great helper. He worked side by side with me in my work for ten years—the flower of his life, the whole blossom of it, as it proved. He was my right hand, one lobe of my brain, and then he died, in a moment. After all the fuss, and miserable activities, after his death, I came back from the funeral, and, for one hour, I believed that somehow, his thoughts, his advice, and his brotherly help, would be mine. I thought it, without any orthodox sentimentality, I assure you. But when the hour was passed the thought was gone."

" Yet my experience is different. I lost a friend—a boyhood friend, when a boy. But to this very day, I believe, I never even back a horse, without consulting him."

" Some have that gift—it is to be cherished."

" I never had a friend so close as these. I had acquaintances and relations, for whom I had plenty of affection, but no exchanging of ideas. I have now, of late years, made friends more than in my more imaginative youth. When I die I am hoping to make new friends. As one gets older, moving about, you meet a friend at one corner, but you don't expect to meet him at the next. In childhood, I recall, wherever I was taken I always expected to find the same people. Just as I brought a toy with me everywhere, or my nurse carried it along for me, so that, when I arrived at the seaside, or wherever we were going, there was my toy horse, or toy donkey, or little cart, or whatever it was, waiting for me."

" Perhaps, when we all reach our second childhood, it will be so with us—expecting our toys to be waiting for us beyond."

" On the Farther Shore."

" In the Promised Land."

" Where we all get our deserts."

" I hope to God not."

" Amen."

" Perhaps they hear us talking ; I mean those that have gone on before."

" Perhaps they wouldn't be bothered."

" I believe they would."

" If we knew they were listening we might amuse them."

" That would make us self-conscious, more self-conscious than we are, and we have plenty of it."

" The mahatmas in the East are all for passing through

self-consciousness, into the unconscious, or into the great consciousness, lost in a kind of filmy state. Put your finger into the mist, the finger makes a hole, withdraw it, and all is mist as before."

" It doesn't appeal to me."

" Nor to me. I am of a fleshly school. I believe that it is possible that the ingredients of the film are within me. But I am solid. As I beat my arm I feel it. My pipe has gone out. I light it again. I hold the match in my hand, flaming. I blow out the flame. It has gone—where to ? Something decarbonised. Or something, has left some minute particles in the air. Now, they have dissolved again. But that flame was, and I'm telling you, as long as any of you live, you will remember that flame, not because it was of any value, as we value things, or because the man, the individual, who struck the match was of any particular value, and not just because I tell you that you will never forget it. But because that flame will insist on being never forgotten by any of you. Oh, just the darkness. The flame shining, you all saw it, the surroundings were suitable ; I was talking my nonsense. But lots of other flames, from matches, you'll see, I hope, for many years, and you'll hear lots more nonsenses, unless we all get too sensible, and dour. But that small flame from that small match has taken the freehold of your memories."

" And yours too."

" How do you mean mine ? "

" You'll always remember it too."

" Oh, yes, I expect so."

> " There's plenty gold,
> So I've been told,
> On the banks of the Sacramento ;

So blow, my bullies, blow,
For California oh,
There's plenty gold,
So I've been told,
On the banks of the Sacramento.

These shanties, I don't think we always hear the best of the old ones. They keep on just at a few."

" You're right, Judge. They sing from books now, not from recalling when they sang them themselves first. We, speaking for myself, who have never been to sea in a sailing vessel, try to reconstruct the scene, and the style of seamen, singing those old working songs aboard a ship. But it won't come."

" It won't come at will, sir. These things recall themselves. We may ask them, but it's the things themselves that come to us, not we who go to them. I'm sure of this, though I couldn't convince you if you don't want to be convinced."

"It's impossible to convince anyone of anything, unless you have agreed before on some rules in a hand-book. The Rules of Archery—if it's a bull, it's a bull."

" That seems simple."

" But in simple there's a catch. This simplicity business is the perfect trap. The perfect fly trap."

" I suppose you can hear them buzzing when they are inside."

" A big, simple bluebottle in a bluebottle trap, buzz, buzz, buzz, buzzing,—that's the idea."

" If simplicity isn't the way, is complication the road to salvation ? "

" There I leave you."

" I am afraid that's what we all must say."

" I think my friend would agree that simplicity is

impossible for us, but desirable. But complication is possible, but undesirable."

" If this was a debating society, we'd have a chairman who would, I'm afraid, be continually calling us to order."

" But it isn't a debating society. It's simply a collection of seven good men, and true, sitting on posts haranguing each other."

" Six sitting, one bird walking."

" Yes, the Judge is in his proper position, standing up. He can have his eye on us, and when he walks up and down, he keeps disappearing into the darkness, and coming back again. Mobile like truth. Truth is like rubber, it can be pulled out long."

" Yes, but it snaps back to the original length and size."

" Not if you nail it down."

" Yes, but if ever you draw the nails, even after the lapse of time, it'll snap back."

" Unless the rubber has perished in the meantime."

" I get you, sir, even truth, kept stretched too long, loses its virtue."

" We're talking like books."

" They don't write books like this nowadays."

" Well, they used to."

" Come, come, my friends, have any of you got a cigar on you ? I believe I would like to smoke one."

" A cigarette."

" A nice Havana cigarette."

" No, thank you. I thought I'd like to try smoking a cigar, if there was one in the crowd. I thought I'd like to try smoking one in the dark. They said that tobacco is not the same thing in the dark as in the light."

" Well, it isn't, but the habit goes on."

" Yes, I suppose so. I suppose it would be possible to have no habits to break, each day, the habits begun yesterday. It would be very original."

" How about the habit of speech."

" Yes, certainly, it may be said to be habitual with many."

" But it's dying out. I don't mean just ' good talk ' as people like to call it. Of the existence of ' good talk ' even I have my severe doubts. But talk, even for giving information, or for pure statement, is losing ground—going backwards."

" Very few people now care to listen to comment. They think that given a photograph of a fact, with a phonograph accompaniment, that they'll be able to make what comment they like themselves. But they won't, for a long while yet. A race of supermen may be able to make their own comments without reading newspapers, or reviews, or books."

" Which is as good as saying we are supermen, for we, some of us, have been making comments to-night, indeed I have myself."

" Well, we are supermen."

" Us sitting round here on these old posts supermen ! "

" If there are any supermen anywhere why not here. The time and the place is excellent. The moon is in the flush of the third quarter—or will be when she rises."

" I've noticed some light creeping into the sky, just a little."

" Ah, yes, but when she comes up, she'll come up with a cloudy face, and to-morrow will be a dirty day. There may be wind, but I don't think so."

" What did the paper say about it ? "

" Yesterday's paper, it didn't say anything about the future, it was non-committal. Anyway, I don't suppose our friend, if he's a prophet, read the papers. I always read one paper a day, pretty well through, and I never know what's going to happen until it arrives, and not always then."

" I expect you agree with me—we'll know soon enough."

" Speculators, they like to think they know what's coming along, and invest their money accordingly."

" But do they ?—they talk about it and give reasons, I know. But if they do, they'll .be some of the last left talking, in the abomination of desolation when the bottom's fallen out of the last market."

" I don't think they'll be talking with their lips. I think they'll be making signs with their fingers."

" Well, I must say I think the end of the world is a more cheerful subject for conversation than death, individual. When pirates walked a plank, they mostly walked it alone. But at the Last Day, all together, a good company, doesn't look so dreadful just at the moment. Though I daresay I'd be able to face it better after I've had my dinner. I had a very light lunch to-day. I came in late, and just took a biscuit, and a bit of cheese. I feel a bit lost, and that's a fact. I don't think I'll smoke any more, it makes my head ache. Has anyone got the time ? "

" Yes, but we don't want to know it ; it's not dinner-time yet—I know that."

" And we mustn't begin talking about what's likely to be for dinner. Though those ducks last night were very good. I like country produce. I don't want imitation *table d'hôte*, all out of tins, without the labels. If you dine out of tins, you should have the labels served up, with the grub. For, after all, it was the labels the housekeeper saw when she bought the stuff, and she's thinking of the label when she's giving you the dish. But, if you haven't seen the label, you're at a disadvantage. Good grub never did anyone any harm. Everyone who has reached years of discretion ought to have some, or if they haven't, they ought to know how to make allowances. We mustn't talk about what's to be for dinner, or we'll be imagining miasmas in the sand heaps, like the starving arabs in the desert."

" That's what we've been doing about this death business. It isn't death-time, and we've been anticipating death. It's taken, without cocktails before it, often, and most would like to have it without *hors d'œuvre*. A quick death and a happy one is the wish of most. I'm not asking anyone here what they look for, hope for. I'm not asking myself. I'm not insured ; I've got no one I want to insure for. I live in my boots—I travel light."

" You'd better not let any of these insurance canvassers hear you. These men they rise in the night to try and sell insurance. If they had the courage to risk it, they'd pay burglars to break into houses at night, and leave particulars, what they call ' literature ', about insurance. They are a menace to the peace of mind of the uninsured, and they know men's resistance is weakest in the still hours of nights. Do you know that clever, unscrupulous men have learnt to acquire, as a mask, the expression of the fully insured man."

" Like a man crossing a frontier with an I-am-rich-and-powerful-not-to-be-annoyed-and-have-a-passport-in-perfect-order-in-my-wallet-in-my-breast-pocket-book — that took a long breath."

" Sir, pearl divers learn to make the breath last, and you certainly brought a pearl from the depths."

" I thank you, kind sir, I do my best."

" Sirs, that moon we heard about doesn't seem to be coming up at all. It has perhaps turned back, unwilling to shine on seven just men, who cannot bear the moon-light to interrupt their symposium. For when we heard, just now, that the moon was coming, we all looked over our shoulders, without a spirit of welcome. And yet, I think we'd look well all sitting around, endorsing the shape of this old ship, six figure-heads, all bristling round her sides, and the chief figure-head marching up and down her deck of sand, from his quarterdeck to his fore-castle, and lord and chief of all."

" Hear, hear."

" All of us, I think, are only here because the Judge thinks we are here. If he was to stop thinking about us, we'd vanish, as the poet says, ' like the baseless fabric of a dream '. Don't all ask me now where we'd all vanish to. I hope to a good place, but we didn't get much forrader when we enlarged ourselves around the compass that has no rim."

" On the contrary, my friends, it is you all who have made the Judge. In the earth, anyway, one can't help many, but many can help one."

" When we think of you, Judge, we are not counting heads. We are weighing, by a scales that weighs earth, air, water, feathers, and lead."

" You are very good to me."

" Not at all, Judge, we are good to ourselves."

" The Judge knows and understands. He has to remember his manners, but let him forget them."

" Them—who invented him."

" Say, ' who imagined him '. I am not any wooden

man, and I can imagine now, sitting here, on a weather-beaten stick, with my feet in a dry sand, a dripping cliff clothed with evergreen trees, foliage dripping, and water falling and rushing from heights above. And I can smell fern moss, in my imagination. I can smell the brown mountain water too. I could, if I didn't hold my hand, lift it to wipe the spray, I have imagined, from my forehead, and cannot I myself, and you all, imagine the Judge. So that he is our own Judge, and then he, in return, imagines us."

" Oh, begob, that's clear enough, and a better judge I never saw. He loves us, and we love him."

" Who said we were afraid of the moon. Just now, did he speak for himself or did he speak of us all ? "

" And I was right ; you're afraid of the moon, yourself, this moment."

" I don't know about that."

" I'm not saying you're so afraid that it makes you cower. But I'm saying ; you'd sooner have any light shine on us now, but moonlight."

" An artificial light he wouldn't mind. If one of us had a torch, an electric torch, and shone it round on us all, he would not be put out, as he would be under the moon."

" Why would he afraid of the moon ? Am I afraid of the moon ? "

" You are, sir."

" Afraid, afraid is a term that should be qualified. I would say all he meant was that you, Judge, and our friend on the stern-post, if the moon came up making shadows, that you would prefer to sit in the shadow, than in the light."

" That is because we think, as erring men, that the

light of the moon is analytical, while her shadows protect us from her."

" I'm glad you recognise he meant us all and not just the Judge, and our friend on the stern-post, if he hasn't shifted."

" No, I'm still here."

" By contrast, the shadows, the moon shadows, are more friendly than the light."

" And that's not so with all shadows. I would say that a red light, old-fashioned gas, or firelight, coming from a doorway, in a town street, at night, was encouraging. But a white electric light, not so. Walking along the terrace, above the river, I often spotted Mars and Venus sailing in the sky. It's about all the astronomy I know, and I always thought there was something bluff about red Mars, and something questioning about pale blue Venus. ' Stand on your defence well,' both of them said that. A ruby to a diamond. But I always loved a diamond, the cattlemen playing nap always said, ' Keep a diamond.' I don't know why. They thought it lucky perhaps. Perhaps they were afraid of the colours of moonlight."

" Perhaps it was with them a reminder of the days when, I hear, that to be a moonlighter wasn't so good if you were caught at it."

" Oh, it's older than that."

" As moonlight is to sunlight, as water is to wine."

" As water is to wine."

" In this country the poteen is of a moonlight tinge. So that song doesn't go here."

" And of course in America, the stuff, the tangle leg they made in the mountains, was called moonshine."

" And of course these cattlemen when they said ' keep a diamond ' weren't thinking of the colour ;

they were thinking of the diamond shape of the pip. The colour would be red."

" How could you tell what they thought of, first, at any rate. How the hell can we be certain that when they said diamond, the first thing that flew into their minds wasn't a shining bright stone in a ring."

" They wouldn't know much about diamond rings."

" Aren't you very innocent. The cattlemen knew about everything that was good—to themselves."

" Ah, why was Mars so red ? Is it because blood is the colour of war, and yet red is also the colour of sunsets. Good ones ; it may light the edges of a bivouac on a road of peace."

" I think, with all respect to you, that a bivouac can only be used for a camp on a road of war."

" You're wrong, I think. I think you'll find that the word bivouac can apply to a peaceable camp so long as it is temporary, for a night."

" Well, there's some who never bunked in peace, and never hope to ; they sleep with arms beside them, and they are jealous of the sleep."

" They are foolish men."

" That's what you say."

" Don't you ? "

" What I say is of no consequence."

" It isn't what the one says that matters, it's the echoes that count ; there's a reason for that."

" I think we have enough of reasoning for one night."

" It's early yet, and no heads broken."

" Reason is a dangerous commodity."

" Would you have men live without it ? "

" I'd have them live for it, but not by it."

" Just the reverse for me."

" I can't smoke, by reason that I have forgotten to get a packet before I came out."

" Have some of mine."

" No, thank you. That kind you smoke is all right, but it's too hot for me. Anyway, I smoke too much."

" It blows away in the sea wind ; it doesn't do you any harm."

" At the same time, it's slavery ; though I could give it up. I do, from time to time, but I come at it again, harder than ever."

" You can cure yourself of any habit by keeping at it, steadily, until it bores you."

" But you might die before the cure was completed."

" That's true."

" I've never cured myself of anything. I was always from five to ten minutes late at the office in the morning, and I often made up my mind to break the habit by coming early one morning, if only once. Then the office closed. It was final. I never went to it again, except during the winding up, and then I was more or less my own master. I had just spoilt some of my time, quietly fretting, just a little, over a habit ; while I believe the truth was, I just wanted to do something I'd never done before. Some impulse within me to strike out for myself, and I was barking up the wrong tree all the time, thinking I wanted to be virtuous. It's a sad world, and I daresay if we had two goes at every day of it, we wouldn't manage it any better. If I still want to do something I'd never done before, I could strip off, and pelt down to the sea, and bathe. That would be a new one for me. I never bathed at this time of night, in the dark."

" I wouldn't do it now, I'd be against it, cold, and uncertain, the effect. You'd have to walk in a good way before you'd get any depth of water, so it would be creeping up on you, chilling you by degrees."

"Well, I won't do it."

"Your suggestion of doing something we have never done before is going to cause anxiety to our loved ones. The seed you have sown will take root, and every now and again will be trying to do something quite new, coming down to breakfast by the balcony, and the creepers, or something like that."

"Imperturbability should be taught in the schools, and then we would all get away with a quantity of actions, which, owing to the excitement we know it would now cause us, we have to forgo."

"And that's the way the world loses a lot of what really should belong to it."

"I'm all for freedom and scope, and let the by-standers stand back and pass no remarks."

"But still I like to think they are there. Long ago, when scene painters were cheaper than supers, when they wanted a large crowd they'd have them painted on the back-cloth, and alone on the stage, with the curtain down, I'll tell you an old actor, looking up at them in rows, felt something like a dying gladiator on a bad Monday."

"You mean thumbs down, Judge. Well, this back-cloth here, the darkness about us, has no thumbs down for us. By it we live, by it we die. Here we sit, in the shape of a ship, and what we say, and what we think, are two different things. We live in the little light that rises from the colour of the sands, and in the darkness so deep round us. And our ideas and feelings cross about, and make a basket-work formed to hold us all. And then it lifts us, some wildness lifts us, and our basket rises, till the superfluous nonsense of our thoughts gushes away, through the opening in the basket-work, and we are lifted, like glittering fish, with feathered scales, for land, or sea, air, or nothingness."

" You said the darkness around us was outside our feelings, and it is indeed dark now, as dark as it has been at any time since we rested ourselves here."

" Never mind what I said ; if the darkness around us is dark enough. If the darkness is thick enough, it isolates us, waiting for our moon admirer to produce the light. If the darkest hour is before the dawn, the same should apply about the moon. And we soon should be seeing each other for what we are, more or less. That is what we are, not at home, in the hotel, but out here, on the sands, sitting on our timber ends, waiting for the Captain, in the centre, to call out ' Moon on the port quarter, dim and mousy looking '. Till then, let us hold our ground, stay where we are. Number, beginning here on my left—number one say it."

" Number one."

" Two."

" Three."

" Four."

That's sounding right from the stern, I believe.

" Five."

Only one to starboard. Then here's myself—six and the skipper.

" Annso."

Seven all told—a lucky number. Some of them, I know, think I'm going to try and work some strange incantation. One, I'm sure, is saying inside his mouth " hocus pocus ". I wonder, if I was a trained mesmeriser, could I make any of these go through any ridiculous paces. Of course, they can't see me now. The idea is always, it appears, to focus—focus—pocus. The lad's eye on some one bright object. The Easterns look at their navels, not so very bright. I wonder when a sea-gull turns his beak into his chest, and fixes his view, is he looking in his ignorance, in the wrong place for his navel. And of course he never had one, I forgot that. What a good thing it is that thoughts are not yet public property, by any process of listening in. When they are, how careful we will be to think as little as possible. It will bring a revival in handwork of all kinds. I so hate the word craft, and handicraft, worst of all, that I would go a long way round in circumlocutionary talk not to use the word. But how about it when I let slip that I was thinking in " craft ". Ah well, we'll all move away in time. When our surroundings become too complicated for our machinery it falls down, and we skip off among the ghosties, where all machinery goes. If I had time, and a good listener, I would be able to discourse on the beauty of this language. " When all machinery goes ", mean equally well that the machinery goes round in that bright spot. That it " goes " in the way that all the angels will stand for it. And then it can mean that all machinery goes to the ghosts in its latter end. Oh, if the Good God would send me a good listener, or one that looked like a good listener, I would be willing to fool myself for my own pleasure. I'd be able to imagine a listener from just a resemblance to one. But no, here, on these sands, at this moment, I believe, or hope, or bow my head before the cold shower of what must be, that from this onwards, the whole seven of us, will be able to draw the breath of the spirit, without depending on any kind of a dummy listener.

I like being here—a kind of sympathy flows round the outline of the ship, from the others and through me. It is a light sympathy ; it has a quality of buoyancy. I could imagine, if I had within myself the fires of this world a little more damped down, floating into the air, and sitting a few feet nearer the sky, above my timber seat. If I imagine myself now floating upwards, rising slowly, not coming up quickly like a cork, rising, I should be able to imagine myself looking over the sandhills, and seeing the first glint of the moon dawn. These simple fancyings of mine are my own affair, because I believe I can detect the links in the chain. If there were no links, I might think the thoughts had slid into my mind from one of these other boys. But these fancies, even apart from links, are the kind of thing I've idled my pate with before. But still, that proves nothing, one way or the other, because when I thought this sort of foolishness before I may have been catching it from someone else. If I was an adept it would be fun to send off a thought, of my own invention, letting it sail into number one on my left, with a riding suggestion to pass it along with the sun to number two. And after a few minutes, or seconds, whack, in on the right-hand side of the hopper of my brain comes back my dear little thought to me. All covered I hope, with fresh garniture. There was a gossiping game one time like that.

The Judge, or the Captain, is walking up and down. The air is so still, and we are all so quiet, that I can hear the slight crunch his shoes make as they touch the sand. He is walking very slowly, he is feeling this waiting on the moon more than any of the rest. Number two moved once ; he's turned himself more towards the point where the moon should show itself.

He's, I am sure, the one who had most to say about this lingering shiner.

If she out-Joshuad Joshua, I am sure it was Joshua who stood the sun still, and never came up at all, but after shining away on the inhabitants and Coromandel Coast a while, slewed herself round. That would worry her introducer. With any open praise this evening, he'd make himself what the music-hall people call the " compère ". He is a man who has been supressed not so very long ago, I'm sure ; I feel certain that if he is who I think he is, the man with the Haggard Face, with a little kindly admiration his face would round itself, colour would come into his cheeks, and brightness into his eyes. I wish I could think out something short, and very agreeable, to say to him. I might go in for saying agreeable things. It wouldn't cost me anything, except a little study. I might make a list something like the Polite Letter Writer—only more brief in style.

Greeting to be used on a successful business man. Greeting to be used on a student, who has failed in an examination and cannot go in again, having reached the age limit. I ought to be able to get a good one for that easily ; I might just let people say nice things to myself, and then I could use them on other people, with a small alteration here or there.

" The moon—the moon."

It is the voice of Sitter on the Stern—he's not sitting now ; he's jumped up, I know, his voice is coming from higher in the air than when he answered to his number four. Now, Haggard Cheek, number two, says, " Yes, there it is." He's a little put out at not spotting his own moon first. I believe, trying to be gentle and nice, if I had seen it first, as the Stern Man did, just because he was farther out from the sandhills, I would have kept it to myself, so as to let Haggard Cheek get his effect. A lot of trouble about kind hearts is not thinking of ways to show the hearts how to speak. The moon is nothing yet, from where we are, but the spell of silence is broken, and everyone is moving about. Their voices coming from all about me. One minute a thin squeal on my right ear. Another a reverberating chest shout beats against my chest. I'm standing up ; it's the only thing to do. These moonstruck creatures would be colliding with me, if I wasn't ready to step quickly to one side. The Judge, I'm sure, is in some place of safety, probably standing with the top of a timber before him, so that they'll run into that, before they can barge into him.

Now we're all up, I suppose we'll begin moving away to meet the moonshine. We'll never have the courage to sit down again and discuss anything, certainly not the moon, before her face.

Here we are marching off ; not all abreast, the way we came into this sandy country, but two and two. I'm not going to be odd man out, for I find the hound-voiced comrade beside me. Perhaps the odd man will be, *ex officio*, the Judge. No, he's just behind me, and he's talking with Small Voice. But here is Haggard Cheek ranging about, the man who invented the moon. I daresay he likes it better so ; it will give him a chance to draw our attention to the style of his protégé, or is it the other way round ? That leaves Woolly and Thin Stern the leading pair. I'll try to see that we don't walk on their heels, and that Small Voice behind me doesn't step on mine, but he won't ; he's too ways wise for that.

Haggard Cheek is backing his fancy to the last. He keeps saying, "When we see her she'll have a dirty face, all in a tattered cloud."

Woolly is walking carefully, keeping a good watch out for the first opening in the sandhills, or at any rate, a way through, that will not have us climbing up a high slope of slithering sand. Getting our shoes full of it. I suppose most of us wear shoes, though the Judge has boots, laced up well.

I can make out Haggard Cheek's shoes; they are brown shoes, and would have a nice shine, if the sand hadn't rubbed them dull. He has been rather smart looking each time I have seen him, and now it is right that he should be better turned out than the rest—he, the moon's page.

Woolly stops the cavalcade. He doesn't give much warning, but I pulled up in style, and avoided treading on his tender heels. I am sure they are tender. Woolly people are generally tender about the heels. Old Haggard Cheek is wiry built, you could step on his heels. He'd pretend to feel it, but he wouldn't.

Woolly is going to smoke; he fills and lights his pipe. It's one of those hanging-down ones with a curved mouthpiece. The mixture he is smoking smells with a full contrast to the smell of the bent and the sand, and old black seaweeds. His tobacco has Latakia in it, I'm sure. It's odd I hadn't noticed any of the smells about our marching, until Woolly began to loose his tobacco scent. Another time he would take a pride in getting his pipe blowing with one match only, now he has just used his third. But he is producing plenty of smoke. Great bundles of it are coming about our heads. Just here, in the shelter of the sandhills, the air must be very stagnant, for, though Woolly produced the cloud of tobacco, it wasn't until we stepped off anew that we walked our heads into it. No one else wants to smoke, not even Thin Stern, next to Woolly. And he, I should think, was rather a heavy cigarette smoker, in ordinary times. However, it's only by the greatest experience and a profound knowledge of our fellow-men that any person could be certain of what others were like in ordinary times, when he'd only seen them on a holiday.

Woolly is walking rather fast now. Haggard Cheek has just ranged up on his left hand, and told him that any moment now an opening might show the moon with her cloudy face. Woolly goes ahead, fast indeed. I'm almost at the trot to keep up with him. Another sudden stop ; he nearly overshot his mark. He's going in over the sandhills, well up on a short, steep heap, a piece of grey wreckage, perhaps broken away from our old coaster, lying at a slope, has caught his eye.

Right ahead of us the sandhills part themselves and there before us, over the top of distant low hills, is the moon, clear of the land, but clouded over with ragged clouds, broken and irresolute looking, as though they would hold to her and detain her, but had no reason they could give. Haggard Face is delighted that he should be right about her ; I feel he is very glad that having the courage of his fancy he has proved him right this time. I think he remembers when having the courage of his fancy left him in the wrong, time after time, he believes his luck has turned.

We are all brought to a stand, in good order, looking at the moon, and congratulating her introducer. If he had a long pole he'd point on her like a lecturer who has a magic-lantern picture thrown on a screen above him. As he ranges about trying to focus her better for us, he steps into a pool of water, where some accidental clayeyness in the ground had held the rain in a small pond. The water must have gone over the sides of the low shoe. But it doesn't matter at all. He didn't make any splash stepping into the water. Nothing of a splutter to make an anti-climax to the moon. He just stepped quickly into the pond, and out again. He thinks that the clouds are not packing more densely about the moon. But, ever so little, they appear to get nearer to the texture of old black lace. He foretells that, as he has already said, to-morrow will be a bad day, but the day after will be better, much better. It amuses me to find us all discussing these moon clouds, as if they were arching about it. When, of course, I know that they are within quite ordinary measurable distance ; in fact, if we had sky boots, we could walk to them, in no time, while the moon is immeasurably far away, well, not immeasurably, for the distance is known, exactly, but a darned long walk.

We are walking still, two and two, diagonally across uneven sod, towards the road, and some way off, the hotel lights.

Haggard Cheek is well ahead of us ; he stands and turns his face away from the moon, to look out to the sea, where she will disappear, her night's journey ended. His face is silhouetted against the light, and it is a fine classical profile, a wreath of laurels, sloping upwards, would become his shapely defined brow, nose and chin. He looks long at the selvage edge of the sea. He is trying to squeeze every drop out of these moments of his importance. He is not thinking so much of the rest of us now. We were but the doorway to a place of confidence in himself. He knows this place of surety, and ease, and peace, will last but a little while, and be blown away, by something of the slightest. A bustling little chatter from a bird in a bush, would make him again just an ordinary tourist, on a visit to a country which he has never visited before. But he knows that these moments, where his hollow cheek was lighted, by the moon's round orb, will always remain with him, not as a memory, which one recalls at will, every now and then, but as an actual figure in his brain, always standing by.

He has turned his head again full to the moon and is marching on. A boy rises out of a piece of low land the far side of the road, and, crossing the road, stops Haggard Cheek on the grass edge. He has something in his hand ; he is showing it to Haggard Cheek. We all know, perfectly well, what it is, because I, on my last visit, and the others either to-day, or yesterday, were stopped by this boy. This small merchant, he has a small electric torch, and with it he is illuminating his merchandise. It is a pearl. There is a river, not far away, where a few small pearls are harvested from mussel shells. Haggard Cheek is buying the pearl ; I am glad he is. That boy has been carrying it about so often, and it would be so easy for him to drop it, and never find it again.

Hound Voice, on my right, has noted the sale of the pearl. The boy has turned quickly back on the way he came. I think now, that is the way with those who win a piece of good fortune, they have no longing to stand about where they were lucky. They are, perhaps, afraid of a ground where the magic wish came true. Those you see standing about a wishing-well are not those who have had a wish granted. Those ones I do not believe ever return ; they don't want to turn their feet. When the rest of us go straggling up the hill to an old ruin, where, on a stone, between the ivy, we must rest our flat hand, as we wish. They stay behind. They would appear to be superior to superstition. Once bit—twice shy! No, but once fondled with a lucky tongue, shy for ever.

And it's the same, when we go swaying down the glen to the well, as we look back, we can see them against a round of blue sky, where we came under the curved branches on the well path.

Hound Voice says to me : " Alexander, I'm glad that pearl has found a good home at last. We had a lecture here, the other day, from one of the visitors. He'd never heard an r so lively in a pearl before. And another visitor gave him another lecture, all to himself. He said Cleopatra didn't drink the powdered remains of something between a 'pal' and a 'pail'. My ear isn't very pure, Alexander, but that was as near as I could get myself to the way the first lad pronounced it."

I hear the Judge kick an old shell along the grass. He is pleased that Hound Voice does not call me Hector. He likes to think that Hector is for him alone to use.

We are all on the road now, during the delay of the pearl, we crept up, and are now right on Haggard Cheek's heels. He doesn't stop and show us his new geegaw, and why should he. We have all refused it, and it would take a man insensitive where even he is sensitive, to show six grown men, untrained in dainty politeness, a pearl just bought from a sea urchin, under the light of the moon, and an electric torch. I am trying to be ready, for perhaps he will not feel shy with me alone. He may take me into a corner of the landing at the hotel, where the geraniums are resting on their wire frame, and show me his pearl. I want to be ready, with something to say. I am rejecting everything " chaste " " pure light " " lovely " " well shaped " "but how translucent" "the best of all the gems" "what lustre" "how cold it is to the touch". I like that, it suggests an aloofness; "So dazzling with light of life, and yet as far from us as the echoless stratosphere". I wonder, when it's a common thing to go ballooning there, will they bring back Thermos flasks full of the stuff, and when people come to your evening party, you take off the cup, and pull at the cork, and people crowd round you and your little card table, where you are giving the display. And those on the outside say: "What is it?" And those nearer say: "Stratosphere, wonderful!" And they'll move their hands about where they think it is sitting in the hot air of your drawing-room and they'll say "clammy" or just "very queer". And the day may come when, when the young now alive, may see the travellers at the races in the West, selling little lead tubes of it for threepence. "Genuine stratosphere—take it home," but there'll be no guarantees that it isn't just the Coombe. I must be very empty in my stomach, that I'm being thought-led so far, far away. Hound Voice, I believe, is hungry too, but he would like to talk; he doesn't care about walking beside a man who is wrapped in thoughts of his own. I believe we are all hungry, even the man with the pearl. Perhaps that is why we walk slowly; shaking makes hunger greater, and we won't get any dinner for some little time yet. There's a dressing-bell, though we don't dress for dinner at this hotel, but most men, I remember, make some sort of a quarter toilet as their fancy takes them. It may be more subdued than their clothing of the day, and it may be more gay. Hound Voice bays a couple of times and then says: "As Mrs. Catteryama said—'All is not yet.' Hayden has prepared a surprise for us." He speaks loudly, so that all of us can hear ; he doesn't speak for my ear alone. He's tired of my ear. " You ought to all know so as to be prepared ; Hayden is standing by the hotel door now with the surprise by his side. The way it was my friends was thus : One of the dance band is left behind. When the rest left, this one—Willy is his Christian name, and Prendergast is his surname—was left *hors de combat*. It appears, feeling chilled still from the wetting he got yesterday, this morning he went for a walk amongst the hills and hollows. And every now and then he'd stop and shiver, and then start on again. Well, he was a good way from the hotel, and was just going to turn for home, but, before doing so, he sat down on a wall. As soon as he sat down he began to shiver, and that brought down some of the stones out of the wall. Well, the man who owned the wall, living hard by, heard the stones rattling down, and he thought it was a goat, or a bullock, so he came up through the little potato patch, and there was William shivering very lively.

The man's heart was touched to see any young man quaking so quickly, so he brought Willy down to his own house, and he got out a bottle and it was a dark bottle, so you couldn't see what the liquid in it was up to the inside, and he threw some of the stuff into a mug, and gave it to Willy and saw that he finished it. Well, it appears now the stuff was left over from the races, and it was a kind of " twenty-four hours " as they call it, made of blue stone, and some other things. Well, it took the horizontal shivering from Prendergast, but it gave him a kind of upright jump. And he came away from the Kind Man's house taking walls as if he was on stilts. But he'd only gone about a quarter of a mile when he came down on his knees and vomited. That saved his life. He got the rest of the way back to the hotel crawling. The man that gave him the medicine never saw him after he'd given him the dose. He fired the rocket, and then he shut the door, and went in, and sat by the fireside. Prendergast was all tucked up, coming into the hotel, through the back door. But Hayden saw him and put him to bed, and let him have darkness, and quiet, and kept him behind when the rest of the band sailed away.

Hayden says he never saw a man so frightened. And it appears to me that it wasn't the vomiting that frightened him, but the highfalutin state of grandeur he felt he was in, when first the stuff was working through his nerves. Now, this is what is coming our way. This Prendergast, it appears, is quite himself again now, and anxious to make himself obliging, and to show Hayden some respect. So, what do you think he's going to do ? After dinner to-night, he's going to entertain us. He's able to do a whole band himself. Imitate all the instruments. But it's worse than that ; he's able to do imitations of all sorts of international characters. Oh, he's gifted, and he can twist up his face to look like any of the leading film stars." " Oh, I don't mind," says Small Voice, " it will pass the time." Thin Stern and Woolly both pretend to be looking forward to this one-man show, or perhaps it's just good nature, and they don't like not to accept this young man's offer of entertainment in the spirit in which it comes. I'm not giving any opinion just now. I don't want to be unkind to this son of Bacchus from outside the blanket. And I don't suppose the man who owned the wall is to blame ; he did the best he could, if he had had the noblest and oldest nectar from the distillery, he would have given it, I am sure. And, anyway, he was an instrument of fate, and we are fated to be the audience for this young man's one-man concert to-night.

I am making up my mind that it is going to be a success, and after all, we must consider the ladies. This woebegone chicken, with his entertainment, will draw out their mothering instincts. I'm sure he's a decent young fellow, and worthy of our support. I don't know that I saw all the band, but all I did see looked to me very decent, intelligent-looking men, all, I would say, artists in their different lines.

Well, our troubles, if they are to be troubles, will soon be in sight, for here we are almost at the hotel. The door is hidden by the outward jutting end of the square bay. But now we have rounded that, and before us, in the doorway, is Hayden, with a pale, unassertive, young man, dressed in a neat black suit, its darkness cheered by a pale blue silk tie with long wide ends. Perhaps his entertainment will be above our heads. Perhaps it will be about people we never heard of. Suppose it should turn out after all that he isn't a young man member of a band at all, but some famous film star young woman. I don't remember all their names. Perhaps she met the original Willy Prendergast and changed clothes with him. This lad has certainly a rather girlish look. But this is ridiculous, I'm telling myself " Wouldn't it be fun if——" stories.

If she changed clothes with Prendergast, was it before, or after, the adventure with the spirit of blue stone, or was the whole adventure the figment of her brain? And where is Prendergast? Well, that's easy ; he's just hopped off after the rest of the band. He'd walk a bit, and get a lift on a bread van.

I'll keep my suspicions to myself. Hayden tells us how Prendergast is so fond of the Pride that he stayed after the others left. And now he's going to give this amusement for us to-night after dinner.

Will he have dinner with us, I wonder? If so, I'll watch carefully for any feminine gestures with the knife, the fork, and the spoon. But I expect she'll have her dinner in the back parlour before we sit down in the big dining-room. These actors and actresses have to eat some time before a performance.

Hayden is quite flushed. As a rule his colour is a mat yellowy brown. He's been anxious about, first, the Judge and myself, and then about all the rest, when they didn't get back. Not that he would believe any ordinary accident could have swept us all, but now we are safe home, he doesn't, even by a hint, attempt to upbraid us for bothering him. Naturally, a man couldn't run an hotel, if every time a visitor was behind time, you gave him the black look. Dead, or alive, when the visitor returns to his hotel, he has to be let in. I fancy that's the law of it. But come to think of it, I'm not very sure. The laws about hotels are, I think, very fixed. But I think I'll go up to my room now. If the dressing-bell hasn't gone in our absence, it'll be going very soon. I'll change into my darker, and more easy, clothes, and I'll put on a clean collar and my dark necktie, and my patent shoes. The bell must have gone because there's the hot-water can in the basin. I think now it would be a good idea to get the day's paper, and have some intelligent opinions to offer, during dinner, to the ladies on each side of me.

I've got the paper, and I am sitting on a truly comfortable little armchair in my room and reading any foreign news I can find. That's the safest stuff to talk about. But I saw something just now that's spoilt my sensational female film star romance just when I'd invented it. I saw Prendergast with a tube of shaving cream and a brush in one hand and a razor in the other, and he was making for the bathroom, and I noticed what I hadn't noticed at the door as I should have, if I hadn't been up in my cloudland—that he hadn't shaved yesterday, for he's got an eighth of an inch black stubble round the edges of his chin. I could have noticed it easily too, for his face is white. Well, good luck to him, and good luck to Bowsie, and where is Bowsie now? I expect he's in an hotel near his office-to-be. He'd go to an hotel instead of to his old lodgings, because an hotel is more used to getting people up punctual in the morning, and he believes that he must be absolutely punctual to-morrow. He's certain of that, and he's at his old game of taking no chances. " If man cannot achieve punctuality, he can deserve it." And very likely, he didn't have his dinner on the train because he was drinking whiskey, fair enough, but cautiously, with men who might be of importance, and who would not let dining interfere with drinking whiskey. So, Bowsie is now, I expect, having his chop, and chipped potatoes, at his hotel. And, presently, he will go to the second house at the variety show, and if the men sitting next him are strangers to Dublin, he will allow himself to be led into conversation with them, and he will tell them some dreadful lies about the sights of Dublin. And now, I hear the bell sing of dinner. I am glad I resisted the idea of having a cocktail, and munching some biscuits, down below. I have my hunger, full tiptoed, I believe. I don't believe anything could take it from me now.

I am in my place. I have a young woman sitting on my left, an elderly woman, Mama perhaps, on my right. No, it isn't Mama, because the young woman called her " Mrs."—I don't know what. I didn't catch it.

We have plates of soup before us, and dabble, dabble, go the spoons. It's my favourite here, duck soup. I have three good mouthfuls, and make a remark about the price of gold to the old lady on my right. She snuffles, not a reply ; it's no more than " I heard you ". I turn my nose downward towards the young woman. She answers some news about a yacht race in Australia with a wave of her soup spoon. I have made up my mind. I will not bother about conversation. I will just be funny with myself, so I look across the table ; we are all at one great table, and I look at the row of human beings opposite, and I begin to name them, from fancy, beginning on the left, Mrs. Wan Lee——

THE END